To Don Williamsburg

This copy from my early
press run — before
the recall went out.

Regards —

Jerry D. Little

Oct 26 '82

THE
BOMBING
OFFICER

THE
BOMBING
OFFICER

■
■
■

Jerome Doolittle

E. P. DUTTON ■ NEW YORK

Published in the United States by E. P. Dutton, Inc., 2 Park Avenue, New York, N.Y. 10016

Library of Congress Cataloging in Publication Data

Doolittle, Jerome.
    The bombing officer.
    I. Title.
PS3554.O584B6 1982   813'.54   82-5136
ISBN: 0-525-24105-1   AACR2

Published simultaneously in Canada by Clarke, Irwin & Company Limited, Toronto and Vancouver

10 9 8 7 6 5 4 3 2 1

First Edition

To Gretchen

THE
BOMBING
OFFICER

The sky was hazy from the dry season's dust and the smoke of the fires the hill tribes set to clear new ricefields. Fred Upson could see well enough straight down below the plane, but it was harder to see to the sides, or ahead. He hadn't noticed the effect until the Air America pilot pointed it out. It was as if the haze had afflicted the two men with tunnel vision, from the plane to the ground below. The tunnel had no sharp boundaries; the landscape just became less and less sharply focused as you raised your eyes toward the horizon, until the mountains rimming the Plain of Jars seemed only blurs. And yet the sunlight in the cloudless blue sky was brilliant and brutal.

The bare plain rolled gently below, dun-colored from the drought. Its surface was mottled with bomb craters, scattered in the emptiness where there seemed to be no possible targets. Upson tried to picture what must have been down there when the bombs hit—what Soviet-made tanks, what concentrations of North Vietnamese troops, what communist supply dumps. The plane passed over several small buildings, not much more than sheds with tin roofs. Three neat lines of bomb craters ran toward and past the buildings in different directions. But none of the bombs had hit the targets.

"How come they were trying to bomb the village?" Upson shouted over the roar of the plane's engine.

The pilot pushed his headset off one ear. "Say what?" he shouted back.

"The little village. How come they were trying to hit it?"

"Shit, who knows? They send 'em up here to drop bombs, so they drop bombs. Bring your bombs back home with you, you lose brownie points."

Upson smiled and nodded, to show he had heard, and the pilot shoved his earphone back in place. A moment later, the plane went into a diving turn so sharp that at first Upson thought something was wrong. But the pilot was holding the wheel loosely and casually, with the fingertips of his left hand, while he waved with his right at a collection of tents and huts. "Lima Lima," he shouted. "There's the Gunfighter, waiting on us." The small figure of a man stood by a pile of brown bales. There was no landing strip marked out, just a patch of fairly flat ground near where the man stood. The pilot cut the throttle, and Upson could hear the whistle of the wind the plane made as it settled through the air. This was the first time he had heard that sound, his first time in a small plane. The ground came up frighteningly fast. The pilot raised the plane's long nose till it blocked the onrushing ground from sight, till it seemed he was trying to stand the aircraft on its tail. There was a bump and a squeal from the tires, and in an impossibly short distance the plane came to a stop.

"Door-to-door," the pilot said. "You call, we haul." He leaned over to show Upson how the door on the passenger side unlatched. The man waiting near the plane for them was perhaps a year or two older than Upson, who was twenty-nine. Upson liked him and envied him on sight. The man had a black, drooping gunfighter's mustache. He was tall and lanky and broad-shouldered, whereas Upson was of medium, unremarkable height and weight. The man had eyes of vivid reddish brown; Upson's eyes were a nondescript hazel, and had needed glasses since second grade. Upson wore a permanent press sports shirt, with slacks and desert boots; the man beside the plane wore a filthy tennis hat, a khaki shirt with the sleeves torn off at the armholes, faded Levi's, and sneakers with no socks. "Dick Lindsay," the man said.

"Hi, Dick. I'm Fred Upson."

"Shit, call him Gunfighter," the pilot said. "Look at that damn womb-broom on him."

"What kind of talk is that, Harry?" Lindsay said. "What if I told your momma you knew words like that?"

"She'd be proud of me. She never went to school and learned those fancy words for it."

"Listen, Harry, can you carry a few of my people here over to Ban Leng with you? Some of them wouldn't be able to make the hike."

"Long as you pick 'em out, babes. I'm not going to be the prick that won't let their twenty-five uncles and aunts onto the plane." Lindsay nodded, and went off towards a group of peasants nearby. "Ol' Gunfighter talks Lao like he was born here," the pilot said as he watched the American with the peasants. "Hard to believe that scruffy-looking son of a bitch studied archeology at Yale. He's a good old boy, though, Gunfighter is."

Upson had gone to the University of Pennsylvania, and nobody had ever called him a good old boy. Maybe the State Department personnel office had made him into a good old boy ex officio, he thought, just by assigning him to Laos. In Morocco, his only other overseas posting, people would have condescended to a good old boy. There the main business of the American embassy was the transfer of American money and technology to Morocco, and the production of cables to Washington. The work had been agreeable enough, and had even seemed important. But, even in Upson's short time in Laos, his service in Morocco had come to seem trivial. There the Americans were spectators; here, they were actors. In Morocco the embassy officials had been cautious and passive; here they seemed aggressive, masculine, confident. In Laos the American mission commanded an air force, an army, the economy—an entire country, really. Upson had never doubted his ability to handle his job in Rabat's political section; he was not so confident that he could measure up to the demands of wartime Laos. He had never made the varsity in high school and had not bothered to try in college. Now, he thought, I have made the team at last. As if the coach mistook me for some natural athlete with the same name. The question is whether I'm good enough to take advantage of the break and keep my place on the squad.

Lindsay was bringing the group of refugees over toward the plane. There were women and children and old people, but no young men. Some were barefoot and some wore rubber sandals, like shower sandals. Both men and women wore skirts of checked cotton, knotted in front. Some of the women wore cotton blouses; some wore nothing above the waist but brassieres that made their breasts look conical. The small children wore only shirts. Upson was the only one who paid any attention when a little boy squatting near his mother peed into the dust, watching as the dark patch grew in front of him. Lindsay was talking sternly to the villagers, like a father trying to hold his temper. Finally several old men and women and a sick child

3

went to the plane, where the pilot helped them up through the cabin's sliding door. "How many more can you take?" Lindsay called.

"Many as you can cram in," Harry said. "Just fill the son of a bitch up, and I'll get it off the ground somehow."

Lindsay sent more of the old people over to the plane, where they boarded without protest. But one last lame old man refused to go. Finally Lindsay half dragged him to the plane, boosted him aboard, and slid the door shut behind him. The roar of the plane's 340-horsepower engine filled the air and the plane started to move, its propeller boiling up a thick cloud of dust. By the time the cloud had cleared enough so that Upson could see again, the plane was far away, climbing heavily. An old woman was in front of Lindsay, her head bowed and her palms pressed together in an attitude of prayer. "Poor old lady," Lindsay said. "The old guy didn't want to leave without her, but he could never had walked out with the bad leg he has."

"What was she saying just then?" Upson asked.

"She was thanking me for giving her husband the chance to live, even though she knows she'll never see him again."

"She won't?"

"Probably she will, sure. Down in the refugee camps. But she doesn't know that. None of these people know what the hell is going to happen to them. Some of them believe what the NVA have been telling them. That we're going to push them out of airplanes and take over their land."

"What's the NVA?"

"North Vietnamese Army."

"I thought everybody wanted to leave, to get away from the communists. That's what they said at the embassy."

"Did they say the people were voting with their feet?"

"No."

"Sometimes they say that, too, at the embassy. The thing is, at the embassy they don't know their ass from second base. A lot of these folks would rather stay here no matter what's going to happen, so I sort of give them the impression they don't have any choice. What else can I do? In a few days the NVA will retake the area, and the whole goddamned PDJ will be one big free-fire zone."

Upson didn't have to ask what PDJ meant. He had learned a

few of the acronyms already: PDJ for the Plain of Jars, from the French *Plaine des Jarres;* RLAF, pronounced Arlaf, for the Royal Lao Air Force; PL for Pathet Lao; RLG for the Royal Lao Government.

"From the air coming in, it looked like it must have been a free-fire zone before," Upson said. "So they must have lived through it once . . ."

"Sure, but this time the NVA is coming, too. So they'll have both the bombing and the soldiers to contend with."

Upson explained what he had seen on the way up—the lines of bomb craters that had approached and missed the little village. "How could they miss it three times running?" he asked. "And why were they trying to hit it in the first place? I thought inhabited villages were off limits."

"Maybe they had intelligence it was an arms dump and the civilian population had left. Maybe they just bombed it anyway. That's what the air force does. May not hit, but it bombs. The old prop planes, the A-1Es and the T-28s, they can hit what they aim at. But the fast-movers, forget it."

"Really? You get the impression it's precision bombing . . ."

"Sure it is. Once I was showing a movie outdoors, eight miles inside an area that wasn't validated, where they weren't supposed to bomb. Before I could get through on the radio to call the bastards off, a couple of F-105s made four passes at a lighted screen, probably the only light in fifty miles. Missed us every time."

"Why didn't you turn off the projector?"

"When I went to cut the generator, the villagers said to leave it running and stay where we were. Their theory was the planes were sure to miss whatever they were aiming at. If we cut the lights they'd have to guess where we were, and maybe they'd hit us by mistake."

Upson thought of the maps in his new office down in Vientiane, with their precise markings and carefully drawn overlays, showing where bombing was permitted and where it was forbidden under the rules of engagement. "How could they have been eight miles into an unvalidated zone?" he asked.

"Not much of a mistake," the refugee worker said. "It's dark, you see a target of opportunity. At those speeds, you cover eight miles in less than a minute. Besides, those guys figure as

5

soon as they cross the Mekong, they're in Indian territory. So basically, deep down inside, why give a shit about a bunch of rules of engagement? The only person who cares is you, babes. The Mad Bomber."

"The what?"

"Aren't you taking over from Thompson as the new Mad Bomber?"

"I guess so. Air force liaison officer."

"Right. Lots of luck. It's a kamikaze job. Do it right and you go down in flames, like Thompson."

An old man came up to them, leading a delegation of Lao. He asked a question, and then Lindsay went into a long explanation of something. Everyone listened humbly and politely. At the end an old woman went off to the huts and returned carrying a gas can. Lindsay opened the can, sniffed at it, and sloshed the contents around.

"Do you have any *kip* on you?" he asked Upson.

"Yes, some."

"There's probably five hundred kip worth of kerosene in here. How about giving her fifteen hundred for it, and I'll pay you back tonight? If you've got any extra, in fact, maybe you could exchange some of their PL money for RLG money. Send it to the folks back home as a souvenir or something. Just don't tell the ambassador."

"Why not?" Upson asked, starting to count the Royal Lao Government currency in his wallet.

"He figures that if we won't change their communist money for them, they'll learn that they can't count on the PL. So now their life savings are worthless."

"But wouldn't that just discourage other people from coming over to the government side?"

"You tell the ambassador. It didn't work when we did."

Upson had about twenty thousand kip, forty dollars at the official rate. The black market rate was just about the same, because the kip was freely interchangeable with the dollar. It was an extension of the dollar, really, as Upson had learned in the round of briefings set up for him when he joined the embassy staff the week before.

When Lindsay explained that the American stranger was

6

willing to pay government currency for their Pathet Lao savings, the refugees began to rummage through their bundles and clothing for money. "I told them you'd only take two for one," Lindsay said. "That way, more people will get at least a little something. And the stuff may be worthless, but it's kind of pretty, really. Take a look at the five-hundred-kip note."

It showed happy Pathet Lao workers in an underground factory, safe from the bombers. "They're making aluminum cooking pots out of the American planes they shoot down. They make little ashtrays, too, with inscriptions saying it came from the thousandth American plane shot down over Laos. They give them to communist bloc visitors as souvenirs."

"A thousand sounds awful high."

"Sure it is. They lie just like us. Maybe they've shot down a couple hundred, mostly in the trail area."

When the transactions were over, Lindsay pulled a small hunting knife from its sheath and began to slash at the burlap-wrapped bales piled near the improvised landing strip. Rice ran from the cuts he made.

"How about that?" Lindsay said, letting a handful run through his fingers to the ground. "Three weeks ago we airlifted this stuff in, and now we don't have the aircraft to take it back. So I'm supposed to burn it to keep it from the NVA. Shit."

When Lindsay had slashed all the bales on the outside of the pile, he poured kerosene around and touched it off with a lighter. After the first big whoof, oily black smoke began to rise straight up into the still air. The sun was so bright that the flames themselves were almost invisible.

"That's something they never teach you in school," Lindsay said. "How to burn rice. Burns itself out after a while, and most of it'll still be left. Probably it's ruined by the smoke or the kerosene or something, but I don't really know. It's like the rest of this war, kind of an out-of-town tryout. Next time we get into a guerrilla war in a fifteenth-century rural culture we'll have it all worked out, how to burn rice."

The Lao stood around the rice dump, watching without expression as it burned. Now and then a child would run toward the fire till it got too hot, and then run laughing back to its mother.

"Harry's got to make a swing to a bunch of other sites," Lindsay said. "Gives us time to grab something to eat, then walk out to the ridgeline over there. The Vietnamese will have the whole damned PDJ again within a few weeks, so it's the only chance you'll ever have to look at the jars."

"You're an archeologist, the pilot said?"

"I was going to be, once, and then I got tied up with this. I did a monograph on the jars a couple of years ago, but the fact is nobody knows what the hell they were for, or where they came from, or how they got them here."

Lindsay took them into an open-fronted shelter with a corrugated iron roof and walls made of woven grass. An old woman was squatting flat on her heels inside the shop, tapping with a knife to make little cuts along the length of a green papaya. When she had worked her way all around it, she shaved the fruit from top to bottom. With each shallow slice, slivers of papaya fell into the enamel bowl between her knees.

"She's making kind of a salad, with lemon juice and hot peppers," Lindsay said. "Pretty sour. I'd try one of these things instead."

He handed Upson one of several green cubes which were hanging by strings from the rooftree. Upson undid the banana leaf covering, as intricately folded as an origami construction. Inside was a pink cube almost two inches square. "What is it?" he asked.

"Pork rind and a little meat, all chopped into little slivers. Sort of a square sausage with a banana leaf for skin. In the middle there's a hot pepper and a clove of garlic."

"Raw meat?"

"The only way to make it up here is just go ahead and eat the food and drink the water, and then get the shits and shakes and the cold sweats for a week. Once you're through that, the local bugs don't bother you too much anymore. Start to worry about the sanitation, you'd go nuts."

Lindsay laughed. "Jesus, I remember one kid they sent up to us, his first overseas tour. I took him out overnight to a Meo village where we had a rice demonstration project. Next morning he went out to crap in the bushes and when he came back he grabbed a ride on the next plane to Vientiane. What happened,

8

he squatted down and when he looked up there was a big circle of dogs and pigs around him, waiting. Soon as he finished they rushed in, all the dogs and pigs fighting over his turds."

"I'll say one thing for you, Dick," Upson said. "You really know how to whet a guy's appetite." But, of course, now he had to eat the raw meat. The red pepper in the center gave him no trouble; he had got used to hot peppers during his tour in Morocco. With the food they had warm Filipino beer, two brown bottles of San Miguel. The woman who kept the food stall had her entire stock laid out on a plank on the ground: wicker containers of sticky rice; enamel bowls of sauces and pastes, crawling with flies; a pot of grayish stew, a kettle of tea, orange soda, and three more bottles of San Miguel.

"How do you get beer from the Philippines to the Plain of Jars in the middle of a war?" Upson asked.

"Black market from our PXs in Vietnam. The stuff finds its way to North Vietnam, and then they bring it down here. A lot of the people up here are ethnic Chinese, and they'd find some way to do business in the middle of a firefight. You know Harry, the pilot who brought you in? He's a silent partner in a bar down in Vientiane, and the rent money goes to the owner in Hanoi. God knows how it gets there, but it does."

When they went outside again, the sun beat down so heavily that it seemed to have a force you could measure, like a wind or a waterfall. Lindsay didn't look as if he was walking fast as they headed for the distant ridgeline, but Upson found himself slightly out of breath keeping up. A dark patch of sweat began on the back of Lindsay's khaki shirt and grew larger as they walked. Upson could see the rime of salt crystals on the sun-bleached khaki, marking the limit that earlier patches had reached. Maybe this one would be a record. As they began to climb, though, Upson stopped thinking about anything but keeping up.

At the top of the hill were the jars—huge things that had settled into the ground over the centuries and now tilted like the gravestones in an old cemetery. They were in no particular pattern or relationship to each other that Upson could make out. Some were only knee-high; some were as tall as a man. They were of light gray stone so rough and soft that bits crumbled off when he picked at it. Upson saw nothing inside them but a little windblown sand and dust at the bottom. He could barely reach his arms around the biggest of the jars.

"Take a good look," Lindsay said. "We're likely to be the last Americans to see these for a good long while."

"Nobody has any idea what they were for?"

"Some say funeral urns, but nobody knows for sure. People up here are afraid of them, keep away from the place. They know there's no stone like that in the whole area, and they can't figure out how the things got here."

The Plain of Jars was the only place in Laos Upson had ever heard of, before he had received orders six weeks ago assigning him directly to Vientiane, with no home leave. He had only found out that Vientiane was the administrative capital of Laos by looking it up; at first he had the vague idea that it was someplace in sub-Saharan Africa. Now he was on what the newspapers liked to call the "strategic Plain of Jars," among the jars themselves. No bombs had hit anywhere near; the locations of the jars were marked on the maps in Upson's new office, off limits to the air force. There was no litter around, no path leading to this particular collection of jars, no hint that anyone had ever visited them before today. The closest sign of man was Ban Lat Sen, from which they had walked, and the settlement was far enough away to be indistinct. The smoke from the burning rice was still rising straight up, until it blended into the general haze.

"We better head on back," Lindsay said. "Don't want to keep Harry waiting. Every plane we've got is busy on the airlift."

They had only been back in Ban Lat Sen for a few minutes when a buzzing came from the sky. Lindsay glanced towards the west and said, "There's Harry." Upson saw nothing at first, but at last he caught sight of the small shape of the plane coming back for them. "I better get out there and start playing God again," Lindsay said. "We can carry another half dozen or so folks over with us to Ban Leng, save them the walk."

He went off to talk with the village elders about who should go, while Upson watched the plane, a Swiss-designed Porter Pilatus, make its final approach. The nose was enormously long, to make room for the over-powered engine. It was a solid, inelegant working craft made for mountain flying, with nothing nonfunctional about it. The pilot landed in the same startlingly short distance as before, cut his engine, and climbed out. "Just you coming?" he called. "Where's the Gunfighter?"

"He's picking out another bunch to go out with us to Ban Leng," Upson answered. "Here he comes now."

"That all you got for me, babes?" the pilot said to Lindsay. "I can take one or two more than that even, if you got any small ones."

"The rest of them are in pretty good shape. They can make the walk to Ban Leng all right."

"You're the boss, babes."

As the Porter Pilatus approached Ban Leng, Upson could see that there was no airstrip there, either—just a long and fairly level place between two lines of low hills. A C-130 four-engine transport plane was on the ground, small as a toy in the distance. Its propellers blew a huge plume of dust out behind the plane, along the ground and then rising into the air in yellow billows. Hundreds of tiny people stood well clear of the clouds. "I don't know if I got enough room to grease her in without getting us all dusty or not," the pilot said. "Looks like I either go into the dust or I chop up a few Meo."

The Meo refugees spotted the light plane as it was making its final approach, and began to scatter out of its path, pulling children and animals along behind them. Upson thought the plane was going to hit a bale of possessions someone had left behind, but the left wheel passed six feet from it. "Nice work," he said when the plane stopped. "Jesus."

"Not as hairy as it looked," the pilot shouted. "Groundloop was the worst thing that could have happened to us."

The noise was terrible, a steady roar that made normal talking impossible. When the Air America pilot took off again, the plane seemed to rise away from them silently, its noise lost in the larger din. Dust covered Upson's skin and made a paste on his teeth; when he rubbed them with his forefinger, brown, gummy stuff came off. Lindsay was in the worst of the dust, his black mustache now a reddish yellow. He was shouting noiselessly at the refugees, urging them up the ramp into the huge belly of the plane.

Upson wanted to be useful, but he didn't know what to do. The three or four other Americans around were all so busy that he was afraid to bother them. He stood off among the waiting refugees, feeling useless and left out. Both men and women wore loose, black turbans. The babies, slung on their mothers' backs, wore cloth caps decorated with silver coins and elaborate embroidery. Many of the families had pigs with them, tied up in cloth and cord so that their legs were squeezed against their bodies and they looked like huge wieners. Only the heads were free, with the eyes wide and staring, paralyzed beyond fear. Every family had bags and wicker baskets and bales and old cardboard suitcases held together with twine, and net bags of vegetables Upson couldn't recognize, and primitive farm implements, like something in a museum. One woman had a foot-powered sewing machine, with *Singer* worked into the ornamental grille of the treadle. Finally, to get away from the dust and the noise, Upson walked to the top of a slight rise nearby and sat down. The four giant airplane engines roared, and the dust roiled so high that Upson could barely make out the U.S. Air Force markings on the tail of the C-130. The original plan, as he had learned on his first day on the job, only a week ago, had been to paint out the military insignia . . .

That first day, Jerry Brautigan had taken him to the daily ops meeting, held in the embassy's bubble. "You didn't have a bubble in Morocco?" asked Brautigan, the deputy chief of mission. "No, I guess not. You wouldn't have had the same security problems." The bubble was behind a small, locked door on the third floor of the embassy. To make the door open, Brautigan pushed the buttons on a cipher lock in a certain sequence. Inside, the bubble hung in the air—a room hanging within a room. The bubble was made of transparent plastic, like a giant Lego-block construction. Clear plastic tubing, a foot or more across, carried fresh air into the floating room. A low, sighing sound filled the air. Upson supposed later that the transparent room must have been supported as well as suspended, but at the moment all his attention was on the bubble itself.

Inside it was a long boardroom table of polished wood. Fifteen or twenty men sat around the table in chairs of Scandinavian design, upholstered in bright orange. Upson could see the men's lips move as they talked, but no sound came out of the bubble. The larger room that enclosed the bubble was dark, while the bubble was brilliantly lit—a transparent boardroom floating in the night. Brautigan explained that the bubble was designed to baffle any known listening device. "Recording devices couldn't pick up anything inside anyway," he said. "That low background hum is white noise. We'd better go on in; the ambassador's about due."

They went up four stairs into the floating room. The deputy chief of mission showed Upson to a place at one end of the table, and himself went to one of the two empty chairs at the other end. Pads of yellow paper and sharpened pencils had been laid out at each place around the table. Upson had barely sat down and introduced himself to his neighbor when everybody got up. "Good morning, Mr. Ambassador," they all said, nearly in unison.

"Good morning, gentlemen, good morning."

The ambassador was a spare man of middle height. The veins were prominent in his hands and neck, and even his temples. He wore a freshly pressed tan summer-weight suit. His iron gray hair was just longer than a crewcut. He was the kind of man who looks natural with a whistle around his neck—a coach, a counselor, a ranger, a drill instructor. The ambassador walked briskly to the seat beside Brautigan and sat down, allowing everyone else to sit down.

The ambassador began by going around the table, asking each member of the operations group for his report. Much of it meant nothing to Upson—discussion of Lima sites, SGUs, POL, LOCs, ravens, Steel Tiger, Barrel Roll, Arc Light missions. But he began to understand once the military and intelligence people finished and Brautigan took over. The deputy chief of mission was laying out the plans for airlifting some twenty thousand refugees—the entire remaining population—off the Plain of Jars. Any day now, apparently, the North Vietnamese were expected to recapture the Plain from the forces of the Meo guerrilla commander, General Vang Pao.

"We're going to have C-130s going in and out of Wattay

Airport all day long," the DCM said, "so we'll have a security problem with the newsies. We'll probably have to paint out the air force insignia and put on Air America markings. Air America doesn't have enough C-130 qualified pilots, so that's another difficulty. But I guess we can have the air force guys leave their uniforms back at Udorn, and we'll rustle up some Air America caps or something for them. You'll take care of that, won't you, Mike?"

Mike, who had seemed to be the air force representative, made a note to himself to take care of it.

"Let me ask you something, Jerry," said the man next to Upson, who had introduced himself at the start of the meeting as Phil Casey, the press attaché. He was balding, overweight, middle-aged, and had smoked three cigarettes since the meeting began.

"You have a problem with that, Phil?" asked Brautigan.

"I guess I do. What am I going to say when the reporters ask me how Air America just sprouted a fleet of C-130s overnight?"

"Can't you just stonewall the bastards?" the ambassador said.

"It would only make it worse, Mr. Ambassador. Every reporter in Southeast Asia knows that Air America doesn't fly C-130s. So they'd write that, and they'd tack on that the American embassy refused comment. We wouldn't just look like liars, we'd look like clumsy liars."

"What do you suggest, then, Phil?" the DCM asked.

"Well, all we're doing is getting innocent people out of the line of fire, isn't it? Why can't the air force take on a noncombatant mission of mercy in-country? We admit the air force flies reconnaissance missions here. If that doesn't violate the Geneva Accords, why should a refugee airlift?"

"You'd just run them in with air force markings, and uniformed pilots?" asked the deputy chief of mission.

"I don't see why not. They're unarmed cargo planes. Hell, we could even take reporters up and let them cover the airlift. Give us some positive coverage for a change, instead of all the secret war stuff."

"It might just work," the DCM said. "What do you think, Mr. Ambassador?"

"Why the hell not? It *is* a mission of mercy."

"All right, Mike. If you'd make a note of that," Brautigan said. The air force man made a note.

Under his breath, Casey said to Upson, "Telling the truth is generally the last thing that occurs to these guys." Upson smiled with automatic politeness, but he was surprised that the press attaché would say something so incautious to a man he had just met.

After the meeting, Brautigan beckoned Upson over. "This is our new air force liaison officer, Mr. Ambassador," the DCM said. "Fred Upson."

"Glad to have you on the team, Fred. What do you think of our little war so far?"

"Pretty confusing, sir."

"Well, it'll all sort itself out quick enough. Remember the central goal of the U.S. Mission here, and all the rest will fall into place."

"Yes, sir?"

"We're here to take the pressure off our boys in South Vietnam. Every commie our little guys can tie down here is one less commie shooting at American boys in Vietnam."

"Yes, sir."

"Got him fixed up to meet everybody, Jerry? AIRA, and ARMA, and CAS?"

"Yes, sir."

"Why not shoot him up to take a look at the airlift when it starts? Do him good to see the PDJ with his own eyes. He'll be seeing enough photos of it, God knows, once the commies move back in."

Finally Lindsay and the other Americans got the last batch of refugees up the ramp and the cargo door rose like a huge lower jaw, clamping the refugees inside. The Americans ran clear as the engines roared even louder and the giant cargo

15

plane lumbered into motion, lost in its own dust. A moment later the plane reappeared out of the red cloud, lifting heavily into the air at the end of the valley.

Upson saw Lindsay walking toward him, with an M-16 rifle he had picked up somewhere. "Would you mind holding onto this for me?" he said, his voice sounding unnaturally loud in the sudden silence. "Too much dust down there." The rifle had a plastic stock and a red plastic sleeve over the muzzle, to keep the barrel clean. It was much lighter than the M-1s Upson remembered from his one year in ROTC. "The next flight will be in a few minutes," Lindsay said. "Casey's on it, the press attaché. He's got a bunch of reporters with him. I thought I'd bring them up here on the hill out of the noise."

"What papers are they from?"

"There's Bill Bailey, and the others I don't know."

"Who's Bill Bailey?"

"The Vientiane stringer for the *New York Times,* and I think *Time* or *Newsweek,* too. One of them. Basically kind of a prick, I guess, but he's the only journalist here who ever bothered to learn Lao, I'll say that for him. Tass and the *L.A. Times* and Agence France Presse have full-time, paid correspondents. Everybody else uses stringers, or sends in guys now and then from Saigon or Bangkok. All the out-of-town tourists write pretty much the same stories. Casey got up a phony press kit once to save everybody time. "Laos, the Land That Time Forgot," I remember that one. It starts out, 'This tiny, landlocked jungle kingdom, slashed by giant, Guam-based B-52s.' He's got ones on the CIA, too, and the bombing, the opium, the gold. One or two others. Fucking Casey, he's too much."

Another C-130 approached from the south. They were on half-hour schedules as long as daylight lasted, one full and one empty plane always in the air and others on the ground, loading or unloading. The engines were shut down only back in Vientiane at the end of the day, when it got too dark to land in the little valley where the refugees waited.

"The reporters will have fun flying back with one hundred fifty, two hundred refugees," Lindsay said. "It's the first time in a plane for most of them. They're scared to death, airsick all over the place. First thing the Air America maintenance crews do every night is hose the puke out of the cargo bay."

The C-130 rolled to a stop way past the crowd of refugees. It turned ponderously around, taxied back, and turned around again to be in position for takeoff. The cargo ramp dropped and five small figures came down it, a ludicrous load for so huge a plane. Upson recognized Casey's thick-bodied figure and bald head. The press attaché was out of breath when he finished the short climb up the hill where Upson and Lindsay waited. "Damn," Casey said. "I'm much too old for this guerrilla warfare shit." The press attaché blotted the top of his head dry with a handerkerchief, and turned to the reporters who followed him. "Okay, gents," he said, "this is Fred Upson from the embassy, and Richard Worthington Lindsay the Third, who is a living legend. The gently bred scion of a fabulously wealthy New Canaan stockbroker, Lindsay has chosen to spend the past eight years living the life of a fourteenth-century hog. Author of numerous scholarly monographs, this modest young refugee worker . . ."

"Cut the crap, will you, Phil," said a reporter with an English accent.

"I'm sorry, I was forgetting myself," Casey said. "Gentlemen, may I present Ian Carmichael of the *London Daily Telegraph?*"

"Exactly what is it you *do* at the embassy?" Carmichael asked.

"Pretty much like the man says," Lindsay answered. "Refugee relief work for USAID."

"Not you. Mr. Upson."

"Me? Well, nothing, really. I mean, I'm assigned to the political section, but I just got here last week, and I haven't really started yet."

"Is that why you haven't got your gold ID bracelet and your Wellington boots yet?"

"I don't follow you."

"Most of your colleagues who work vaguely for the embassy seem to wear gold ID bracelets and Wellington boots."

Carmichael took a camera no bigger than a cigarette pack from the breast pocket of his blue green safari shirt and snapped two pictures of Upson.

"Come on, Ian," Casey said. "Fred's just going to be the new air force liaison officer. He's not with Air America or CAS."

"What's 'cass,' and how do you spell it?" Now the British reporter had his notebook out, and a ballpoint pen ready like an offensive weapon.

"Capital *C*, capital *A*, capital *S*. In Laos, it's kind of an all-purpose acronym. It can mean Continental Air Services, which is a subsidiary of Continental Airlines and does the same work as Air America. It also means Close Air Support. But the way I was using it, it refers to the CIA."

"Does it, now?" What do the letters stand for?"

"Officially, nothing. It's a nickname, whatever you want to call it, for the Agency. The tradition is that it stands for Confidential American Sources."

Carmichael noted this down, looked up at Casey, and said, "I thought you told us there were no CIA operations here."

"No, I told you that I wouldn't be at liberty to discuss CIA operations, if there were any here."

"Isn't that a distinction without a difference, as the lawyers say?"

"Ian, a big boy would understand exactly what I was saying. And I bet you're a big boy."

"Let me see if I've got this straight. If there was a CIA in Laos, you would refer to it as CAS, if you were at liberty to refer to it at all."

"Which I would not be."

"Which you would not be. I think I've got it straight now."

"I think you have. Now, are there any substantive questions on the airlift for Richard Worthington Lindsay the Third, the living legend?"

"Dick," said a very tall, very thin young American, "how extensive was the bombing on the PDJ?"

"Pretty extensive."

"How does that square with the official line that all you do is fly armed reconnaissance missions?"

"I don't know, Bill. I work for USAID. Probably RLAF did some of the bombing."

"What's 'arlaf'?" the Englishman asked. "What's 'yousaid,' as far as that goes?"

"Arlaf is RLAF, The Royal Lao Air Force," Lindsay said. "USAID is the U.S. Agency for International Development."

"U.S. is the United States," Casey said. "Short for the United States of America."

"United States of America," Carmichael repeated, making a show of writing it down in his notebook. "Thank you, Phil. Now, if we can return to Mr. Lindsay for a moment. Mr. Lindsay, do you expect us to believe that one of the most massive bombing campaigns in the history of warfare is being carried out by the Royal Lao Air Force?"

"No, I'm just saying I don't know for a certainty who did the bombing. I wasn't there. I do refugee relief."

The tall American reporter said, "Regardless of who did the bombing, Dick, it was done. And the civilian population of the PDJ was there while it was being done, or there wouldn't be anybody for you to airlift out. Right?"

"Right."

"Two questions, then. First, how heavy were civilian casualties?"

"Apparently very light. I've only come across two people wounded."

"How do you reconcile that with the intensity of the bombing?"

"They learn pretty quickly to deal with the bombing. Just be sure you're always near a hole. Generally you have some warning when a strike is coming, because of the FACs."

"What facts?" the English reporter asked.

"Forward Air Controllers. Little light spotter planes."

"I see. You use them to call in the reconnaissance missions, do you?"

"I don't use them for anything. My job is just to pick up afterward."

"Let me just get back to my question, Ian," the tall American reporter said. "What you're saying in effect, then, Dick, is that it doesn't take a Lao peasant long to get smarter than the U.S. Air Force?"

"That isn't quite the way I'd put it for publication, but I wouldn't argue with you if you did."

"My second question is this. We were perfectly willing to bomb the civilian population in support of General Vang Pao when he marched onto the PDJ just a few months ago. So why don't we just leave the poor bastards in their villages and bomb them again when the Vietnamese push Vang Pao back off the Plain?"

"I would assume that we didn't want to bomb them in the first place, Bill, but then we didn't have any way to get them out of there. Now we do. *Jesus Christ, don't touch that thing!*"

One of the reporters stopped motionless, one foot raised and drawn back a little. In front of his foot was a red metal canister, something like a seltzer bottle cartridge, but much bigger and fatter. "What's your name?" Lindsay asked the man.

"Wilkie Oliphant, *Boston Globe*."

"Look, Oliphant, do me a favor. Anything you don't know what it is out here, don't touch it. Kick that son of a bitch and we'd all be hamburger. That's a CBU."

Oliphant lowered his foot to the ground and backed away. "A mine?" he said.

"Cluster bomb unit. It's full of little ball bearings."

"They go off if you touch them?"

"They're supposed to go off when they're dropped, but a lot of them don't. So they lay around like that, and eventually sink into the ground in the rainy season. When the fuses get old, sometimes any little touch sets them off."

"Antipersonnel bombs, are they?" the English reporter asked.

"Is there some other kind?"

"I mean, are they something specifically designed to make the U.S. Air Force smarter than the peasants? The peasant gets out of his hole after the raid, feeling very pleased with himself, and then he steps on one of these little buggers?"

Lindsay looked at the reporter an uncomfortably long time, saying nothing. At last he answered, "If you mean does it happen that way sometimes, it probably does. If you mean did the United States intend for it to happen that way, is it a tool designed to kill the civilian population, the answer is no. And you're full of shit."

"Oh, really? May I quote you on that?"

"I hope you do."

"Just let me have your name again."

"Richard Lindsay. L-I-N-D-S-A-Y. Get the spelling right."

"Not to worry. I shall. And you're Mr. Upson, is it? Spelled the usual way?"

"That's right."

"And you're the embassy's new air force liaison officer. Why would the air force liaison officer carry an M-16?"

"Dick asked me to keep it out of the dust while he was loading the refugees."

"Oh, Dick gave it to you, did he? Why would a refugee relief officer carry an M-16?"

"To shoot assholes with," Lindsay said. "You get a lot of assholes up here in the hills, this time of year."

"And may I quote you on that, too?"

"Lindsay, spelled the usual way. Look, Phil, this shit is getting a little old. I'm going to get on back to work, if you don't need me for anything."

"One thing before you go," said Wilkie Oliphant, the *Globe* reporter. "As I understand it, we're in the foothills near the Plain of Jars, not really on the Plain?"

"That's right. The plain proper starts a little to the northeast."

"Can you see it from the ridgeline there?"

"Nothing much to see, but yeah, you can see it."

"Would it be okay if we hiked up there and had a look?"

"Okay with me if it's okay with Phil. Just don't wander off the path. Those goddamned CBUs are seeded all over the place, and there was a PL ambush last night only a klick and a half from here."

"Thanks a lot, Dick," Phil Casey said.

"No problem. So long, gents, Carmichael. Look, Carmichael, you see anything interesting lying around the ground, just give it a kick." Lindsay turned and walked back down the hill.

"Friendly fellow," the English reporter said to the press attaché.

"Come on, Ian," Casey said. "You started it."

"Me? What did I say?"

"This'll probably come as a surprise to you, Ian, but some people are so unbelievably thin-skinned that they get offended when you suggest that their country is deliberately targeting civilians."

"Then they should get into some other line of work, shouldn't they?"

"I'm not going to argue with you like Dick. I'm too old and tired to bother."

"Can we go on up to the ridgeline, then?"

"Go ahead, Ian. Don't be too long, that's all. We have to catch this last flight back. If we miss it, I'll have to lay on a special plane and bill you guys for it."

"You're not coming with us, Phil?" the *Boston Globe* man asked.

"No, I'm too old and tired for that, too. The climb would kill me." The long ridgeline was a half mile away, and hundreds of feet high. The hillside was bare except for a few small bushes along the gulleys.

"You guys go ahead," the tall reporter named Bill said. "I think I'll hang around down here and talk to some of the refugees."

"How nice for you, to be able to speak their curious native tongue," Carmichael said. "Well, come on then, fellows."

When the other four reporters had left, the tall American turned to Upson. "We haven't really met," he said. "I'm Bill Bailey, for the *New York Times*. I'd like to come around and talk to you once you've been in the job a few months."

"Be happy to," Upson said, flattered. No one had ever been interested in interviewing him before. Bailey smiled, and headed down the hillside toward the crowd of refugees.

"Some job you have," Upson said to the press attaché. "Is it always like this?"

"To some extent. Ian comes on stronger than most, but they've all got their roles to play and so do we. You can't take it personally. They pick on us because they can't get to the guys who really blow people up—the spooks and the air force. And after all, we're part of the machinery. Once a kid, a stringer for the *Bangkok Post*, told me that the USAID refugee guys like Dick were like medics in an SS division. I told him he was full of shit, sort of." Upson wondered about the "sort of," but said nothing.

Ten minutes later the four reporters were hardly visible. They had reached the ridgeline and were moving slowly southward along it. Bill Bailey came back up from the valley, as red from the dust as Lindsay had been. "Well, what did you find out?" Casey asked.

"This and that."

"You blew it, Bill. The other guys will have firsthand descriptions of the legendary Plain of Jars. Regular prose poems."

"There's no story on the PDJ any more. Just craters in a piece of empty real estate. The only story left in Laos is the bombing. Vang Pao captures the PDJ with massive U.S. air support, and he's about to be pushed off it in spite of massive U.S. air support. There's a factor in that equation that works out to be zero. I'd think the embassy would be interested in studying that question."

"Why?" Casey asked. "Why would we risk finding out that the bombing is useless, when the bombing is all we have left?"

"Interesting idea," the reporter said. "I wonder if that could be it. That would explain why Kissinger doesn't allow coverage of the air war, when the whole world knows it's going on. If reporters went along on air strikes, the stories would make Fat Henry face the truth. That the last card left in his hand only works against civilians—and not even very well against them, if Lindsay is right. Thanks for the idea, Phil."

"You're very welcome, I'm sure. If you quote me, credit it to 'confidential American sources.'"

Upson wondered if this sort of discussion between a government official and a reporter could be normal out here. He felt uneasy, as if he were being made to overhear a conversation that should be private. "You can't see them anymore," he said, to change the subject.

"Who?" asked Casey. "Oh, our explorer scouts. They must be on the other side of the ridge."

"You won't see them for a good long while," Bailey said. "They're trying to walk to Lima Lima, to see if they can spot a real, live CIA case officer."

"There's nobody left at Lima Lima. How the hell did they know it was there, anyway?"

"I told them."

"Thanks a lot, Bill."

"I'm on their side, Phil. Not yours."

"Jesus, don't I know it," Casey said to the reporter. "Look, I don't want to call in a chopper and have it turn out they're just on the other side of the ridge. Would you do a favor for an old man, Bill? Would you hike up to the ridgeline and have a look? If you spot them, hold your arms out to your sides. If they're out of sight, wave your arms over your head so I can radio for a chopper to find them. Okay?"

"Sure."

Bailey took off quickly, in a long stride that was almost a run. "I could have gone," Upson said.

"Why should we do the humping?" said the press attaché. "Bailey feels guilty about getting me in trouble, so let him buy absolution. Won't hurt him. He ran the two-mile at Harvard."

The distant roar of the engines changed its note as the C-130 in the valley began its takeoff roll. The big plane went along and along, looking too slow and heavy to leave the ground. At last it heaved itself into the air. From their angle on the hillside, it looked as if the C-130 would crash into the rising ground at the end of the valley, but the plane kept going and finally the noise died away to a distant buzz. Then the buzz grew louder, and turned into the roar of another C-130, the last of the day, coming in from Vientiane.

"Do you think Bailey will actually do the kind of story you were talking about?" Upson asked. "About how the bombing is ineffective?"

"I don't know. I hope so, though. The *New York Times* is the only way I've got to get a message through to Kissinger and Nixon. Not that they'll pay any attention."

"You could get a message to the ambassador, certainly."

"The ambassador likes the bombing. He likes anything that makes a loud noise."

Upson was surprised, as he had been in the ops meeting, at Casey's willingness to show disloyalty before someone he barely knew. Upson was mildly offended by the press attaché's assumption that they shared a low opinion of the ambassador. The ambassador might not be an intellectual, certainly, but he was a decisive, energetic, and aggressive man in an operational job that required just those qualities. His DCM, Jerry Brautigan, was more than capable of taking up any intellectual slack. Upson thought how lucky he had been to have had so many really first-

24

rate people placed over him in his life: Miss Wray and Mr. Tait in high school, Professor Ward and Dean Jaeger, Chauncey Morrison in the Rabat embassy. Jerry Brautigan was the most impressive of them all—a diplomat capable of both action and reflection, a self-assured Hamlet. And if Brautigan didn't say things about the ambassador behind his back, then Upson wouldn't either.

"Bailey made it to the top," he said instead, seeing the reporter's tiny figure silhouetted against the sky. Bailey was making his way along the ridgeline, stopping now and then to scan whatever was on the other side. At last he turned toward the two men watching him, and waved his arms over his head.

"Damn," the press attaché said. "Let's go find a radio."

It took more than an hour for the helicopter to arrive, to find the four reporters, and to bring them back to the valley. "The last C-130 is long gone," Casey said once the helicopter had taken off and it was quiet enough to talk. "A Porter is coming in a few minutes to haul your asses back to Vientiane, at your expense. The chopper goes on your bill, too. It rents for four hundred fifty bucks an hour."

"We didn't ask to be looked for," Ian Carmichael said.

"Bullshit. You weren't going to spend the night all by yourselves in Indian country. You knew Mommy would come around to pick up after you. Children know that kind of thing instinctively."

"Come on, Phil," the *Boston Globe* reporter said. "We have our jobs to do."

"No, you were just playing a trick on the grownups. Come on, Fred, let's take a walk."

When they were out of the reporters' hearing, Casey stopped. "I wanted to cool off a little," the press attaché said, mopping at his head as if the problem were the just-setting sun. "I only get mad once or twice a year, and I have to be careful I don't go too far. I used to have trouble before I learned to walk away. You know something, Fred? The main trouble with being against this war is the company you have to keep. Can you imagine being lumped in with a collection of assholes like Mary McCarthy, Noam Chomsky, and Ian Carmichael?"

Upson was surprised at this line of thought, and would have asked Casey to pursue it. But he felt he owed it to Brautigan and the ambassador not to show approval of the disloyal Casey, even by entering into an extended conversation with him. It was hard to keep on disliking Casey, though—mainly because the rumpled, sweating, cynical press attaché didn't seem to give a damn whether you did or not.

Enough light to aim by came from inside the house and from the moon. Upson's porch looked over the Mekong, but now in the dry season the river had cut its way out of sight into the sand of the pale and moonlit riverbed, far out. Over on the Thai side, tiny sparkles of light showed from villages hidden in the trees by day.

Upson sat without moving on his porch. The smells of Asia were still new to him—cooking from the nearby houses, unknown flowers out in the hot dark. An acrid scent came from the mosquito coil Somchan had put under his chair before he took up his watch. The smoke from the coil rose straight in the still, heavy night. The mosquitoes came anyway. Whenever Upson saw one land, he moved his free hand very slowly to chase it away. In the dim light, the borrowed pellet gun in his other hand looked real. It was as heavy as a real pistol, and made of the same blued steel. The pistol had to be pumped up after each shot, so that the first shot had to count. Till now, Upson had always missed. The evening before, one of the misses had buried itself almost all the way into a porch rail. Upson had been surprised that the compressed air charge could bury a pellet in such dense, hard wood.

He could hear the music from Somchan's tiny green plastic radio. He had heard Asian music before, in movies and in Chinese restaurants. But to find people really listening to it was still strange, like first hearing children speak a language you have only studied in school. There was no real need for Somchan to stay around in the evening. She could have gone to her maids' quarters behind the house, or to a movie, or done whatever she did with her free time. But he had no way to tell her that, and the truth was he liked having her company.

At last Upson heard the scrabbling sound of the rat, climbing the dry vines that covered the porch pillars. The animal appeared all at once, in a rush, and stopped on the floor a few feet from the railing. Its head moved in nervous little jerks, scanning for danger. Satisfied, the rat moved another few feet and stopped again, heading away from Upson.

Upson lifted the gun very slowly, freezing twice when the rat turned its head. He tried to keep the bobbing front sight in the notch of the rear sight. He could hardly see the gray rat in the gloom. He tried to squeeze the trigger, not jerk it.

The gun went off with its odd, clanging sound. The rat shot straight up into the air and landed on its belly. The animal's shattered nervous system flashed out violent, random signals that made the limbs spasm while the body went nowhere.

"Damn," Upson said. As soon as he saw the hit, he wished he had missed. All he could think of to end the rat's agony was to load the gun again. He was trying to get a new pellet out of the box when Somchan came onto the porch. When she saw the rat, she pointed at the gun and then at Upson, and smiled.

"You number one," she said.

Upson tried to smile back. His fingers fumbled and he dropped a pellet. It rolled along the floor toward the rat, which was still lashing and jerking in torment. Before Upson could reload, Somchan picked up a Thai-English dictionary he had bought so he could show her what he wanted from the morning market. She put one end of the heavy book on the rat's head, put her heel on the other end, and rocked her weight forward, heel to toe. The skull broke with a pop, and the thrashing body went still.

Somchan picked up the rat by its tail and went down the porch steps to the yard. He heard her call out to the family that lived in the tin-roofed shed next door. Then she was telling them something, and at the end everybody laughed. Upson knew they were laughing at her story and not at him. He wondered why he was so sure of that—that she hadn't made them laugh at him.

He remembered Somchan's bare foot, protected from the

rat's teeth by the dictionary. Her toes were slightly splayed and wide at the ends, from going barefoot so long. One day he had gone for a drive and seen dozens of little children jumping off a high bluff into the Mekong where it came up to the Lao bank, further south. They would scramble back to shore like puppies, and climb all brown and gleaming back up the bluff to jump again.

Somchan must have done that once, he thought.

When Somchan came back, she brought a fresh glass of ginger ale to replace the warm, half-empty one that had been sweating a puddle beside Upson during his wait for the rat. He gestured for her to sit down in a chair near his, but she just stood there smiling, unwilling or not understanding. He got to his feet and made her sit down, pressing lightly on her shoulders. He had never touched her before; she felt solid and strong.

"*Chak noi,*" he said, one of the few Lao phrases he knew. It meant, "Wait a minute." He went to the kitchen and made her a glass of ginger ale and ice, like his. When she saw that he had waited on her, she started to get up. But he motioned for her to stay still, the way a photographer does to show his model she is in just the right pose. And she sat there obediently while he went back to his own chair. He wondered why he had waited on her. Was it a naïve democratic gesture, or was it because this seemed to be the proper way for a young man to behave with a young woman?

"Let's talk," he said. "I can tell you about my day at the office, or something. I never knew my father to talk to my mother, not really. Not unless they did it at night, after I went to bed. Never knew him to talk to me, either. Or anybody talk to anybody. Apparently Americans used to be able to. You can see signs of it in some of the literature and correspondence, some of the nineteenth-century stuff. Young men would talk to each other about their ambitions, their love lives, even private things like their fears. They would lay themselves open to each other. Well, that's over. We just don't do it any more.

"But it should be easy to talk to you. You don't understand, after all. You don't, do you? Let me try. Did you know you have lovely dark eyes, miss, and lovely, long, black, thick hair? There's a part in the Bible where a woman dries a man's feet with her long hair. My father would remember. He's a minister, even if he can't talk to his own family. You're passing my test, aren't you? You do nothing but sit there looking pretty and confused when I talk about your lovely eyes and hair. You don't understand a word. We can speak freely, Somchan."

She cocked her head a little when she heard her name, as if trying to make out what he wanted her to do.

"I'll have to watch that, won't I?" Upson said. "I can't use your name, or it would spoil everything. I'll call you Susie. That way we can keep any jarring notes out of our communication, so that it will be purely soothing noise. Did you know we have a bubble at the American embassy, and that it's full of white noise? True. Nobody from the outside can hear anything that's going on inside the bubble. Nobody inside can hear anything from outside, either, although that point wasn't particularly emphasized during my orientation. Anyway, Susie, let me tell you about my day at the office."

Since Upson's arrival in Laos eight weeks before, his days at the office had left him with tired, burning eyes and a headache. Today's headache still lingered a little. He rubbed hard at his eyes and fell silent, remembering his first day at the embassy. Somchan sat quietly, moving only to sip at her ginger ale or brush away a mosquito . . .

The embassy had put him up in the Laan Xang Hotel till his house was ready. The way from there to the embassy took him down Samsenthai Street, where the shops were just opening. Indian merchants stood on the sidewalk outside their stores, very polite, very humble. They all said, "Hello, sir," as Upson walked by. He turned off the business street and onto a smaller dirt road that led to a black, crumbling monument. The hotel clerk had given this to him as a landmark along the way—the *That Dam,* he had called it. The heat was already heavy. A dog lay in the dust near the monument, in the total limpness of death. As Upson walked past, the dog opened an eye, examined him, and let the eye fall shut again.

Just a few more yards down the road was the embassy, an unimpressive three-story structure painted white. The building was windowless, giving it a bunkerlike appearance. But there were no sandbags or sentries with machine guns, or any other sign that Laos was a country at war. An unarmed Indian guard in a blue gray uniform said, "Hello, sir," just like the merchants downtown. Inside, a pretty Lao receptionist took his name and invited him to wait in the small room behind her. A bookcase against one wall was empty except for a set of volumes of the U.S. Code. The waiting room table held back copies of *Time, Newsweek,* the *Bangkok Post,* and the *Far Eastern Economic Review.* Upson had just begun to look the collection over when the receptionist said, "Mr. Brautigan will see you now."

The deputy chief of mission was a big man, with beefy, freckled forearms. His sandy hair was tousled, as if he had just run his hand through it. His face was wide and open and pleasant, the face of an older brother you can always depend on. He smiled when he saw Upson—a smile that somehow made the younger man feel that the DCM wanted nothing more fervently than to welcome him aboard.

"Well, here you are," the DCM said. "Good to see you, Fred."

"Nice to meet you, Mr. Brautigan."

"Jerry. Things are pretty informal here. You'll see most of our people wearing sports shirts to work, with no tie. Here in our office we like to wear ties and slip on a jacket when we go out, but the USAID and military types, hell. As long as they don't frighten the horses. Well, Fred, it's wonderful to see you. We're counting on you to clear up a little problem area in the operation. Did they tell you anything about the job when you went through Washington?"

"Not very much. They said it would be coordinating with the air force, but they didn't go into detail."

"I'll start at the beginning, then. Since 1964, the United States, at the request of the Lao government, has been conducting reconnaissance flights over Laos. These planes are armed, and have the right to return fire if fired upon. For public consumption, that's all we say about our part in the biggest air war in history. Did you know that? Tonnage dropped, missions flown, by any measure you use, the air war in Indochina is bigger than World War II and Korea, put together."

"No, I didn't." Upson thought of the vast airborne armadas in the old World War II newsreels—the ranks of bombers filling the skies, the swarms of fighter planes.

"Anyway," Brautigan went on, "we try to keep a fig leaf on the air war the best way we can, so as not to officially admit to any violations of the Geneva Accords. Both sides have been violating the hell out of the accords since they were signed, but they're still the most viable structure to build a peace on when the time comes. Which, in my private opinion, will be in about two years. Once President Nixon is safely reelected."

"I don't see the connection," Upson said.

"If he ends the war in his first term, the right wings of both parties will see to it he doesn't get a second term. So he's got to keep it going till he gets reelected, and then we'll fold our tents and silently steal away."

"Interesting thesis," Upson said neutrally.

"Not that getting President Nixon reelected matters to me one way or another," the DCM said. "The country of Laos does, though. Wonderful, gentle people, but hopelessly unable to take care of themselves. Thailand on one side and Vietnam on the other, and both of them in the habit of snatching off pieces of Laos whenever they get a chance. So what I'm working toward, Fred, is to see Laos come out of this mess with some kind of internationally guaranteed neutrality and territorial integrity. As far as I'm concerned, that's the whole justification for what we're doing out here. Your job and mine. Everything."

"Um, I see." Upson had learned, from watching his father deal with parishioners of all political persuasions, to listen without offering his own opinion. Later, when he knew more of the political and military background, would be time enough to take sides.

"That's what justifies the agency presence, the military presence," Brautigan continued. "And that's why we need a dominant State Department presence, to keep the military and paramilitary sides of the mission under firm control and channel our overall effort toward diplomatic ends. As the air force liaison officer, you embody that diplomatic presence. The American effort in Laos is run by the ambassador. Not the station chief, not MACV in Saigon or MACTHAI in Bangkok, not some Seventh Air Force general sitting down in Udorn. The ambassador has the responsibility of approving or disapproving every single air strike carried out by U.S. forces in this country. And he exercises that responsibility through you, Fred."

"I see," Upson said, although he didn't yet see at all.

"**B**ut after eight weeks of this," Upson said on the darkened porch, "now I'm beginning to see." The light from the moon left Somchan's features dim. "Susie, my dear, I am the enforcer for something called the 'rules of engagement.' Funny, I never called anyone 'my dear' before. Talking to you is sort of like being the Shadow. When I was a kid, I used to think about how the Shadow could take his clothes off right in the middle of the street and no one would ever know. He could jump up and down in front of the girls and wave it at them if he wanted to. And never worry about whether it was too small.

"Anyway, anyway . . . Under the rules of engagement, Laos is carved up into little patchwork pieces. Here you can bomb, here you can't. Here you can bomb sometimes with some kinds of bombs, but not other times. Over here you can dump your bombs in this patch of empty jungle, if you weren't able to drop them on your target. Apparently the pilots would just as soon not land with a full bomb load, because if there's an accident or a hard landing or something you blow yourself up. So those are the rules of engagement. Funny term, isn't it? You think of two armies coming together, under some sort of minimally civilized rules. No mustard gas and don't shoot the wounded, that kind of thing. But somehow you don't think of somebody dropping a bomb as being engaged with the people down below."

He paused, and Somchan pointed at his empty glass. He waggled his finger at her and made a "tch-tch" noise with his tongue, the way you signified polite refusal in Morocco. Then he thought how absurd that was, as if the noise and gesture would mean anything more to her than Arabic itself. But she seemed to understand. Maybe the French, like him, had brought the mannerism with them from North Africa.

32

"What I do at the office all day, my dear, is approve or disapprove requests for bombing strikes, depending on whether they fall within the rules of engagement, in my mature judgment as a man with one year of ROTC under his belt. Requests for permission to bomb are called 'requirements,' as in 'requirement for air support.' Casey was the one who pointed out to me how the air force manages to load the dice before the game even starts. What reasonable man could refuse permission for a 'requirement'?

"God knows how Casey gets away with saying these things. Nobody seems to mind, no matter how outrageous he gets. Maybe they think he's kidding. Maybe he is, for all I know. A hard man to understand. He's on nobody's side. Not the press's, and not the mission's, either. The other day he said, 'How's the job coming along?' and I said fine. 'Really?' he said. 'My own feeling is that if a job isn't worth doing, it isn't worth doing right.' And then he wandered off. Now what the hell am I supposed to make of that, Susie, my dear?

"The job is worth doing all right, but if Phil asked me how I knew that, I wouldn't dare give him the answer. Which is that I know it's worth doing because Jerry Brautigan says it is, and I trust his moral judgment. Try telling that one to Casey. He'd tell you he understood perfectly, he used to feel the same way about the tooth fairy. Well, the hell with Casey. I'll go with Jerry till something better comes along.

"Still, it's a hard job to do, Susie. I'm the bureaucratic equivalent of Zeus. But the bombing was going on before I came, and it will probably go on after I leave. If I gave the job up, somebody else would just become the bombing officer. Maybe he would be less conscientious about it than I am, and more people would get killed who shouldn't. Or maybe he'd be better. How can I know? What can I do, except keep on working away at it the best I can? And sometimes you win a little bureaucratic victory that might even have saved a few lives, for all you know . . ."

It could be day or night outside, sunny or stormy, but inside Upson's office the fluorescent lights gave off the same cold, flickering illumination and the humming air conditioner kept the temperature at the same 72 degrees. The only opening in the outer wall was the one filled by the air conditioner, which was chained, for security reasons, to bolts inside. The whole office was classified secret, because of the maps of Laos which covered the walls. Overlays showed which areas were unvalidated, partially validated, or fully validated under the rules of engagement. Unvalidated areas were those where there were temples, hospitals, POW camps, friendly troops, inhabited villages. In these, no bombing was allowed. In partially validated areas, the air force needed permission for some types of bombing but not for others. Fully validated areas, mostly along the Ho Chi Minh trail down south, were basically free-fire zones.

The tools of Upson's new trade were the huge Army Map Service topographic maps on the wall, grease pencils, compasses and protractors, files holding photographs and the documents which comprised the rules of engagement, and a large light-table on which to examine the reconnaissance photos. There were crank handles to move the film back and forth and a stereoscopic viewer to make the pictures three-dimensional. He had a small shredder, too, so that he could avoid being buried by the hundreds of classified messages that came to him every day. After-action reports on every strike listed the type of airplane used, the call signs, the time, the weather, ordnance dropped, what the air force believed the target to be, and results of the strike. Other reports gave the location of friendly troops and of teams behind enemy lines. Still others listed what the ground troops—Thai, Meo, Special Guerrilla Units, the Royal Lao Army—needed in the way of air support. Upson filed whatever he thought might be of later use, but most of the paperwork was stuff that would be out-of-date in days or even hours. It went through the shredder, to become billowing piles of paper vermicelli.

Upson had been waiting for the series of photographs on his light-table. They showed several buildings, little more than huts, that he had refused to validate as a target a week before. The strike request had been accompanied by other photographs, showing an indistinct line from one of the structures to the forest nearby. The air force had insisted the line was communications wire, which suggested a military target. Upson thought the line might just as easily be a footpath, in which case the structures might well be active. "Active" meant used by human beings—men, women, children. Nobody bombed or strafed people in the air war. Ordnance was delivered on active structures. The air force described its war in a language which suggested that nothing much, really, was going on at all.

When the air attaché appealed Upson's disapproval of the strike request, the matter came to the ambassador's attention. He directed the air force to take new reconnaissance photos, from a lower altitude—and he bet Colonel Mike Costikyan, the air attaché, twenty dollars that the new pictures would prove Upson was right. At first Upson took this as an uncomplicated expression of support for the home team. Later he wondered if it wasn't the ambassador's way of saying that all his trust was in Upson, and that Upson better, goddamnit, be right when he tangled with the air force.

Upson looked away from the stereoscopic viewer for a moment to rest his eyes, and then examined the photos again. What he saw relieved him enormously; the twenty-dollar bet had raised a minor difference of interpretation to policy level. Since he had good news to deliver, he walked the few steps to the ambassador's office instead of phoning. He found the ambassador where he often was—contemplating the pins and unit flags on the war map that covered one wall of his office. "I just got the photos we asked for last week, Mr. Ambassador," Upson said. "No doubt about it this time. Couldn't possibly be communications wire."

"That's my boy," the ambassador said. "Listen, Mike is coming over on something else in an hour. Have the secretary let you know when he comes, okay? And then you just wander in by accident with the photos. We'll teach him to fuck with the Lone Ranger."

"**I** guess that was a victory, anyway," Upson said to Somchan, sitting there in the dimness. "State Department One, Air Force zip, the way the ambassador saw it. Villagers one, Air Force zip, the way I guess I saw it. Not that it wasn't fun seeing Costikyan pay over the twenty bucks. He's kind of a domineering type, and it was fun to see him dominated.

"Well, this must be fascinating for you, Susie, my dear. All this gossip. But what about you? Tell me about yourself. You can't, of course, but maybe you could express a general attitude by purring or something. Think how pleasant an animal's life must be. Most of the things that divide people would be gone without language, wouldn't they? You couldn't very well have a war unless somebody told you who to hate. And you wouldn't know whether anybody was more charming or boring, or dumb or smart, than anybody else. You couldn't tell whether people were upper-class or lower-class, native or foreign. I guess nobody would be pretty or homely any more, would they? There'd be no way for everybody to agree on which was which."

Upson remembered that his father had once preached a sermon on the text, "And now nothing will be restrained from them, which they have imagined to do." It was from the Genesis story of the tower of Babel, and his father had used it to lead into a discussion of the atom bomb, on the theory that physicists, by developing a common language, had been able to intrude into God's province. God had had the right idea when he confounded the language of all the earth, Upson thought, but perhaps he hadn't gone far enough. Perhaps he should have struck us all dumb.

"Well, enough foolishness," Upson said. "Time to go to bed."

The pain hit him like an electric shock when he moved to get up. He sat there leaning slightly forward, not daring to budge for fear it would come back. Sitting for so long in one position had caused it—the long wait for the rat. The back pain was in the same place it always hit, over near the spine and just above the right hip. He got up from his chair as carefully as an old man, but still the pain flashed through him once before he got fully to his feet. He gasped and stopped, and then was able to straighten up all the way. Somchan made a little cry of sympathy and came over to help him.

"It's okay now," he said. "I can get around all right once I'm up. It's just getting from sitting to standing. Damn, damn, damn." From the severity of the first spasm, he knew he was in for a week or more of pain, with the worst of it coming tomorrow and the day after.

Somchan was trying to explain something to him, but of course he could understand nothing but the concern and sympathy in her voice. She was gesturing toward his back, and making other gestures he couldn't follow. Finally she beckoned him toward the bedroom. He walked without moving his torso, as if he were balancing something on his head. He sat down in the same careful way, on the bed where she indicated. "Off with the shirt?" he asked, in reply to a gesture of hers. He was shy about taking his shirt off in front of people, because he didn't think much of his physique. But he did it, and then eased himself carefully onto his stomach as she seemed to want him to do.

Somchan got on top of him, her knees straddling his hips. He felt her fingers brush here and there over his back, as if studying how it was put together. The fingers stopped when they came to the place where the pain was, and probed very delicately. Upson wondered how she could have found precisely the right spot without being told. Perhaps the muscles had knotted, and felt different. The middle of his body was held tight under her warm weight. Her strong hands began to work on his shoulders, and then the upper part of his back, and finally down each vertebra and to the lower back where the pain was. She used her knuckles and her thumbs hard, almost hurting him. She seemed to be separating each muscle out, working it till it was loose, and laying it back into place again. All the while her hands kneaded and pressed, Somchan was talking softly. Upson lay like the dead, his muscles all unstrung, as her voice went on.

He was half asleep when the voice and the hands both stopped. Then all of a sudden she tickled him under the ribs, saying a word at the same time, and her warm weight was gone from him. She switched off the light by the bedroom door and

37

stood for a moment silhouetted in the doorway. Her head inclined, and Upson guessed she was making a *wai*, the Lao bow of respect, with joined hands. Then she giggled like a little girl and ran off. Upson heard her pulling the back door firmly shut so it would lock, on her way out to her quarters. He took his pants off carefully and went to sleep almost at once, feeling content.

His back stiffened up overnight, but it was better next morning than he had thought it would be. Somchan nodded and smiled when he tried to get that fact across to her. The embassy car arrived for him just as he was finishing the boiled eggs, toast, and coffee she had made. From the door, he said, "So long, Somchan." The girl said the same word she had said the night before and then laughed with her hand over her mouth, as if surprised at her own boldness.

In the car, Upson asked the driver, "What does *nakadiem* mean?"

"Oh, Lao word," the driver said. "Mean ticklish. Thai people say *chakati*, Lao people say *nakadiem*."

The political section was to the left of the embassy entrance; straight ahead, stairs led to the second floor, where the CIA had its offices; to the right was the suite of offices the ambassador shared with the DCM, Upson, and two secretaries. The ambassador's secretary, Louise Bogan, was small, frightened, and shy. The DCM's secretary, Annie Cutler, was unafraid of the ambassador, the DCM, or anybody else. She had an air of being secretly amused by all men.

"Good morning, Fred," Annie said. "Now that you're here, the First Team is complete." The ambassador liked to refer to the two thousand Americans assigned to the mission as the First Team, smaller than the U.S. Mission in Saigon, but more selective. In Morocco, as a junior political officer, Upson had only seen his ambassador at occasional meetings, fleetingly in receptions, or now and then in the embassy halls. But here he worked directly every day with both the ambassador and the DCM—not just on the team, but almost one of the coaching staff. He had seen very quickly that certain people in the embassy were insiders, and part of things, while others weren't. If you were in, the other people who were in spoke to you a little bit differently. There was an assumption of shared secrets and shared viewpoints. On the inside were the ambassador, Jerry Brautigan, Upson himself, the CIA station chief and his top staff, the army and air attachés and their ranking officers; on the outside were the U.S. Information Service, the Agency for International Development, and the political section—which, in a peacetime embassy, would have been the most inside of all. These were the general outlines, although there were many individual exceptions. A man like Dick Lindsay was in both camps. Some of the CIA analysts were closer in attitudes to the political section than they were to the case officers in the field.

Upson began to go through the mail in his box. "You didn't happen to see a big envelope from AIRA, did you?" he asked Annie Cutler. AIRA was the air attaché, Colonel Mike Costikyan.

"No, I didn't. What's he supposed to send over?"

"A batch of photos. There was a strike a couple of days ago that I had some doubts about, but I let it go through because the AIRA guys said their intelligence was exceptionally good on the thing. Afterwards, Colonel Costikyan said they got a whole bunch of secondary explosions and so I asked them to send over the poststrike photography for me to take a look at. He said somebody would hand-carry them over yesterday afternoon, and they're still not here."

"I wouldn't hold my breath till they come, Fred."

"Why not?"

"Well, when Gus Thompson had your job, he used to ask for the poststrike photos all the time, and mostly they'd get lost in transit, or they'd lose them down in Udorn, or there was no film in the camera, or they forgot to take the lens cap off."

"Do they have lens caps on wing cameras?"

"I don't know. I just know there'd always be something."

Back at his desk, Upson telephoned the air attaché's office. "AIRA ops," a voice answered. "Pierpoint speaking."

"Good morning, Sarge. Fred Upson."

"Yes, sir. What can I do for you this fine morning?"

"I just wondered what happened to those poststrike photos I thought you guys were sending over to me yesterday, Sarge."

"Yes, sir. Well, let me inquire of the colonel on that, and we'll get back to you."

"Appreciate it, Sarge."

Colonel Costikyan called twenty minutes later. "Goddamnit, Fred," he said, "how they hangin' anyway?"

The first time, Upson had been surprised by the colonel's greeting, but by now he was used to it. "Just fine, Mike," he said. "How about you?"

"They're dragging, boy, dragging. I went by Loulou's last night to get my pipes cleaned out, then some of us sat around the ARMA house telling lies till two A.M. What can I do for you? Oh, I remember. The poststrike photos. Listen, I can't send them over because we don't have them, and the reason we don't have them is because we're dumb sons of bitches, is what we are. The guys on that one went back on another pass, for the poststrike photos, and they said it was like the Fourth of July. Must have been an ammo dump under those hooches. Secondary explosions all over the place, fires, the works. Shit was still blowing up when they turned for home. Then son of a bitch if they don't find out next day the goddamn camera had misfunctioned. The guys were really pissed."

"I can see where they would be."

"The humidity gets to those goddamn cameras. The fact is they aren't worth a shit, anyway. I could strap a Kodak onto the goddamn wing and take pictures better than you can with the shit they give us for cameras. Anyway, I'm sorry as hell, Fred. I'll chew a little ass down there and we'll try to do better next time."

"No sweat, Mike. It happens."

No sweat, Mike. It happens. As soon as the words were out of his mouth, Upson felt silly. Had things come to the point where he was trying to sound like Mike Costikyan?

"Did you ever run down those photos you were after?" Annie Cutler asked Upson later in the morning.

"They had a camera misfunction."

"Surprise, surprise."

"Colonel Costikyan said they have problems with the cameras in this humidity."

"Oh, it's terrible. This humidity."

"What did Thompson used to do?"

"He'd call and bitch all the time, ask them why they couldn't get him a simple photo. They loved him over at the AIRA office, all right. Once he told Colonel Costikyan he was going down to Udorn and tie a Kodak onto the wings."

Upson went back to his light-table, disturbed. He didn't want to think that the air attaché might be lying to him. Weren't they on the same team? The stereoscopic viewer tired his eyes, the way the microscope had during biology class. But the worst of the eyestrain and the headache wouldn't come until later in the day. From the photos, Upson tried to imagine what the jungles and mountains might look like from the ground. Through the viewer the jungle looked like an endless bed of broccoli flowerets. Was the forest green at this time of year? Or was it like the trees around Vientiane, whose leaves had lost their greenness and were dulled with dust? There were tigers out where the planes flew. These were supposed to be good times for tigers, Upson had heard. They fed on the bodies after the battles. These were supposed to be bad times for tigers, he had also heard. Now the villagers could go hunting with AK-47s and M-16s, instead of muzzleloaders and crossbows. Sometimes Upson could see water buffalo in the reconnaissance photos. Dick Lindsay claimed that General Vang Pao's guerrillas had rustled more than twenty-five hundred buffalo during Operation About Face, the government's conquest of the Plain of Jars.

Upson forced himself back to contemplation of the photo in front of him. He noted the eight-digit coordinates of the target area, and went over to locate them on the wall map—checking one representation of reality against another. Then he checked them against the lines of the map overlay, which represented no real thing at all, but only the areas where bombs could be dropped or not dropped under the rules of engagement. The strike request fell well within a validated zone, and so he sent it along with his approval. An occasional request would be for an invalidated zone, but those were no trouble to handle. Upson merely refused to sign off on them, and attached a note giving his reason. He never heard back from AIRA on any of them. The requests were just quietly withdrawn, unless they were slipped in again later and got by him. This was possible, since the flow was so great every day that the best he could do was spot-check, more or less at random. But he didn't think it happened.

The disputes came over questions of interpretation. Was a village inhabited or not? The Lao built "day huts" in fields far from the village, to lie up in during the heat of the day. Were these little structures, hardly more than lean-tos, villages under rules of engagement that defined a village as one or more structures? Was that smudge on a photo smoke from a cooking fire, or a shadow? Was that broken shape, partly visible through the trees, a *wat* or an ammunition dump? Upson studied till the images began to blur, and then closed his eyes to rest them for a few minutes.

When he opened them, Phil Casey was standing in the door. "Don't let me interrupt your nap," the press attaché said. "I just stuck my head in to say hello."

"I need more than a nap," Upson said. "This damned job is driving me blind. What brings you over here, Phil?"

"I'm playing nursemaid for Harrison Bottsford."

"The columnist?"

"That's the one. He's over taking a firsthand look at his little war. At the moment, the ambassador's filling in his old Skull and Bones pal, or whatever the equivalent is at Princeton. They both graced the class of 1939."

"I thought you were supposed to sit in on all interviews."

"That's a safeguard. Simmonds doesn't need a safeguard when he's among friends, guys like Alsop, Shaplen, Evans and Novak. He wouldn't want me sitting around and watching while they're making ideological love. Actually, I'm surprised they bothered to tell me Bottsford was in town. Usually the ambassador picks guys like him up at the airport and carries them straight out to the residence. Next day he flies them up to Long Cheng so they can see an honest-to-God, secret CIA base, and the first I know about it all is a few days later when the real reporters pick up on it and start to beat on my head about the preferential treatment. And I look like an asshole once again."

"Must help your credibility with the press, all right."

"Actually it does. The real reporters figure if the ambassador doesn't trust me, I can't be all bad. Besides, they know he hands the same shit out to Bottsford he does to them. They know it because Bottsford, unlike them, will print it. The only difference is that, with a warlover, the ambassador admits the CIA is here. He even lets them meet a couple of real case officers up at 20-Alternate. For an Ivy League intellectual of Bottsford's particularly repellent type, Green Berets and case officers are the equivalent of rough trade."

Upson smiled at Casey's notion. He could never make out, though, whether the bald press attaché was bitter and defeated, or defiant and undefeated. "It's obviously none of my business, Phil," Upson said, "but I'll ask anyway. Feeling as strongly as you do, why don't you ask for reassignment?"

"Because I can't afford to go back to Washington. I pay alimony and child support. I've got two kids in college and another who needs special care. The only way I can keep the payments up is to stay overseas where I get free rent, hardship pay, cost of living allowance, and the living is cheap."

"I'm sorry. It was none of my business."

"Don't feel sorry for me. I knew what I was looking for when I quit the newspaper business eighteen years ago to work for USIS. And mostly I got it."

Upson was uneasy at the personal turn the conversation was taking, and moved to change the subject. "The thing that seems to me to justify our presence here," he said, "is that the country would fall to the North Vietnamese in six months if we left."

"Are you kidding?" the press attaché said. He went over to one of Upson's maps and began pointing, like a briefing officer. "Here's the Tha Tam Bleung area, just north of Long Cheng. Here's Sam Thong. Here's the 335th North Vietnamese Regiment. Here's the 866th. Here's the 312th. Here's the 316th. Maybe twelve thousand men altogether. Here's what's left of our tigers. Task Force Alpha. Bravo. Charlie. Echo. Eleven- and twelve-year-old kids, a lot of them, not even as tall as their rifles. I wouldn't give Laos six months, without American support. More like six weeks."

"But you can't want to see that happen. Can you, Phil?"

"I'd hate like hell to see it happen. And if we were going to garrison this place forever, I'd say fine. There are worse things than being an American colony. Being a Vietnamese colony, for instance. But the fact is we're going to get out of here sooner or later, and leave these people helpless. The quicker we do it, the fewer people get killed."

"You can't be sure, Phil. Maybe the bloodbath people aren't right, but what if they are?"

"If there's going to be a bloodbath, it'll happen whether we leave two weeks from now or two years from now."

Upson sat wondering after the press attaché had gone. Casey made him think of a glib, sarcastic college classmate who had been editor of the college paper and was now in the movie business, a producer-director whose name was in the papers. The refugee worker, Dick Lindsay, reminded Upson of a boy a year ahead of him in high school who had been president of the senior class and had later gone to Alaska to work as a geologist. Upson would have liked to be friends with both boys, but he didn't move in their circles.

Now Upson felt he was being courted, for some reason he couldn't make out—both by Lindsay and by Casey. Even Annie Cutler, the DCM's secretary, seemed to be after him to do something. What they all wanted wasn't clear to Upson, except that it had to do with his job. They seemed to think that Gus Thompson had taken the right approach to the job, although Upson didn't see that his own approach was much different. If he turned down so many requests that his office became a bottleneck, he would only be squeezed out of the job. And the next man might be much worse. Upson thought of Hartz and Mears, in his class at the Foreign Service Institute. Once men like that discovered that the judgment of the bombing officer could only come into question if he turned down a strike request, they would take the safe course of approving practically everything.

Voices came from the hall, and the ambassador opened the door. Harrison Bottsford was with him. The columnist was a narrow-shouldered man with a boneless look, much older than his picture in the paper. He had the face of a divinity student grown old and sour, his soft little mouth turned nasty.

"Harrison," the ambassador said, "I'd like you to meet Fred Upson. Fred keeps the air force honest for me. He's new with us, but he's going to be all right."

"I'm sure he will."

"Fred won me twenty bucks off Mike Costikyan, my air attaché. I bet Mike a twenty-dollar bill his guys were wrong and Fred was right about interpreting a recon photo."

"You've got a very responsible job, Fred," the columnist said.

"Yes, sir."

"And I'm sure you do it very well."

"I'm really still learning, sir."

"Good manners, too. I like that in a young man."

Annie Cutler came to the door. "Mr. Ambassador," she said, "Louise has finally got through to 20-Alternate. The reception has been so bad this morning that I thought you'd want to be interrupted, now that she has a decent connection at last."

"I better take it, Harrison," the ambassador said; "20-Alternate is Long Cheng. Be right back."

"Now tell me all about what you do, Fred," Bottsford said when the ambassador had gone.

"Essentially, I monitor air force activities in Laos for the ambassador. The way the operation is structured organizationally . . ."

"Is there something wrong with your back?"

"It's a little sore, yes."

"I thought so, from the way you moved just then."

"It's a chronic thing. Comes and goes."

"Don't I know. Lower back pain, I've had it for years. Massage is the only thing. I have this marvelous man back in Washington who comes in and does me. He came over with the Swedish ambassador years ago, and liked Washington so much he just stayed on. Of course, you don't get the real therapeutic massage over here."

"No, I suppose . . ."

"Not that there isn't plenty of massage of a certain type. I imagine you've been to the famous massage parlors of Bangkok?"

"No, actually I haven't . . ."

"Not that you'd have to. I'm sure you manage to find plenty of interested young ladies among the embassy secretaries . . ." The columnist stopped and changed tone. "Ah, the good ambassador, back already. Are we all set for Long Cheng then, Buck?"

"We've got a Helio standing by out at the airport."

"Good, fine."

"I told the guys up at Alternate they didn't have to stand down."

"Stand down?"

"Normally we stand down when there are journalists in the

area. All my round-eyes stop their support activities and make themselves invisible for a while. But there's no sense cleaning everything up when it's just family, I told the guys."

"No, of course not. I'd like to talk to some of them, anyway. Well, goodbye, Fred. I'm sorry I have to run off, but Buck is a hard taskmaster. Maybe someday we can sit down together and finish our little chat."

When they had gone, Upson looked in on Annie Cutler. "What does the *B* in the ambassador's name stand for?" he asked.

"Bruce. The full name is Bruce Kingdon Simmonds."

"This guy Bottsford called him Buck."

"It's from the *B. K.* I always figured that's why he used his initials in his signature."

"I never heard the 'Buck' before."

"All his old friends call him Buck. Mr. Brautigan calls him Buck when there's no one around. Maybe someday he'll tell you to call him Buck."

"Did he tell Thompson to?"

"Gus? You've got to be kidding." Just then a pain hit Upson, making him draw his breath in sharply. "Something wrong?" Annie Cutler asked.

"My back went out last night."

"You should go home and rest."

"No use. It lasts three or four days no matter what I do."

The back got worse through the afternoon, and he did leave a half-hour early. Back home, Somchan said things that sounded sympathetic. While he was eating the frozen dinner she had heated for him, she sat outside on the landing of the kitchen stairs. She was eating something wrapped in a banana leaf. She never seemed to sit down to a proper meal, but always had something around to nibble on.

Somchan hurried to him when she saw he was beginning to get up from the table. She took his arm while he straightened up cautiously and helped him into the bedroom. She led him over to the bed, took off his shirt and shoes, and all the while she was chattering away, just as if he understood every word. This must be how a baby feels, he thought. A warm, friendly, incomprehensible noise, and clever, strong hands to undress you for bed. She alarmed him by undoing the top button of his pants as well, but she stopped there and made him turn over on his stomach. Her hands began to work the pain away from his spasmed muscle, to spread it out and finally to dissipate it until only soreness was left. Her strong hands kept working. She moved up to his neck and shoulders, and then to his arms; she pulled his loosened pants down a little and massaged the base of his spine. He felt her warm weight on the back of his thighs as she worked, and he grew slowly hard. He was glad he was on his stomach, so that she wouldn't notice.

But then she shifted off him and rolled him over, so smoothly and naturally that he didn't think to stop himself from turning. She saw right away what had happened to him, and she did a thing so unexpected that he forgot to be embarrassed.

She laughed. The laugh included him, as if he must see the joke, too. Then she barely touched him there with the tip of one finger for an instant, the way she might have touched an iron to see if it was hot. And she giggled, a little girl who had done something daring. Upson looked up, at first too astonished to move. She was flushed from the work of massaging him; tendrils of short, fine hair stuck to her forehead and temples. "Som-chan," he whispered, "you're beautiful." He reached for her hands, but quick as a cat she was out of his grasp and standing by the bed still laughing, daring him to come get her. Then she seemed to remember that he couldn't, and her expression changed from playfulness to sympathy. She moved back toward him, turning off the light by the bed.

He heard the rustle of cloth in the dark. He was trying to work his way out of his pants without hurting his back when he felt her hands on his clothing, and then on him. All he could see of her in the sudden darkness was a dim shape as she lowered herself on top of him in the effortless way Lao women had of sinking into a crouch. He felt her guiding fingers on him. She had become excited from the massage, too, because she was wet and smooth. He reached up and found that she had taken off only her sarong. She still wore her blouse and her sturdy brassiere. When he went to move with her, she made him lie still while she rose and sank, slowly and then faster and faster. It was longer than he had ever lasted with a woman when he felt the tension build in him and spend itself convulsively. She felt it, too. She moved even faster, till in a moment she threw her head back and made a small, mewing sound. The girl settled down on him all the way and sat still while her breathing slowed. Then she slipped off the bed.

"Somchan, don't go," he said, reaching in the dark.

She touched his cheek. *"Pai nawn,"* she said. *"Taan bo sabai."* He saw her standing in the doorway, as she had the night before, and then she was gone. He lay there in wonder, repeating her words to himself so that he could ask tomorrow what they meant.

Phil Casey stood on the levee in front of Upson's house, stalling because he was on his way to do something he didn't want to do. The light in Upson's bedroom window had gone out twenty minutes before—only a little after nine o'clock. Casey wondered how anybody could get to sleep so early, but clearly he couldn't very well drop in on Upson. Visiting Upson had only been a passing idea anyway, and not a very good one. The press attaché couldn't have explained what he happened to be doing in the neighborhood without saying that he lived in it, just a few hundred feet away. But only a handful of Americans—Dick Lindsay and one or two Air America pilots—knew about Casey's living arrangements. There was no reason for the whole world to know that he was living in an old-style Lao house, hidden in the trees, with a French-Vietnamese woman who had been a bargirl in the old Vieng Ratry when he found her three years ago. The reasons Casey had given Upson for not wanting to leave Laos were real ones, but Claudine was the biggest reason. At fifty-three, he knew perfectly well that she was the last young woman he would ever live with. And he couldn't take her back to America, because he knew just as well that she would leave him if he did. She was fond of him, he was pretty sure, and she was certainly kind to him. But it would be too much to expect a beautiful thirty-two-year-old woman, back in the land of the big PX, to stay with an old, fat, broke and bald pensioner just because he loved her.

48

Casey lit a cigarette from his third pack of the day and turned to look across the sandy bed of the Mekong, silvery in the moon, at the scattering of lights on the Thai side. Over there, the villagers terraced the river banks every dry season and planted vegetables, carrying up the water for them bucket by bucket. Then they ferried the vegetables across and sold them in the markets of Vientiane. Here on the Lao side there was no terracing, no gardens, nothing but steep, bare banks down to the dry riverbed. This was supposed to show that the Thai were hard workers and natural businessmen, while the Lao were affable idlers. Casey didn't know whether it showed this, or what it showed. "But at least I know the limitless extent of my ignorance," he said, half-aloud. He flipped his unfinished cigarette off into the dark and went to do what he had to do. Or had agreed to do, to be brutally accurate.

He turned left a few blocks above the Laan Xang Hotel, up an unmarked and unlighted street of small wooden houses. The White Rose was a little larger than the others, with a single line of Christmas-tree lights strung across the front. If Casey liked a visiting newsman and felt like showing him the town, he would start the tour here. Every American journalist in Southeast Asia knew about the White Rose, where a tall, Thai bargirl named Aw did the dance of the eleven cigarettes for four dollars. Casey went through the door into a large, dimly lit room with a service bar at the far end. The walls were of bamboo matting, varnished dark brown. A bargirl was dancing naked for a group of Frenchmen in one corner. In one of the booths, another naked girl was sitting on an American's lap, keeping time with the music by slapping him softly in the face with her breasts, back and forth. Casey walked all the way to the rear of the room looking at the customers on one side, and then walked back toward the front looking at everybody on the other. As far as he could tell in the semi-darkness, there was nobody he knew in the place. And so that was all right, at least. He didn't want anybody he knew to wander outside and spot him at what he was about to do. He nodded goodnight to the Vietnamese woman who ran the White Rose, and went back out into the street.

Three of the pedicabs called *samlors* were parked outside, in the green and blue and red light of the Christmas-tree bulbs. The drivers, identically dressed in straw hats, cheap cotton shirts, shorts, and high sneakers, were smoking and talking with a young woman who wore heavy make-up.

"Samlor, sir?" one of the men asked. "Number one, cheap-cheap."

"No, thanks, I'm walking," Casey said in poor Lao. He had tried to get Claudine to teach him the language, but they hadn't got far. It was hard work for him at his age, and they both spoke French.

"I'm looking for a woman," Casey went on. "Do you know any?"

This made the three men laugh, as he had known it would. One of them pointed to the tall girl with them. "Doesn't she look like a woman?" he asked, and everyone laughed again. Casey told the girl that there was an old man at the Laan Xang Hotel, as old as himself but not so fat, who was looking for a woman like her. Did she like old men? She was very fond of old men, she said, and everybody laughed again. The samlor drivers offered to take them to the hotel, but Casey said they would walk. It was only a few blocks, and he was damned if he'd spend even a nickel of his own money on this business. They walked in silence to the hotel.

Casey nodded at the desk clerk, whom he had known for a long time. The press attaché took the woman upstairs to the room number the deputy chief of mission had given him. He knocked more heavily than he had to, hoping to be mistaken for a cop, and waited.

Harrison Bottsford, dressed in a red silk robe with gold dragons on it, opened the door. "Why, hello, Mr. Casey," he said. There was a tiny pause in his voice, a barely perceptible change of gears when he caught sight of the woman behind the press attaché. "Oh, I didn't mean for *you* to bother yourself with this," the columnist went on. "Jerry could have just got one of the embassy drivers to do it."

"He probably didn't want it to get around among the local employees," Casey said. "There could be a misunderstanding. Conceivably."

"Yes, I guess there could be," Bottsford said. "Well, anyway, thank you for your trouble, Mr. Casey."

"No trouble, Mr. Bottsford." Casey was pleased to see the columnist's expression tighten with irritation at the mimicry, and then smooth out as he presumably realized he was in no position to indulge his famous temper. "One thing I should tell you," Casey went on. "She's expecting a little present for the interview."

"Of course. I expected that, too."

In Lao, Casey told the girl to go on in, that the old man was rich and would pay her plenty.

"What was that you told her?" Bottsford asked.

"I said you were an important journalist, and it was okay to answer all your questions honestly. Even if they were about the police or local laws or something, she could speak freely. Because nobody would ever know she had been interviewed by you. Except me."

"I see," Bottsford said slowly. "Well, good night, then."

"And a very good night to you."

It should have been funny, Casey thought as he went back downstairs. It should have been funny when the bastard's lips tightened and his eyes went narrow and he looked like a vicious rabbit, wanting to attack but helpless. Casey walked heavily down the stairs and up to the desk.

"You know that girl I just took upstairs, Deng?" he asked. "She *is* a *khateui*, isn't she?"

"Oh, yes. I thought you knew."

"I thought I did, too, but I just wanted to be sure."

Casey went to the rear of the lobby and out a little door which led to the hotel's garden and swimming pool. He sat in one of the poolside chairs and looked at the absolutely still water and at the huge, fan-shaped palms, black against the moon.

Jerry Brautigan had telephoned him to come over toward the end of the afternoon and he went, wondering. Most of the time, neither the DCM nor the ambassador paid much attention to the press attaché's functions. The ambassador was happy as long as the press was kept away from him; the DCM figured reporters came with the territory, like mosquitos, and nobody could do much to keep them from biting. Casey found the DCM at his desk, scratching at his sandy hair as if he were totally baffled by the papers in front of him. "Sit down, Phil," Brautigan said. "I'm almost finished here." He ran down a column of figures, making checks here and there with a black, government-issue ballpoint that looked tiny in his big, freckled hand.

"There," he said. "Out of the way for a few weeks, anyway. Till I get the final estimates back. Phil, you can thank your lucky stars you're not somebody's deputy. The real purpose of having a deputy is so you can make him do the budget instead of you."

Casey smiled and said nothing. They both knew that the true power in any bureaucracy lay with the man who controlled the budget. "I wonder if you could help me with something, Phil," the DCM went on. "You know those Lao transvestites, what do they call them?"

"Khateui."

"Right. Anyway, Harrison Bottsford thought they might make a feature story. Local color, or something. He wants to interview one before he leaves the country tomorrow on the early flight."

"Well, why doesn't he?"

"He doesn't know how to go about finding one."

"Tell him anything standing outside the White Rose after dark that looks like a woman, isn't."

"He's afraid it might be misunderstood. And he's kind of a public personality, after all."

"But nobody would recognize me? Is that it?"

"Come on, Phil. It's in all of our interests to make him happy. He can do a lot for the cause back in Washington. Not just through his column, but on the Hill and in the White House. I can't tell you to do it, Phil, and I won't. I'm asking you as a favor because you're the only one who really knows his way around the town that I can trust on something like this. You can do it with discretion."

"Oh, I can do it," Casey said, and paused to consider it for a moment. "In fact, I even think I will."

"That's terrific. He'll be in Room 108 at the Laan Xang all evening. Listen, I really appreciate this."

"Did Bottsford tell the ambassador about his feature story idea, Jerry?"

"No, he didn't want to bother him with it."

"I'll bet he didn't. They were probably in the same dining club at Princeton."

Brautigan came out from behind his desk and clasped Casey's shoulder with his big hand. "Listen, Phil," he said, "thanks again."

52

"Any time. Want me to round up an interpreter, too? You know, for the interview?"

"Phil, leave an old man with his illusions."

"I'm the old man, not you. And I haven't got any."

Not quite true of course, the press attaché thought as he sat by the pool at the Laan Xang. For example I have the illusion that I am an agent who has penetrated the establishment, whereas I have probably been turned by it long since. Casey got heavily to his feet and went over to the left of the pool, over by the garden's edge where a cage was hidden in the shadows. The cage held one of the small black bears that lived in the mountains of Laos. The chunky animal was lying on its side. Its head moved a little as it picked up Casey's approach.

"Well, bear," Casey said. "How do you like it in that goddamned cage?"

Upson was still awake, too full of questions to sleep. His limited experience of women had always before been spoiled in one way or another. The women were parting reluctantly with something of great value, so that a great debt had been created. Or they had the air of doing something that they didn't really want to do, to accommodate his unwholesome demands. He had made them drink too much, and so had taken advantage of them. Or his great charms had made them lose their helpless heads, which was nonsense. Upson was under no illusions as to his charms, which were average. So were the girls he had slept with. He had never, until Somchan, succeeded with a really attractive woman. Always, until Somchan, he had associated the process with regrets, recriminations, tears, inadequacy, incompetence, passivity, anxiety. There had never been anything natural or unforced or—and it came to him that this was the important thing—innocent about it. Perhaps he had done so well, for once, because she had taken him by surprise before he had time to get worried. She made it seem simple and friendly, part of the treatment and nothing that anybody could possibly get worried about. There had been heavy breathing and moans and thrashing around with women in the past, but he suspected that they were put on for his benefit—possibly to get him to stop. Yet this time he was sure that Somchan's little cry had meant a true orgasm. Was it possible for a woman to wait for a man the way she had, though, and then make herself come?

But most of all, he wondered why she had done it. What could she have seen in him? Was it just a social gesture in Laos, something that meant very little? Was it to cheer up an invalid, like a get-well card or a box of candy? How should he act toward her tomorrow? How would she act toward him?

At last he went to sleep.

Next morning, Somchan acted exactly as she did every morning. She gave no hint that anything at all had happened between them. He guessed he was glad of that—except for the fear that it might mean last night had been an accident not to be repeated. He was going to ask the motor pool driver the meaning of the words she had said on leaving his bed, in case there might be a clue in them. But then he thought that they might mean something intimate and that it would be better to ask Annie Cutler at the office. She would know basic phrases from the Lao lessons she was taking, but would be unlikely to know any endearments.

"Pai nawn, taan bo sabai?" Annie repeated when he asked her. "It means, 'Go to sleep, you're sick.' "

"That's all? You're sure?"

"That's all. *Pai nawn* is what my maid always says when she puts Johnny down for his nap."

Annie Cutler was divorced, with a four-year-old son.

Phil Casey was giving Upson a ride to the Brautigans' Christmas Eve party. Back home in Pawling, New York, Upson thought, the moon would be glistening off the snow in the fields. The fencerows and forest would be black, and the old, gentle hills of Dutchess County would bristle with a stubble of bare trees. The shops would be open late, with Christmas carols playing. Houses, stores, and evergreens would be hung with the blue, green, red, and yellow lights.

Here the banana trees and the palms were still green, but it was an old, dusty green. The lawn in front of the deputy chief of mission's residence was a brighter green, kept alive into the dry season by a sprinkler system that ran all night. The drops of water sparkled in the flickering light of smudgepots set on poles all around the lawn. Two mission guards in blue gray uniforms were posted at the entrance to open car doors.

"Hi, Sergeant Bounlek," Casey said to one of them—a big man for an Asian, so solidly built that he seemed to be on the point of exploding his uniform.

"Hi, boss," the guard answered.

"That's Mancuso's pet gorilla," Casey said. "You know Mancuso, the idiot who runs the mission guard service? 'Hi, Boss,' is all the English he knows. Maybe it's all he knows in any language. Fine figure of a man, huh? That's another difference between us and the countries that understand colonialism. The French wouldn't guard the DCM's residence with a couple Thais dressed in uniforms that look like work clothes from J. C. Penney's. They'd have a couple of goddamned six-foot Senegalese, with tribal scars and red tunics and sabers."

The DCM's wife had come out of the door to greet them. "Phil," she said, "I'm so glad you could come. And Fred Upson. We met at the Costikyans the other week."

"Good evening, Mrs. Brautigan. Thanks very much for having me."

"Jane, for heaven's sake."

"I see your Christmas orchids are out," the press attaché said.

"Aren't they lovely? Last year they didn't come out until after Christmas, and I was so disappointed. Do you know about the Christmas orchids, Fred?"

"I'm afraid I don't, no."

"These here," Casey said. "They're sort of the local equivalent of holly."

A plant with broad, straplike leaves was growing at eye level on the smooth trunk of a tree beside the door. It was anchored by roots as thick as a pencil, flattened against the bark like blunt-

55

tipped tentacles several feet long. Three heavy sprays of blue blossoms hung from the base of the leaves.

"Just smell them," Jane Brautigan said. "Aren't they divine? They bloom every year, around Christmas. The poinsettias are beautiful this year, too."

Upson suddenly realized that the tall, ungainly bushes he was looking at were huge versions of the red-leaved plants he had only seen in pots. Mrs. Brautigan moved away to greet some other guests, and Casey said, "Christmas orchids, can you fucking imagine? What a great country! Once I went to the Independence Day celebration at the South Vietnamese embassy, and the Royal Lao Army Band was playing *'Tiens, voilà du boudin,'* the marching song of the French Foreign Legion. Just that was enough. But you know what it turned out the South Vietnamese celebrate as Independence Day? The day Ngo Dinh Diem was assassinated. Think about that. The band is playing the song of the defeated French colonial forces to celebrate the murder of the guy we installed. Meanwhile, you got the U.S. ambassador talking to the Russian ambassador over here, and the Chinese chargé is standing over in the corner with his little red Mao button on, wondering what they're saying about him. Whole goddamned country is schizoid. Is that the word? Schizoid?"

"I think so." Upson saw what he had not until now: that Casey was already more than a little drunk. The Brautigans' residence was a very large, two-story villa with high ceilings and terrazzo floors. A few pieces of furniture were plainly their own, but Upson recognized most of the pieces as embassy stuff. A firm owned by a Japanese woman had the contract for all embassy furniture, and so everybody's quarters looked the same. The style was Swedish modern, upholstered in brightly patterned Thai cotton. Upson could read the Brautigans' past postings from the artifacts they had collected: nineteenth-century brass railroad lanterns from a tour in India, masks from West Africa somewhere, icons from Russia. From Laos there were two fine Kha drums of bronze, used as end tables, a heavy silver necklace of the kind Upson had seen on Meo women during his visit to the Plain of Jars, and a crossbow from the mountain tribes.

"Dick Lindsay says they still kill bears with those crossbows," said Jane Brautigan, who had come up beside him. "The kids keep wanting to try it out, but fortunately they don't know how to make it work."

"Where are the kids?"

"I gave them early supper and sent them upstairs. The *amah* has strict orders not to let them down till dawn tomorrow— predawn, if I know Petey and Susan. We decorate the tree after they've gone upstairs, so it'll be a surprise in the morning. My parents always did that with me. Then we keep it up through New Year's."

"Where did you find a real tree, anyway?" Upson asked. "All the other ones I've seen here have been those terrible plastic ones."

"Isn't it wonderful? Apparently they grow in the mountains up north. One of the agency people brought it with him when he flew down yesterday. It doesn't really look like our spruces and firs, does it? But I don't think it looks too awful now that it's decorated, do you? It was a little hectic, trying to get ready for the party and trimming the tree at the same time, after the children had gone upstairs."

"I can imagine."

"But it's worth it, just to see their faces Christmas morning."

Jane Brautigan moved away, a tall, handsome woman going a little thick at the waist.

Upson thought of how Somchan would look in Pawling at Christmastime. He imagined her shopping at the last minute, in a heavy, olive green loden coat like the one his mother wore. Snow whirling in the Christmas lights, nesting in her jet-black hair. She would be buying dolls or a teddy bear for the kids. Or an electric train. She wouldn't know where to look for an electric train, or how to ask for one. She wouldn't even know what one was, actually. But he could buy her one, and watch her laugh when it ran around and around, tooting.

A retired colonel in Pawling was married to a Chinese woman with an elegant British accent. Her face was covered with small, soft wrinkles. Why did it seem unnatural for an old man to be married to a wrinkled Chinese woman? Lindsay and one of the USIS officers were married to young Thai women, and Upson didn't see anything peculiar in that.

Upson went over to the bar to join Phil Casey and his boss, Earl Punderson, the public affairs officer. "How are you, Fred?"

he said. "Merry Christmas, Fred." Punderson repeated names Dale Carnegie–fashion, but he did it so relentlessly that the effect was irritating rather than flattering.

"Merry Christmas."

"Fred, I was just kidding Phil that he should stop slipping those tanks onto the PDJ without telling us about it."

"What tanks?"

"The sixty Russian PT-76s that showed up right outside Lima 22 yesterday morning, Fred, and nobody ever spotted them all the way across the plain. It was in the papers, Fred. Did the convoy show up in any of your recon photos?"

"I don't know. I can tell by the coordinates when the request is on the PDJ, and I don't even bother to look at the photos. The whole area is validated now."

"I damned sure didn't know about any sixty-tank convoy moving across the Plain," Casey said. "Even if they missed them in aerial surveillance, you'd think some of their fancy detection devices should have picked up a movement that big."

"What did AIRA say?" Upson asked the press attaché.

"Well, when I asked Brother Costikyan, he said, quote, Beats the shit out of me, end quote."

A little later, Upson came across the air attaché and asked him how sixty tanks had managed to get through the electronic detection net, escaping the bombers. "They didn't get through," Colonel Costikyan said. "We tracked them every foot of the way."

"Phil said you didn't know how they got through."

"Look at it this way, Fred. When Phil doesn't know something, he can honestly tell the *New York Times* he doesn't know. Makes it easier on him."

"Maybe I'm slow, Mike, but I still don't understand," said Upson, who felt flattered that the air attaché would trust him with information that he kept from Casey. "If your guys knew a column of tanks was moving onto the PDJ, why didn't they bomb it right at the start?"

"I didn't say my guys knew. I said *we* knew. The people who had a need to know."

"Who needs to know more than the pilots? They're the guys who are supposed to kill tanks."

"Think it through. If the tanks moved by night, we theoretically couldn't spot them from the air, right? As a matter of fact, anything that uses electricity or produces heat out there, we can pinpoint it exactly. But if we used that information for targeting purposes, the enemy would start to wonder how we got it. They'd ask Moscow and Peking, and pretty soon the commies would figure out what we were doing, and work out ways to counter our electronic intelligence sources."

"So somebody knew the tanks were coming, but they never passed it on to the pilots or to the ground troops that might be threatened by the tanks?"

"That's about it. No target in Southeast Asia would be worth compromising the existence of some of our really sophisticated intelligence-gathering systems."

"What good are they, then?"

"We'll need them later on, if we ever get into a war we mean to win. Look, Fred, face it. The fucking politicians aren't going to let us win this one, so we might as well learn what we can out of it."

"Maybe that's why it never seems to end," Upson said.

"I don't follow you on that one."

"Well, no, nothing. I just had a thought that probably doesn't make sense."

The air attaché wandered off, but Upson kept working around in his head the idea of the war as an eternal maneuver with live ammo, a sand table with little lead soldiers that really moved. The little guys, the ambassador always called the Lao and Meo troops. Upson thought of himself years from now, remarkably young for a retired ambassador, before his international relations class at some small but very good college. Middlebury, Reed, Williams . . .

". . . I seldom descend into psychohistory, ladies and gentlemen, but sometimes the temptation becomes irresistible. Can the Thirty Year War—for, after all, the Indochinese conflict lasted in one form or another from 1945 to 1975—be explained in other terms than those of psychology? We could have ended that conflict at any time by the application of sufficient military strength on the ground, in North Vietnam. We could equally have ended it at any time by complete withdrawal. That last word was hardly chosen at random, if the young ladies in the class will pardon me. One of the enduring lessons of Freudian psychology is that the result achieved is the result intended—

59

although the intention often lies buried in the subconscious. The result achieved in Indochina for so many years was neither victory nor defeat, but an extended state of war. Or perhaps it would be more accurate to say war *games* . . ."

The classes were always in the fall semester, with perfect football weather outside. After them he would walk through the fallen leaves and the autumn haze back to his tiny, colonial house. Sometimes friends from the old, wild days would come to visit—spies, diplomats, soldiers. Sometimes a young and pretty graduate student. The faces of the young women were only vaguely imagined, but they were all mature beyond their years, quiet, intent to learn, and very kind. They were musical, too. He would have a piano for them . . .

"Fred, are you there? Is anybody home? Speak to me, Fred."

"Oh, Phil, hi. I'm sorry, I was just thinking about something."

"Don't think," the press attaché said. "It drives you crazy in the end, like masturbation. Don't masturbate, either."

"Phil, do you think this war will ever stop, one way or another? All the way in, or all the way out?"

"Sure. It'll stop as soon as Nixon gets reelected. It's only gone on this long because neither Kennedy nor Johnson made it to his second term. Both those guys knew the war was a piece of shit, and so does Nixon. But losing an election is even worse."

"That's Jerry Brautigan's theory, too. It's a pretty bleak view."

"Pretty bleak world, kid. Wait and see when that puke Kissinger gets reelected, and his trusty sidekick, Tricky. We'll declare victory and haul ass inside of six months."

Casey gestured to illustrate the process, and half of his drink slopped out on the floor. "Look at that dumb son of a bitch," he said. "He can't even keep a drink in his glass and it's only ten-thirty or whatever the hell it is. I've never worn a watch, being a lifelong Democrat. Democrats can take watches or leave 'em. Republicans are the only ones that have to wear watches. You never saw a Republican without a watch, did you? Never will, either. Watches are very important to them."

Upson held Casey's drink while the press attaché mopped at a wet spot on his pants. "Best thing is to drift away from the evidence, let somebody else stand in the puddle," Casey said, starting for the bar. "I should go home. My ex-wife would tell me that if she were here instead of in Framingham playing bingo at Saint Theresa's. Fucking bingo."

"Well, go home if you want, Phil. I can get a ride."

"Can't go home, you know that as a professional diplomat. Protocol requires that I not leave before my master. And the ambassador looks pretty shitface himself and not about to go nowhere. Did you know the son of a bitch cheats at cards?"

"Come on, Phil."

"I saw it. He was playing poker with some of the marine guards. He tossed two and dealt himself three, and then slipped the extra one back into the discards."

"Come on, Phil."

"Don't keep saying, 'Come on, Phil.' There's no goddamned 'Come on, Phil' about it. I was standing right behind him."

"He must have been drinking."

"You mean I must have been. I was. So was he. Only thing is, you can drink without cheating at cards. I do it all the time. So 'Come on, Phil,' my ass, buddy."

Casey stopped for a moment to see what Upson had to say to that. Upson was surprised and hurt by the attack, but he said nothing. "Ah, shit, I'm sorry," the press attaché said. "Okay? I'm sorry. I don't mean to take it out on you. I just feel shitty about something else, nothing to do with you."

Before Upson had to say anything, Casey turned and walked away, moving with the studied precision of a man who knows he is drunk. Upson admired him and was frightened by him at the same time. Was it possible for an FSO-4 in the United States Information Agency to be a tragic figure? Locked by circumstances into a bureaucracy he despised and a war he opposed, Casey could be seen as carrying on with cynical bravery against all odds. But how accurate was that gallant portrait, after all? Wouldn't it be even braver to criticize less and work harder within the system to make it a better one? Upson remembered a quote from Samuel Butler: "If you would do good, you must begin with minute particulars." These had to be particulars over which you had some control, and that meant those of your own job. Surely true courage was meeting your own responsibilities day after day in a conscientious, decent, and moral fashion. Then you had a base from which to offer constructive criticism.

Upson smiled to himself, remembering Casey on the subject of constructive criticism. "Let's say it's mission policy to kick old ladies to death," the press attaché had said during an argument with one of the embassy political officers. "When you suggest that all officers wear jackboots instead of Thom McAns, now that's constructive criticism. Destructive criticism is what you get from that asshole over there in the corner, the one who keeps saying maybe we shouldn't kill the old ladies in the first place."

"Casey, you're too much," the political officer had said. That was the general way of dealing with Casey: by treating his statements as too outrageous to be seriously intended. Brautigan's attitude was different. He indulged Casey, as if the press attaché were a younger brother whose intelligence and wit made up for his being a smart aleck sometimes. But while Brautigan suffered no damage from regarding the press attaché with friendly, amused tolerance, it was a question whether Upson, a junior officer, could get away with tolerating Casey at all. To be seen as close to someone of doubtful loyalty was to put your own loyalty in doubt. Upson regretted now that he had accepted a ride to the party from the press attaché and wondered if he shouldn't try to find some other way home.

"Aren't they attractive?" said Jane Brautigan's voice. Upson had been running his fingers absently along the surface of an oiled teak desk. "The top folds down so that you can make a huge work table out of it, too."

"I know. I have one just like it. Or I will have, once my household goods arrive."

"Do you really? Were you posted to Denmark, or did Justessen's send it out to you?"

"Justessen's sent it out. My only other tour was in Rabat."

"Oh, that must have been wonderful," said the DCM's wife. "We were hoping for Rabat last time out, but we got Bombay instead. Justessen's just saved our lives in India. You couldn't get a thing on the local market. Oh, look, there's Earl Punderson. I must go say hello to him. Their little girl is sick."

Justessen's, a Copenhagen mail-order house that offered everything from furniture to dry breakfast cereal, spread a common culture over all the tiny clusters of official Americans in missions throughout the world. There must be hundreds of desks like his and the Brautigans', Upson thought, in American residences from South Africa to Greenland. Hundreds of identical cartons from Justessen's in kitchens and pantries, each carton separated by cardboard dividers into seventy-two little compartments, and each little compartment holding its plain, seven-ounce glass to be brought out during large parties and receptions. Glittering diplomatic receptions. He remembered the receptions in Rabat: the Johnny Walker the Moroccans favored, the perfumed, repulsive French-brewed beer called Stork, the orange soda called Fanta and the Coca-Cola, both made nauseatingly sweet for the North African taste. The same faces at each party, from the same ministries and embassies. The photographer hired by the host embassy, so that the ambassador could send home proof that he was using his entertainment allowance effectively. The CIA routinely ordered two extra sets of prints from the photographer after each communist bloc reception; presumably the bloc intelligence services did the same when the western embassies held receptions.

Upson was on his way to the bar when he heard Casey's voice, rising above the other conversations in a large study off the main room. "You know what I'm talking about, Jerry," he was saying. "Second generation, all the micks became cops. Third generation, ours, everybody became FBI agents or spooks. Roll a grenade into the Vientiane cathedral any Sunday and you'd get the entire goddamn leadership of CAS."

"I never thought of it that way, Phil," the deputy chief of mission said. "How come you wound up in USIS and me in State, then?"

"You know what my first job was?" Casey asked. "Police reporter for the *Boston Globe*. Now I'm the official spokesman for a CIA war. As for you, Jerry, yeah, goddamnit . . ."

"As for me?" Brautigan's tone was amused and friendly.

"Well, as for you, the U.S. is the policeman of the world and you're in the Southeast Asia division. Listen, Jerry, when you were a kid, did the sisters teach you about the Doctrine of Invincible Ignorance?"

"If they did, I don't remember."

"Yeah, well, it says that if you've never been exposed to the true faith, you can still get to heaven eventually. As long as you've never had a chance to receive instruction. If you're unwitting, as the spooks say."

"I'm lost, then. Not only am I witting, Phil, I left the church to become an Episcopalian."

"That's right, Jerry. You're witting. We're both witting agents, and we goddamn well better watch to our souls."

"If you're talking about the war . . ."

"What do you think I'm talking about?"

"Then I have no problem. You say this is a CIA war, well, that's a hell of a lot better than a Pentagon war. Who do you think kept the Pentagon out, kept this from turning into complete chaos, with a half a million American troops running around? A lot of men in this mission over the years who stayed with jobs they maybe found distasteful or even wrong sometimes, and did them the best way they could. Those are the men who kept the lid on this country, and it's a damned good thing they hung in there. Because there are a hell of a lot of other men waiting in line for these assignments who have a very different idea about how this war should be run."

"And actually some of them have made it to the head of the line, haven't they?" Casey asked, gesturing with his head toward the door, through which the ambassador's loud voice could be heard.

"All right, Phil."

"All right, my ass. You know what you are, Jerry? You're a guy on a runaway railroad train, and you're trying to slow the damned thing down by walking very politely toward the rear, saying excuse me to all the passengers. But that son of a bitch is going to hit anyway, and it'll hit just that tiny bit harder because you and me are still on board."

"That's a cute analogy, Phil, but I don't know how much it has to do with the real world. And I think you might try keeping your voice down. This is my house."

"So it is. Your booze, too."

"My booze, and you've had enough of it."

"Just trying to keep up with the ambassador."

"That's enough, goddamn it, Phil."

64

"No, it isn't. I've got to unwind, you know. I work so hard all week, trying to get good press for the mission. Morning, noon, sometimes even night. You know how far I'll go to get good press, don't you, Jerry?"

"Phil, please. Look, I'm your friend. I know you're tired. Christ, we're all tired . . ."

"Oh, *there* you are, Jerry." Jane Brautigan had been drawn from the other room by the rising voices. "I've been looking all over for you. I want you to explain something to Somphet. He never understands a thing I tell him." She led him off with quick skill, smiling at Casey and the others nearby as if to apologize for breaking up such a stimulating discussion.

Upson started to move away, but the press attaché came after him and caught his arm. "What did you think of that?" he asked. "Pretty brave, huh?"

"I think it's none of my business."

"Pretty goddamn brave, pissing on the DCM's leg. Except that there's nothing the poor bastard can do about it."

"He could have you sent home. It wouldn't surprise me if he did."

"No, he can't."

"All right, then, he can't. Excuse me."

"Certainly. Pretty much all of the time, I excuse everybody. Except myself and one or two other witting agents."

Upson felt shaky as he walked away. He was almost never rude to anybody. He didn't know if that was a virtue, or just a sign that he was afraid of people. But why had Casey been so belligerent earlier, and why had he just now gone out of his way to pick a fight with Brautigan? That he was drunk was neither reason nor excuse; Casey himself had made that point when he talked about the ambassador cheating at cards.

Upson went out into the main room, where the ambassador was sitting on a sofa, surrounded by the air attaché, the air force major who commanded the forward air controllers, one of the assistant army attachés, and the CIA station chief.

"Scoot over, Mike," the ambassador said. "Make room for Fred. Grab yourself a drink, Fred. Hell, it's Christmas. Oh, you've got one. Thought the goddamned thing was full of water. A decent drink ought to be brown."

"The browner the better," said Earl Punderson, who was standing nearby. The ambassador ignored the public affairs officer's attempt at getting into the conversation.

"We were just talking about that goddamned Bailey," the ambassador said.

"Bill Bailey?" Upson asked. "The reporter?"

"Reporter, hell. He just passes along the lies he gets from the North Vietnamese embassy, isn't that right, Chuck?"

"He goes there certainly," said Chuck Hurley, the CIA station chief. "We know a lot that goes on inside there, but we don't know exactly what Pham tells him. Or vice versa."

"Or vice versa, damned right. That's the point, vice versa. Who's Bailey *really* working for?"

"Not just the *New York Times*, that's for sure," Punderson said.

The ambassador went on as if his public affairs officer hadn't spoken. "And the goddamned irony of it all," Simmonds said, "is that Bailey is allowed to stay in this country because of one man. Me. Souvanna wanted to kick him out three months ago and I had to practically get down on bended knee to get him to change his mind."

"Why didn't you just let Souvanna kick the son of a bitch out, Mr. Ambassador?" asked the young air force major.

"Buck, son. Call me Buck. I'll tell you why. The power of the press. Goddamned dangerous thing in a democracy. Jerry and I decided that we couldn't let the prime minister kick Bailey out, or the press would have been all over us like flies on shit. So I find myself pleading with the PM to let the guy stay here, so he can keep on kicking me in the balls. These kids come out here to make a name for themselves, and the bigger lies they write, the better chance they have to get their trash in the paper."

"And then Fulbright reads it and takes it for gospel," Punderson said. This time the ambassador noticed him.

"Goddamn Fulbright," he said. "There's nothing that pisses me off more than a man who will play politics with national security."

"Is he up this time?" the air force major asked, but nobody knew.

"Doesn't really matter," the ambassador said. "A man like that is always running for reelection."

Upson went to get himself a fresh drink as soon as he politely could. More and more, he felt uncomfortable around the ambassador. Upson still found himself looking for excuses when Simmonds talked about things like the danger of a powerful press in a democracy. Since the ambassador couldn't possibly believe what he said, probably he was just playing to an audience he knew was hostile to the press. Or perhaps he meant that the press was becoming too powerful in relation to the other necessary elements of a democracy. The emperor *looked* naked, but he could hardly have got to be an emperor with no clothes at all. Surely a certain mental suppleness and subtlety were necessary to climb to the top of the U.S. Foreign Service? The evidence was building day by day, though, that this was not the case. With Ambassador Simmonds, there seemed to be no nine-tenths submerged. Upson was about ready to concede that what you saw was all there was.

"Hey, Larry's here with the booze," Punderson called out over the noise of the party. "*Lao lao,* the real stuff. Have you ever had lao lao, Mr. Ambassador?"

"Does a bear shit in the woods?" the ambassador said. Everybody sitting with him laughed.

The big Thai sergeant who had been outside was coming toward the ambassador, lugging a heavy earthenware crock nearly the size of a five-gallon can. Behind him was the fat, balding man who was head of the mission guard service, Larry Mancuso. Mancuso wore the colors of Christmas: lime green polyester slacks and a red and white checked jacket. When the big sergeant had set the crock at the ambassador's feet, Mancuso stuck one end of a four-foot-long bamboo tube into the brown substance that filled it, and offered the other to Simmonds. "Have a snort, Mr. Ambassador," Mancuso said.

"Looks prime," Ambassador Simmonds said. "Probably been aging all day." Everyone near enough to hear him smiled or laughed.

"What in God's name is it?" Upson asked Lindsay, who had come up beside him to watch.

"Kind of a rice wine," Lindsay said. "You pour water over sugar and rice and let it ferment a few days under the house. It's ready when it turns brown and starts to stink. You jam the

67

bamboo down to the bottom where the worst of it has settled and suck it right up."

"You sure make it sound tempting."

"It is. Tastes a little like bat piss, only not quite as good."

The ambassador was having trouble with the bamboo tube. "There's nothing coming up, Larry," he said. "What the hell's wrong with this thing?"

Mancuso tried, but nothing came up for him, either. "What the hell is this, Bounlek?" Mancuso said. "Damned thing doesn't work." He gestured for the sergeant to take over. The big Thai stirred the brown mass around with the end of the bamboo, and took his turn. He failed, too. The sergeant straightened up, took three or four deep breaths, emptied the air from his barrel chest, and bent over to try again. His shoulders hunched and big veins stood out in his neck as he sucked, both hands grasping the bamboo. Whatever was blocking the tube gave way so suddenly that some of the brown liquid squirted out of the big Thai's mouth and onto his uniform shirt. "That's my boy," Mancuso said, throwing his arm around the sergeant's beefy shoulders as everyone cheered. Bounlek wiped the end of the tube politely on his sleeve before offering it back to the ambassador. "That's more like it," the ambassador said when he had drawn up a mouthful. "Good man, Sergeant." Mancuso smiled with pride, like a trainer whose bear has just accomplished a particularly difficult trick.

"We better ease on out of here," Lindsay said. "If the ambassador sees us, we'll have to gag some of that swill down. Another Budweiser, on the other hand . . ."

Once safe in the other room, Upson looked around for Casey. The press attaché was nowhere around. Upson wondered whether he had had the sense to go on home before the ambassador anyway, protocol or no protocol. The ambassador's wife was back in Charleston with her family for the holidays, and the ambassador, although it was after midnight, showed no signs of leaving. Simmonds's penetrating voice was sounding even louder than usual. His neat, military appearance seemed slightly out of focus tonight. His features were a little loose, somehow, and his clothes didn't sit on him quite right. His posture was a little lax; his gestures were a little larger than normal.

Upson watched as Jane Brautigan went from group to group, chattering and smiling. He admired the brave and bright way she was working to make the party a success. He imagined her as the cruise director on a doomed ship, the barometer dropping point by point as the passengers danced and blew toy horns. It seemed to Upson that there were omens: the strange, sultry heat at Christmastime, the pine tree that didn't quite look like a pine tree, glittering with decorations and piled underneath with toys, the mysterious confrontation between Casey and Brautigan, the ambassador's growing drunkenness. Many of the guests were drunk by now, Upson realized. He himself was feeling strange.

The ambassador had brought Jerry Brautigan into his group, and was instructing him on big game hunting. "Here the damned war spoils everything now," the loud voice was saying. "But the game's still out there. You know about gaur, Jerry? Like a water buffalo, but bigger. Only a few left in the world, all right in the goddamned middle of Indian territory on the Bolovens Plateau . . ."

Upson felt a numbness in the hinges of his jaw. A few minutes before, he had heard himself saying, "I was have" for "I would have." Nobody had noticed, though, and he didn't think it was because of the drinks anyway. He could probably get by with one more. He had gone to get it when he heard the first ornament go, with the soft pop of a dropped light bulb. Upson turned and saw the ambassador holding a BB gun that had been under the Christmas tree.

"How do you like that?" the ambassador said. "First shot. Go ahead, Jerry. See if you can take out that red one, up top on the left."

Brautigan took the air gun, cocked it, and missed the red ornament. Then the ambassador and the deputy chief of mission took turns missing it again, and finally the ambassador got it. As he looked around in triumph, he caught sight of Upson. "Come on over here, Fred," he said. "We'll show these Pentagon sons of bitches how the State Department can shoot. Waste that green one there."

Upson took the gun and aimed at an indestructible plastic icicle instead. The icicle seemed to be dancing around the front sight, skipping away every time he moved the barrel to find it. The instant he fired he knew he was way off target. And then people were clapping, for some reason.

"Goddamn, Mike, Bill, what did I tell you?" the ambassador said. "That's my tiger. Blew the son of a bitch away." Upson saw he had hit the green ball by mistake, although it was a good foot to the left of the icicle. He managed a sort of smile, and handed the gun back to the ambassador.

"Don't run off, Fred," Simmonds said. "We're just getting warmed up."

"I'll be back, sir. Got to use the facilities."

"Siphon the python, huh? That's what the Aussies say. Ever hear the Aussies say that, Jerry? Siphon the python?" While the ambassador's attention was on his deputy, Upson slipped into the next room for a moment to let his presence be forgotton.

The shooting went on for ten minutes, turn and turn about between the two men, with the ambassador keeping score. Both men missed more than they hit, but the ambassador was slightly the better shot. Once they had smashed all the glass ornaments, they started on the colored light bulbs. Those were harder to break. Unless the BB hit squarely, it would ricochet and leave the bulb undamaged. They were so tricky that the Ambassador finally got bored with his game.

"You know, Jerry," he said when he had put the gun aside, "you're not a bad shot for a novice. You ought to take it up seriously. We'll go out after rice birds some Sunday. Little guys aren't worth eating, but they're good enough to practice on."

Red, green, blue, and silver shards glittered all over the presents piled under the tree, and throughout its branches. The jagged bases of the balls still hung from their wire hooks, looking ugly and dangerous. An illuminated angel had topped the tree; now only the glass and wire of the filament were left. The decorations had helped cover up the alien look of the semitropical pine. But now it was an awful parody of a Christmas tree, its oddness only heightened by the tinsel and the few remaining lights.

The party had stopped during the ruining of the Christmas tree. The ambassador's group and a few other nearby men had cheered and encouraged the marksmen. But most of the men remained silent, and all of the women. The servants stood by, smiling. Upson felt uneasily that they would have the same tolerant, mildly contemptuous smiles if they were watching the clumsy antics of a two-year-old.

Once the shooting stopped, conversation started up again. The servants began to move around to take orders for drinks and to pass the hors d'oeuvres. Jane Brautigan had taught her cook how to wrap bacon around bits of water chestnuts and broil them, and how to devil eggs, and how to toast little rounds of bread with cheese on them. Upson didn't need another drink; he hadn't touched the one he got just before the target practice started. He wished he had had the courage to refuse to take a shot. He didn't want to have to say anything to anyone about what had just happened, and so he went out on the rear patio, empty because the mosquitoes had come out in force. He had just sat down in a chair underneath one of the study windows when he heard the voices of the Brautigans coming out the open window above him.

"Please, Jane, don't be like that. Please, dear."

"Oh, shut up."

Upson couldn't stand up without showing himself to them through the screen. All he could do to escape the embarrassment of discovery was to stay put and hope that they wouldn't come to the window where they could see him sitting below.

"They're your children, too, you know." Her voice was unsteady, on the verge of tears. "When is that man going to leave? Why is he spoiling my party?"

"He'll leave soon, honey. I'll suggest it to him."

"You'll *suggest* it to him?"

"Jane, honey, Jane. What more can I do? He's the ambassador."

"Couldn't you *tell* him, just for once? What can he do? He knows you're the one who really runs the mission."

"No, he doesn't. But I'll tell him to go, Jane. Honestly I will."

"Oh, my God, my God, do you know the worst thing of all? I could have died when I saw what you were doing. You're a beautiful shot, and you were letting him win."

"Honey, Janie, dearest, I wasn't letting him win. It wasn't that way."

"Don't make it worse by saying that. You were missing on purpose, and we both know it."

"It wasn't like letting the boss win at golf, honey, honestly it wasn't. I'd miss so as not to ruin the kids' tree. I was hoping he'd lose interest before it was all ruined."

"You didn't want to ruin the tree. Oh, Jesus Mary Mother of God, listen to the man. Get out of here, Jerry. Just let me alone." She was crying now: hard, ugly gasps.

"Jane. Janie."

"Go, go."

Upson heard the door open and close behind Brautigan. The woman was trying to bring her sobs under control, and Upson could tell by the sound that she had moved back into the room, away from the window. He got up to move off, bent over so that she wouldn't see him. When he was safe he scratched at the bites left by the mosquitoes he had not noticed on him. He wanted to help Jane Brautigan, to take her into his arms like a father and tell her it would be all right, that he would buy her a new tree.

When he went back inside, the ambassador was just leaving. "Say goodnight to your lovely bride," he said to Brautigan at the door. "I'm sorry she isn't feeling well."

"I'll do that, Mr. Ambassador."

"Sure you won't come with us?"

"No, thanks. I've got to be up early, with the kids."

There was a stirring when the ambassador had left with his group. Everyone had been freed at last, and was getting ready to say goodbye. Jane Brautigan reappeared, looking as if nothing had happened. She had set the servants to work cleaning up the mess under the tree right away instead of putting the job off until all the guests had gone. Upson thought the small gesture of protest showed just the right mixture of indignation and good manners.

As Upson was wondering who could give him a ride home, Jerry Brautigan drew him inside. "Can you give me a hand with Phil?" the DCM asked. "He's upstairs asleep and he's in no shape to drive home."

The press attaché was lying on his back in one of the bedrooms, snoring. "Come on, come on, lay off," he mumbled when Brautigan shook him.

"Time to go, Phil."

"Time to go, Phil, time to go, Phil," Casey said back.

"Come on, Phil."

"Let me alone." But the press attaché allowed himself to be helped to a sitting position, and then he stood by himself. He combed at his fringe of rumpled hair, and clumsily rammed his shirt tails back in his pants.

"Fred can drive you home, Phil," Brautigan said.

"Yeah, good idea. I don't like driving anyway. The responsibility of it. I'm a born passenger, Jerry, a goddamned born passenger."

Casey held the railing on his way downstairs, paying close attention to his feet. He went with Upson to the car, gave him the keys, and climbed into the passenger's seat.

"Which way?" Upson asked.

"Go like you're going to your house, and I'll show you from there."

He fell silent for a moment and then said, "Irish cancer."

"What?"

"Fucking Irish cancer. Cirrhosis. I don't dare ask the doctors to look, but I figure I'm lucky if the booze has left me any liver at all."

"The booze did you a favor tonight. You didn't have to watch the U.S. ambassador to Laos and his deputy chief of mission shooting the decorations off the Christmas tree with the kids' BB gun."

"You're shitting me."

"No, I'm not. They ruined the tree."

"Jerry too? Poor bastard, I shouldn't have dumped all over him earlier. He's got enough troubles."

"Why did you, then?"

"I was taking it out on him instead of myself."

"Taking what out?"

"Well, you remember Harrison Bottsford?" And it all came out. The press attaché lost the thread of his story now and then, but for the most part it was coherent. Either his sleep had sobered him up somewhat, or he hadn't been that drunk to begin with. "Yeah, and one more thing," Casey said. "One more little vignette, okay? You know what that nasty little fruitcake travels with? A steamer trunk. I shit you not, Fred. I saw the son of a bitch sitting in his room."

"Why would Jerry even suggest a thing like that to you, Phil?" Upson asked. The story had shocked him.

"Jerry thinks it's because he wanted Bottsford to go back to

Washington and talk up our little war. He doesn't even know why he actually did it. Fortunately I know, and am consequently in a position so I can explain it to you. Bottsford is supposed to be very tight with the secretary of state. Next time Jerry's back in Washingon, he'll have a little lunch with old Bottsford, and old Bottsford will mention to Secretary Rogers some day what a fine ambassador Jerry would make to someplace or another. And Jerry would be absolutely horrified—genuinely, too—if you suggested that there was maybe just the teeniest element of blackmail in the whole thing. It would occur to Bottsford quick enough, because he lives with that kind of fear. But not to Jerry. Basically, Jerry is too decent a guy to know what he's doing most of the time."

At first, Upson thought that Casey had garbled his thought. Then he saw that he hadn't. "How about you, Phil?" he asked. "Are you too decent to know what you're doing?"

"I wish I were. But I know exactly. My God, do I know. I didn't pimp for that bloodthirsty little buttfucker as a favor for Jerry. Or even because it amused me. I did it for the same sort of reason Jerry did, except I knew it. I did it so I would have something on Jerry. So he can't slip around behind me and stab me in the back."

"Does he want to?"

"Not that I know of. But if he ever does, he won't do it."

They drove along in silence for a time. Upson thought that Casey was beginning to sound like the people who think the government is suppressing their inventions, or that the CIA broadcasts secret threats to them. Upson hoped it was the liquor talking.

"Take the car with you," Casey said when he had directed them to his house. "I won't need it tomorrow. I'll be opening presents all day. Egg nog, carols, shit like that. Sure I will."

"I'd just as soon walk," Upson said. "I didn't know we were so close."

"We're not so close. You don't want to be close to me. Tell me, Fred, are you working on a novel?"

"A novel? No, why?"

"I thought you might be. Most of the people I've known, all of my life, they've got a novel under the bed or in the closet."

"I wouldn't even try. I could never write a novel."

"I could. I did, once. Did you know that?"

"No, I didn't." Casey didn't sound drunk, but he was swaying back and forth a little as he stood on the stairs leading up to his house.

"Well, I goddamned well did. I was in Guatemala then. I thought it would make me some go-to-hell money. It sold 932 copies. Not bad, huh? Oddly enough, though, you never hear people talk about Phil Casey, the novelist. No, you spend eighteen years covering your ass, and it's Phil Casey, the bureaucrat."

"Come on, Phil. A bureaucrat is the last thing you are."

"Oh, yeah," came his voice from the shadows at the top of the stairs. "Well, if it walks like a duck and it quacks like a duck, what it is is a goddamn duck."

Upson didn't turn the air conditioning on when he went to bed, since the night was tolerably cool. By Christmas noon, though, the sun streaming through the windows had made the bedroom oppressive. Upson lay tangled in sweaty sheets, his damp pajamas bunched above his knees. Whenever he came near waking, he tried to drive himself back down into sleep so that he wouldn't feel the pain in his head. Finally he couldn't make himself sleep anymore, and just lay there, feeling punk. When Upson's father had a cold he would say he was feeling punk. Upson remembered that there was supposed to be some way of telephoning the United States from Laos, but he didn't know how to go about it. The phone beside the bed was connected only to the phones of the embassy and other American homes. Besides, was it twelve hours earlier or twelve hours later back home? Or a little more, or a little less, because Pawling was in the east? He tried to think of the sun going around the earth, since it was easier to imagine that way. He concluded that it was probably only a little after midnight of Christmas day.

Back home, the ambassador wouldn't even have started shooting at the tree yet. Back home, the Reverend Langhorne Upson would be in bed already, to be fresh for the Christmas day services. Earlier, Upson's father would have gone caroling with the Young People's Fellowship, and conducted the carols and worship at the church. Because of the busy day to come, he would have reluctantly limited himself to three or four eggnogs at the Christmas Eve party the deacons took turns giving every year. It wasn't until his college years that Upson learned enough about drinking to understand that his father was a heavy drinker. Not that Reverend Upson ever got loud or boisterous; it was his way to become vague and pleasant instead.

Upson thought his father looked on the ministry principally as a form of social work. He said grace at table, but he never prayed at home so far as Upson knew. Nor did he talk about God except on those few occasions when his young son asked him about the subject. The Reverend Upson baptized and confirmed his only child, but made no further effort to instruct him in religion. His father never said a word when Upson began missing services during his college years, and finally stopped attending church completely. For a long time Upson had thought that his mild inoculation of religion failed to take at all. But lately he had come to wonder whether there was much difference between the impulses leading a young man to the foreign service and, for example, to missionary work.

Upson sat on the edge of his bed for a long while before he could bring himself to stand up. He hung his damp, limp pajamas on the back of the bathroom door and looked at himself in the mirror. His hair was matted flat on one side and stood out like a wing on the other. It was an in-between brown, neither black nor blond, and growing thinner. He would be partly bald in his thirties as his father had been. He rubbed at the crystals, like particles of brown sugar, that had dried in the corners of his eyes. He was not fat at least, but neither was he wiry or muscular. His eyes were as indefinite in color as his hair—a short of hazel. It seemed to Upson that he looked, at twenty-nine, older than he was. In his forties he would look younger than he was, until one day he would suddenly look and be old, and that would be that.

Upson was disgusted by himself.

He had to settle for a tepid shower instead of the cold one

he needed, because the tap water came from the warm Mekong. His mouth still tasted foul after he finished brushing his teeth. He dug at his palate with his thumb, gouging loose a gummy, brown substance. The fresh clothes he put on felt slightly damp, the way clothes always did in the humidity of Laos.

Luckily Somchan was not around to see his sorry state; he had given her Christmas day off. Upson got out a half-gallon container of imitation ice cream from the American Community Association commissary and began to eat what was left. The label said *Foremost Dairy Pride Frozen Dessert, Artificially Flavored Vanilla, For United States Government Personnel Only.* He read it with distaste, but he was so hungry and thirsty that he kept on eating till it was all gone. Before throwing the container out, he washed it carefully, so as not to draw ants. The ants were everywhere: big, black ones that looked dangerous but weren't, and small pale orange ones that bit like fire. The fire ants made nests in the trees by tying green leaves together into a shelter with strands of some silky substance. The Lao would drop the nests into a pail of water, collect the eggs as they rose to the surface, and eat them. Upson supposed Somchan must have done that. She must have eaten all the things Lao ate: toads, beetles, lizards, grubs. The thought had never occurred to him, the times he had kissed her. Now that it had, it didn't bother him. Anything Somchan did seemed wholesome to him. He was the unwholesome one.

Upson went out to the living room, with the idea of reading. Two Christmas cards, sitting on the coffee table, were the only sign of the season in his house. One was from his parents. The other was from a State Department secretary in Morocco who had let him do everything but sleep with her. This had frustrated him at the time, but now he was grateful. If she had let him into her bed, he suspected, they would have wound up married. They would have done it because they were both lonely in Morocco, but they would have gone on being lonely together. Upson had always felt lonely—at home, at school, in Morocco.

Now for the first time, these past days with Somchan, he was not lonely. Even today, when she was gone, he knew she was somewhere not too far and would be back. He couldn't even imagine the life she led apart from him. Sometimes she didn't spend the nights in her little room in the outbuilding behind the house, but he had no idea where she went. He didn't know if she had a family in town, where they might live, where she was from, whether she had gone to school, how old she was, what other jobs she had had. She might have been married, or even be married now. She might spend her nights away with a lover or lovers. Her language and her life, her past and her future, were so unreal that they had no power to make him jealous. She became real only when she was with him—the evenings on the porch and, regularly now, her visits to his bedroom afterwards.

Upson was thirsty from his hangover, and kept getting up to make himself more iced tea. Finally he put aside the book he had been trying to read, in favor of going for a walk. He headed downstream, on top of the dike which ran along the Mekong bluffs. The dirt path had been baked as hard as stone by the sun. Past the royal palms of the Laan Xang Hotel, he turned away from the river and toward town. The street took him to the Lido Hotel, a three-story wooden building almost a block long. Balconies ran all along the front of the building, with slatted doors giving out on them. Here and there a door stood open, as if the hotel had been suddenly abandoned. Once the building had been the color of dry mustard, but most of the paint had weathered off the plaster walls. Black mildew and pale green moss was taking its place. The hotel seemed to belong in the landscape of dreams—an equatorial riverport, standing deserted in the jungle. Upson was briefly afraid, as if he had woken to find that his nightmare was the world after all. His mind felt detached, like something floating along with him. He turned toward the morning market, to give himself a destination.

Although the morning market was one of the sights of Vientiane, he had never been in it. The building itself was nothing but an enormous pitched roof of red tiles, supported on pillars and open on all sides. The interior was full of stalls, and crisscrossed by alleys. Vendors squatted on the ground outside, their wares spread out on mats. Some had umbrellas to shelter them from the sun; some just sat out in its glare, wearing conical straw hats. Upson moved slowly past the little piles of roots and vegetables. He saw a hedgehog and an armadillo for sale, both rolled into defensive balls. Little sparrowlike birds fluttered inside bamboo cages. He came across a python coiled in a slatted orange crate, a knot of smooth muscle with its head buried deep inside. Catfish kept flipping out of the water in big, enamel pans and crawling away through the dust on their pectoral fins, while the owners went laughing after them. There were piles of marijuana for sale, the blue gray color of dried sage, and little stoves made out of flattened USAID vegetable oil cans, and earthenware jars full of unknown sauces, and burlap bags of spices, and huge vegetables he had never seen before.

Down one of the aisles, by the dried squid and shrimp and salted fish, Upson came across a set of doors. Inside them, he found a long room with dusty windows high up. The light that came through the windows was thin and secondhand, whatever reflected rays were able to get under the market's eaves. The air was thick with the stink of blood and offal. Pools of water from the last hosing stood on the concrete floor and filled the gutters which ran along the aisles. The butchers, all women, worked behind waist-high counters made of cement slabs. There were no neat and proper cuts of meat, the way there had been in the big municipal markets of Morocco. There were no links of sausage or trays of ground meat or displays of well scrubbed pigs' trotters and tripe. No sides of beef or whole animals hung from hooks. What lay heaped on the cement slabs looked like the results of an explosion: random chunks of bleeding flesh that were no recognizable part of a recognizable animal. Baskets under the counters held squishy mounds of organs all thrown in together, lungs and livers and other soft parts, shiny brown or gray or white. The blades and handles of the knives on the counters were gummy with blood, and so were the bare arms of the meatsellers. The women must have seen other Americans look sick in the same way before; they kept calling at him and laughing as he went down the aisle toward the far door. He tried to look as if he weren't hurrying.

The smell stayed in his nose until he had left the market area entirely. Although he still felt disordered and strange, his headache had gone. At some point between leaving the market and arriving at Samsenthai Street, only a few hundred yards away, the pain in his head had become a memory rather than a presence.

The market was Lao; Samsenthai Street was Chinese, Indian, and Vietnamese. Along it were jewelry stores with red and gold fronts, tailor shops, pharmacies and dress shops. There was a row of Indian variety stores: Tolaram's Maison de Confiance, Habeeb Store—General Merchants and Books Sellers, Haja Store, Top in Town. "Good afternoon, sir," the Indian merchants said as Upson walked by. "Merry Christmas, sir." They had the smile of tradesmen, not the mocking smile of the meatsellers. Upson stopped at a store, to look at T-shirts that said *Fly the Friendly Skies of Laos* and *Participant, Southeast Asian War Games, 1960–19??*.

"Very amusing, isn't it?" the shopkeeper said. "Many people buy them to send home." Upson couldn't think of anybody back home who would be amused.

"Is that thing a radio?" Upson asked.

"Yes, sir, a radio. Also very amusing." The shopkeeper took down a plastic Santa Claus, a foot high. The buttons on the tunic were the tuning and volume knobs. The plastic sack on the Santa's back was full of striped candy canes.

"After Christmas you can put anything you like in here, isn't it?" the Indian said. "Flowers or pencils. I have some fine felt pens."

"No thanks," Upson said. "Just the candy canes will be enough."

"There is no charge for the candy canes, sir. But you will need batteries, isn't it?"

Upson had the Santa gift-wrapped. Then, when it was too late to change his mind, he began to wonder if Somchan would think the Santa was funny. Or would she think it was patronizing? Probably not, but wasn't *he* being patronizing to give her such an absurd thing? And if she knew Americans gave each other presents at Christmas, wouldn't she feel embarrassed that she had nothing for him?

Upson had almost decided to chuck the thing out when he heard Dick Lindsay's voice calling to him from an open-fronted café. Upson had never been in the place, but he knew it was run by an American newspaper correspondent and a Lao woman. Orchids, a few of them in bloom, hung over the entrance in pots made of coconut halves. Reproductions of old movie posters were pasted on the walls. At the big table where Lindsay was sitting with several other men there was a chessboard made out of tropical woods and a leather cup for rolling the dice in a

French gambling game. Empty bottles of Singha beer from Thailand covered the rest of the tabletop.

"You're just in time, Fred," said Lindsay. "We're about to go to Loulou's, get these guys' ashes hauled."

"Go boonies beaucoup long time too much," one of the men said. "No hab Susy-Q long time, number ten."

"Turkey farm number one," another man said.

"Tell Fred how come they call Loulou's the turkey farm, Duane," Lindsay said.

"Account of all her girls gobble," Duane said. A burst of voices came from under the table, and it took Upson an instant to figure out that the man was wearing a radio receiver clipped to his belt.

"Why don't you turn that fucking thing off?" one of the men said. "It's fucking Christmas."

"Turn it off, bullshit," Duane said. "I'm afraid if I turn it off the war will end and we'll all have to go home."

Lindsay called out something in Lao and in a minute a woman wearing purple slacks and sweater appeared from a back room with a slip of paper in her hand. She handed it to Lindsay. "You tell me how much," she said. "I only poor Lao woman, never go to school."

"Why do you talk that shit, Malichan? You speak English better than I do." Lindsay said to Upson, "Malichan is illiterate in all of the seven languages she speaks. She's too goddamn lazy to learn to read, aren't you, Malichan?"

"No can do. Only poor Lao woman. You read for me, okay?"

Loulou's turned out to be a one-story house behind a dilapidated picket fence. A tin sign over the front gate read *Rendezvous des Amis,* in painted letters flaked almost away. The doorway was curtained from top to bottom with a faded orange flowered print. Inside, two Lao women were playing cards on a table covered with a tiny mauve rug. One of the women disappeared out back to spread the word that customers had come. The room's plaster walls were painted light blue. A strip of dark brown composition board ran around the room at the height of a seated man's head—evidently a sort of antimacassar to protect the walls from hair oil. Over the doorless entrance to the back room hung faded photographs, greenish in hue, of the king of

Laos. Color photographs of naked white women in the hairdos of the late 1940s decorated the walls. A brown plywood bar stood in one corner, with a silver-colored earthenware jar on top of it, holding dusty plastic flowers. The Lao woman who had left the room came back with four more Lao women and a Frenchwoman in her sixties with dead white skin, heavy makeup, and a blond beehive hairdo. "Monsieur Dick," she said in a heavy accent, "how are you?"

"Merry Christmas, Loulou. I brought you a bunch of losers from upcountry, and then this one important diplomat. He speaks French."

"The gentleman speaks French?" the woman asked Upson in that language.

"I can defend myself, Madame," he said. "My name is Fred Upson."

"Delighted to meet you, monsieur. Come and sit down, and we will talk." She took him to the table with the little mauve rug on it, cleared away the playing cards, and told one of the girls to bring her an anisette. Upson ordered scotch and water. They talked about North Africa, where she had been born. Upson ordered another drink, and they talked some more, and then he had another. The drunkenness of last night came flooding back, so that he began to have trouble finding the right French words. A college classmate from Texas used to describe this sort of happy, relaxed drunkenness as "walking light," Upson remembered. Duane's radio came to life every few minutes. Most of the messages were in Lao; reception was so bad that Upson couldn't even make out the occasional English transmission. Lindsay had introduced Upson to the other Americans back at Malichan's cafe, but the only names he remembered were those of Duane and of one other man. "Odom's the name," the other man had said. "Rhymes with scrotum. Call me 'Bag.' "

Now Bag was getting up to go to a room out back with one of the girls. "Hey, Fred," he called over, "tell Loulou I haven't had a blowjob in so long I'll shoot my wad before this little gal even gets started. Tell her to give me half price, babes."

"He says he has been without a woman so long that he is afraid the experience will be too brief to justify the expense," Upson translated.

"Alors, qu'il passe d'abord au cabinet."

"She says you can jerk off in the men's room beforehand."

Bag went off into a roar of laughter. "Goddamned Loulou's all right, ain't she?" he said when he could talk again. "Got these gals trained up to where they could draw jism out of a jackhandle."

"Is that the specialty of the house?" Upson asked Lindsay as Bag went off with the girl.

"Yeah, the old gal is kind of a missionary, really," said Lindsay, who was sitting at the next table with one of the Lao women. "Oral sex isn't part of the local culture. In fact, it was practically unheard of till Loulou introduced it. And she really taught 'em right, I'll say that for her."

"Don't you see any girls you like, monsieur?" Loulou said, with a timing that suggested she must have known at least a few words of English.

"They are all very pretty," he said politely, although they were all plain. "Perhaps in a moment." To Lindsay he said, under his breath, "Which one do you recommend?"

"The little tiny gal on my right is best," Lindsay said.

"That one there," Upson said in French, and Loulou beckoned to her. The girl came over smiling, and took Upson by the hand. Her own hand was tiny as a child's. "You can use my bedroom," Madame Loulou said, pointing the girl toward a doorway just by their table.

The only furniture apart from the bed was two plywood armoires, an old desk and chair, and a cheap little altar in the corner with Buddha figurines, joss sticks, and a chipped enamel dish for offerings. Upson felt comfortable with the little girl. Although at the beginning he had not planned to go with one of the women, by now he felt crazy enough for anything. The meat market, the ruined Christmas tree, the haunted hotel he had passed, the sense from the crackling radio that a war was going on somewhere at a safe distance, being drunk on Christmas day while sunlight was still coming through the faded curtains—all of it jangled together inside his head.

Upson set his glass and the gift-wrapped Santa Claus radio on Madame Loulou's desk. The girl directed him to sit down on the bed while she knelt at his feet to take off his shoes and socks. While Upson was getting out of the rest of his clothes, she took off her cotton blouse, padded brassiere, and wrap-around, ankle-length skirt. She had only a suggestion of breasts, like a girl just coming into puberty. Although she had a woman's face, her figure was as slim as that of a ten-year-old girl. She talked along easily in Lao while she put him in position on the bed, as if he understood every word. He thought of himself talking to Somchan. But Somchan didn't do—Lindsay was right—what the little girl-woman, her head dipping like a bird's, had begun to do to him. Her touch was so delicate and smooth that soon he closed his eyes and thought of nothing else.

After he had finished she waited for a moment, unmoving. Then she sprang up from the bed as quick and lively as some small animal, ran over to the wall, and crouched down. It was all so unexpected that it took Upson a moment to grasp that she had gone to empty her mouth into a pot by the wall. She came immediately back toward the bed, smiling and chattering away— a friendly, innocent, tiny thing so frail that he felt a surge of protective warmth. "You know what?" he said. "On the other side of the world, it's something called Christmas."

He handed her the gift-wrapped radio and gestured for her to open it up. He would get Somchan another radio, a decent one. When the tiny girl got the wrapping off, she seemed confused by the plastic fat man with the beard and the red and white suit. He turned one of the tunic buttons, so that music came suddenly out of the man's mouth. She almost dropped the radio, but then began to laugh and talk excitedly. She pointed at the radio and then at herself, to ask if it was really a present. "Merry Christmas," Upson said, nodding. She made a deep wai, hands prayerfully together and head bowed. Then she pulled him by the hand back toward the bed. "No tell mama-san," she said.

"Hey, wait a minute," Upson said, and paused to think how to get the idea across. Then he held up two fingers and said, "Two times, no can do."

"Can do," the small girl said. He knew she was wrong, but she turned out not to be. When she had succeeded at last, they went back into the main room for her to show off her present. One of the girls unwrapped a candy cane, and in a moment all the others had done the same. There were jokes and broad gestures as they sucked on the striped canes, and it all should have seemed coarse. But somehow it reminded Upson instead of the giggly pajama parties his cousin used to have in her early teens.

The drink he had taken into the bedroom was finished, and he had another. The others were talking about experiences everyone but he had shared. The night Mad Dog stumbled out drunk to take a leak and the Meo sentry shot him in the leg. Pouring cans of Carling Black Label down the throats of the three black bears that lived in a cage outside Sky House. The CIA case officers had named them Stokely, H. Rap, and Baby Bear. The time Vang Pao had the Lao reporter buried up to the neck. Forced marches. Airplane crashes. Opium. Through it all Duane's radio crackled with messages from the country up north where these things had happened. Nobody paid any attention to the radio—least of all Duane, who had been muttering to himself and now suddenly spoke up.

"Hey, Gunfighter," he said to Lindsay. "Gunfighter, goddamnit anyway, listen up when I talk to you. I want to know about him. Is he okay?"

"Who?"

"You know. The guy there."

"Fred? Sure. He's the new mad bomber at the embassy, I told you."

"I didn't ask was he at the embassy. I asked was he okay."

"He's okay, babes."

"And he was in Morocco? You were in Morocco, right?"

"In Rabat, yeah," Upson said. "Three years."

"Then you know about the Berbers, huh?"

"Well, a little."

"The Berber conspiracy?"

"What Berber conspiracy?"

"Three years, and they never told you about the Berber conspiracy?"

Upson looked over at Lindsay to see if he had any idea what Duane was talking about, but Lindsay shrugged his shoulders. "The Berbers are the communists in that part of the world," Duane went on. "You know about their headquarters in Baghdad, don't you? Where the chief Berber is? The head communist?"

"I never heard of Berbers in Baghdad, no."

"Three years, and they never told you who the communists

were?" Duane paused to think about it. "Hey, wait a minute," he said. "Maybe you're not cleared. You cleared?"

"Sure, I'm cleared."

"Hey, wait a minute. Maybe you think *I'm* not cleared. Tell him, Gunfighter."

"Sure, Duane is cleared," Lindsay said. "NATO Secret, Atomic Secret, Q-Clearance. You can tell him anything."

"You see? I'm cleared. So they told you about the Berbers, right? The communist conspiracy? Main man in Baghdad, head Berber?"

"I never heard that, no."

"Fuck him," Duane said suddenly and loudly, like a man calling out during a dream. "Don't tell him anything." His head fell back against the wall and his eyes closed. In a minute he was snoring.

Madame Loulou, who had been gone for a time, came back to sit with Upson, Lindsay, and their two girls. "Tell Loulou Merry Christmas from one old-timer to another," Lindsay said. "Tell her that."

Upson translated this, and then her answer: "She says Merry Christmas to you, too, old buddy. Her words. *Vieux copain*—old buddy. But she says you're no old-timer. You only got here eight or ten years ago, she thinks."

"Tell her it isn't how long you've been here, it's how long you're going to stay. Neither of us will leave this dump till they drag us out feet first."

Lindsay's girl sat close beside him, her hand lying in his lap. From time to time her little fingers would move as she fondled him through his pants. Neither the madame with her painted face nor the half-drunk American with his drooping mustaches acted as if anything out of the ordinary was going on. They didn't ignore the girl's hand; they just accepted it as in the natural course of things and went on with the conversation.

"She says she's thinking of going back to France next year, actually," Upson translated for Lindsay.

"She's been saying that every year since I've known her."

"Well, I'm a woman alone, and I have to stay where I can earn my bread," Madame Loulou said before Upson had translated. "It's different for Monsieur Dick. He has a wife and child to think about. He is an educated man, he comes from a good family, he has a future. Without indiscretion, I wonder why he stays here?"

Upson had wondered the same thing, but politeness had kept him from asking. Now he could. "She started out by saying, 'Sans indiscretion,' " he said. "That's what the French say when they're about to be indiscreet. Without indiscretion, Dick, why does a promising young man like you hang around out here, anyway?"

"She knows why, of course," Lindsay said. "She's part of the permanent party, too. All right, though. Why?"

Lindsay was silent for a moment. When he started talking again he seemed to be speaking not to them, but to himself. "When I first came to Vientiane," he said, "people used to keep a jar of water sitting out in their yard, in case anybody walking by happened to be thirsty. There was a Frenchman here then, a doctor. In the evenings he would sit on his porch and shoot stray dogs with a crossbow. It was for rabies, to keep the rabies down. He used to say he did more for public health during the evenings than during the day . . ."

Lindsay finished off his drink, and his girl went to get him another. "I learned to pull teeth here," he went on. "You give them kind of a twist with the pliers, and generally they come right out. Father Jerry taught me how. He taught me how to deliver babies, too. In his leper colony. Lepers have babies, why not? Twice I kept an eye on the leprosarium for him while he was out in the boonies finding more lepers. They'd be tied to a tree, in the forest. Somebody comes out from the village once a day and pushes food to the poor bastard with a stick. I had the dengue here. Malaria, too. Once I got blood poisoning from a leech bite, and the red line was all the way up the inside of my thigh nearly to the groin before I got to penicillin. I was scared that time. Once the PL went under the hut where I was staying and shot up through the floor, but that time I wasn't scared. It happened too fast. By the time I was awake enough to figure out what had happened, they were gone. Through the whole attack there was an RLA squad in the village, and they never fired a shot. Next day General Darasouk lined up the squad, called the squad leader out, and blew his left ear off with a forty-five.

"Twice I walked out of the mountains with my people, in front of the communists. I was there when the survivors walked in from Ban Dang five, six years ago. The NVA and the PL had been marching along beside the refugee column for three days, like wolves following sheep. When they got bored, they'd shoot into the flock, just for fun. Women, children, whoever. Terror. They're worse than we are, that's what guys like Bailey can't understand. They figure because we're bad, Hanoi must be good. Well, I've got news for you, babes. We're both bad. We murder because we're too dumb to understand what we're doing; the communists do it on purpose."

The girl came back with Lindsay's new drink and returned her hand to his lap. Lindsay covered it with his own hand. His tone had become angry and contemptuous when he was speaking about Bailey and the communists. Now it became dreamy again. "I came over here as a Peace Corps volunteer in northeast Thailand," he said. "I didn't know much about women. I learned about them first, really, out in the villages. I go back on home leave now, and I don't see any American women I'd want to go with. Girls I went to school with, girls from home, they all look like cows to me now.

"I'm like Duane. I'm afraid the war will end, too, and we'll all have to go back to the world. The nasty truth is that war is fun, this kind of war is. Except for a few people right on the front edge of it. For the rest of us, it's sort of a safe adventure. Like when you run away, but you know you can always write home for money if things get too tough. When I walked out of the mountains those two times, I didn't have to. The embassy wanted to fly me out, but I said I couldn't leave my people. The truth is, it was more fun to walk. I understand you don't have to be a bullfighter to dodge a bull. Any asshole can do it. To make it look hard, you have to stand your ground."

Lindsay took hold of his temples with the thumb and middle finger of his free hand, squeezing so hard that the fingertip showed white against his tanned skin. "Starting to get dizzy," he said. "Got to go home. Not to America, home here. Where else would I go? What else would I do? This is all I know."

Duane was still asleep when they had settled the bill. They had to carry him out like a dead man and load him aboard a samlor. Upson began to see double on his way home, a thing he had never done before. He tried to make the images come together by concentrating, but they kept straying apart. At his house, he had to hold onto the railing to get up the porch stairs, and was a long time fitting his key into the lock.

"Ho, ho, Merry Christmas," he called out once he was inside. "Santa's going to get you a real radio from the PX, Somchan, and a decent fan and a pear tree." Then it came back to him that she had the day off. He made it to the bedroom and out of his clothes, set the alarm, and managed to turn on the air conditioning. The sun was just going down when he passed out on top of his bed.

Upson had slept through most of the hangover when the alarm woke him the next morning. He felt a little shaky, but even that passed once he had taken a shower and dressed. And Somchan had left a pitcher of iced coffee for him in the refrigerator. He saw her through the window, talking with the mission guard on duty at the house of his CIA neighbor. The homes of all CIA men and military attachés were guarded around the clock, which made some of the embassy wives complain of unfairness. Since the only real danger in Vientiane was from burglars, they argued, why shouldn't everyone be protected?

Somchan took something from the guard's hand and made a small wai. She only bowed her head and curtsied very slightly, but it still hurt Upson that she might consider herself the inferior of a Thai security guard. As she walked back toward the house, she saw him looking out the window and her face brightened with a smile. He waved to her, feeling proud and happy in the knowledge that such a sweet, pretty woman was his lover.

"Sambai di, taan," she said when she came in. Hello, sir.

"Sambai di, Fred," he said. "Fred, Fred. I'm Fred, not *taan*."

"Sambai di, Fed," she said, and laughed. She held out what the guard had handed her, a note printed in careful, awkward letters of uneven size. "Honor Sir," it went, "Somchan ask she can go KM 30 Sunday. Somchan have many familys KM 30. You please write anser."

The main camp for the Plain of Jars refugees, Upson knew, was thirty kilometers north of Vientiane on the Luang Prabang road. He remembered the refugees standing frightened in the storm of dust and noise from the C-130s, and tried to imagine any of them as relatives of Somchan. "Come on," he said, motioning for Somchan to go with him over to where the guard was still standing. The man's blue gray uniform was rumpled, and his nightstick looked too big for him.

"Hello, sir," the guard said, saluting. "What's your trouble?"

Upson was surprised, and then realized that the man must just be repeating something he had heard from an American superior.

"No trouble," Upson said. "I was just wondering about your note. Is KM 30 the refugee camp?"

The guard smiled and nodded to let the American know that the question was an excellent one, and that he had understood every word. Actually, all he had caught were "no trouble," "KM 30," and "refugee." Refugee was the word he had been trying to think of when he wrote the note for the little Lao slut.

"Yes, sir. Many refugee."

"And Somchan's family are refugees at KM 30?"

"I think so, sir. I ask again." In a mixture of Thai and Lao, he asked Somchan, "What is this guy in the camp? Your uncle?"

"Yes, my uncle."

"What's his name?"

"Khammone Rintharamy. He has a bad leg."

"Was he a soldier, then?"

"No, just a farmer."

"Does he have a family?"

"Four kids and his wife, Tongsai. And her parents."

"Your grandparents?"

"No, she's my aunt by marriage."

"What's the name of the old people?"

"Mitsri."

"What's their village?"

"Xieng Dat."

The guard turned to Upson and said, "Yes, sir. Somchan

90

family refugee at KM 30." He made the number sound like "sirty."

"Well, she can have Sunday off to see them, sure." He had wanted to give her Sundays off from the start, but the Chinese local employee who handled housing for the embassy said that servants didn't expect Sundays off in Laos. A day at Lao New Year would be enough, along with a small cash bonus. Upson was glad he had taken the man's advice, because now he and Somchan could spend long, lazy Sundays in bed together.

The guard translated to Somchan: "The taan says you can go see your people Sunday, but be sure you're back on the job Monday."

Somchan smiled and made a wai to Upson. "How is she going to get up there?" he asked the guard.

"Maybe take taxi."

"Would you tell her that I can get a motor pool car and give her a ride up?"

The guard understood *car* and *motor pool*. "Your boss says he'll get you an embassy car," he translated. "You're a lucky little girl. You must be a really good maid to him."

"Don't get smart."

"How about being that good a maid to me sometime?"

"Aren't you satisfied with your water buffalo? The fat thing I saw you with at the movies last month?"

"She say thank you, sir. For car."

When Somchan and Upson had gone, the guard went into the kitchen of the CIA man, Mr. Bancroft, and found a pencil. He tore a piece of paper from a paper bag and wrote down the names: Rintharamy, Khammone and Tongsai; Mitsri; Xieng Dat. When the man got back to mission guard headquarters at the end of his shift, he gave the piece of paper to the sergeant who terrified him so much.

"What's this?" Sergeant Bounlek asked.

"Well, sergeant, you know the house next to the one I guard? The house that belongs to the American who's screwing his maid?"

"How would I know who he's screwing? In fact, how do you know?"

"One day I saw them through the window."

"You saw them screwing?"

"Not exactly. The way the bed is, you can't quite see it from Mr. Bancroft's window. But I saw her get up from the bed and go to the door, and I know the American was in the house."

"How do you know it was the bed she got up from, you complete idiot? You just said you can't see the bed."

"Well, you can see practically the whole rest of the room and you can't see the bed, so the bed has to be in the part you can't see."

"The morons they send me."

"I'm sorry, sergeant. I just thought . . ."

"I'll do the thinking. Now what are these names?"

"The names of the maid's relatives out at KM 30. She had me ask the American if she could visit them Sunday. Xieng Dat is their village. I think the relatives are Pathet Lao."

"Why?"

"Because she said her uncle has a bad leg. Probably he was wounded."

"Maybe a snake bit him. Maybe he fell off a cliff. Maybe a crocodile got him. What's the American's name?"

"I don't know."

"What's the house number?"

"Mekong House, number seven."

The sergeant wrote that down on the brown scrap of paper, under the names. "Is that all you know?" he asked.

"Yes, sergeant."

"Then get out of here."

Sergeant Bounlek thought for a minute about the American with his maid. He would like to see that. Once he had been in the men's locker room of the pool in the USAID compound and seen an American naked. The man was no taller than the sergeant himself, and yet he had a penis easily half again as large as the sergeant's own. A thing like that would make one of these little Lao girls beg for mercy, the sergeant thought with envy. Then the phone rang, and he forgot about the little piece of paper. But Corporal Ouday spotted the note during the office check he made every day after quitting time. He put it away in his own desk, and asked Sergeant Bounlek about it the next morning. Later, when the sergeant was gone, he went to see Mr. Mancuso.

"Make it quick, Ouday," Mr. Mancuso said. "I got this goddamned report to do." The weekly security activities report was the worst thing in Mancuso's life. He hated to write, and yet it was something you just couldn't delegate to a local. Mancuso had tried once, but Corporal Ouday's written English was no damn good. It struck Mancuso all of a sudden that he might try getting the corporal to write the report in Thai, and then have the goddamned thing translated somewhere.

"Yes, sir," the corporal said to his American boss. "All the refugees come from PDJ down here, sir, and many refugees communist, sir. I think maybe somebody have Pathet Lao friend or uncle, something like that, work for Americans, maybe steal papers. So I ask all guards look out. One guard tell me maid for Mr. Upson, Mekong House number seven, she have PL uncle in KM 30."

"How do you know he's PL?"

"Lao Army shoot him in war, sir."

"Shit, the only time the RLA ever shot anybody, maybe they shot one of their own guys in the foot by accident."

"Maybe him not PL, then, sir."

"All right, you got the names or anything?"

"Yes, sir, I type all ready for you, sir."

The only other thing for the weekly security activities report that amounted to a shit, Mancuso thought, was the guard who complained that Bill Rattner's wife, Brenda, was always making the kid jack off in the back yard while she watched from the kitchen window. Mancuso goddamned sure wasn't going to send that in to the DCM. He picked up the sheet of paper Corporal Ouday had left with him and went to work. When he had finished, the item read: "A comprehensive surveillance program was initiated targeting American domestics to indicate the possibility of contact with possible Pathet Lao sympathizers in refugee resettlement areas in the Vientiane area. This comprehensive program has resulted in discovering a potential contact between the domestic employee of Embassy officer Fred Upson and her uncle and several other relatives residing in the refugee resettlement area of KM 30. Subject officer is believed to be providing transportation to his female domestic employee (maid) for purposes of visiting her uncle in referenced resettlement area. Subject uncle is Tongsai Rintharamy and his wife is

Khammone Rintharamy. The uncle's parents have the family name of Mitsri and all of the subjects formerly inhabited the town of Xieng Dat. Investigation revealed that Tongsai Rintharamy is believed to be a wounded veteran of the PL forces. His unit could not be determined."

Mancuso read over what he had written, and scratched out the last sentence. Better to leave it at what you did know; no sense flagging what you didn't know. He took the finished draft of the report to the office of his boss, the chief of embassy security, for typing. The secretary there got around to it the next morning. The morning after that, copies went to the embassy administrative officer and the CIA station chief. The original was addressed to the ambassador, although it never got farther than the deputy chief of mission. The other addressees glanced at the report just long enough to be sure that nothing in it required action, and then put it in the out box, marked for filing. Jerry Brautigan paused for a few seconds longer over the report, because Mancuso's tortured prose sometimes amused him. Upson's name caught the DCM's eye, but he saw right away that the item didn't amount to anything. Everybody in Laos had relatives who sympathized with the Pathet Lao, or had been forced to cooperate with the PL, or had been drafted into PL service as soldiers or porters. Brautigan noticed that the name of the maid's uncle was supposed to be Tongsai. General Sirisouk's wife was called Tongsai, and so plainly it was a woman's name; the rest of the report was probably wrong as well. Brautigan, too, marked the report for filing and tossed it into his outbox. He turned to the latest correspondence from Washington on the embassy's request to authorize construction of a bombproof shelter for key mission personnel in the basement of the ambassador's residence. Washington probably knew as well as Brautigan that the facility would take the form of an elaborate bar and game room, but the paper trail had to look at least vaguely convincing. Brautigan remembered something Phil Casey had once said at a meeting: "If you don't want it on the front page of the *Times,* then just don't do it."

If only life were that simple.

When Upson asked directions to the KM 30 camp, Dick Lindsay offered to drive them up Sunday in his own car—a gray Jeepster that had been auctioned off as unserviceable by USAID. Much of the paint was worn off, the body was dented, and the passenger door was wired shut. Somchan went to get into the back, but Lindsay spoke to her in Lao and she stopped. "We better all sit in front," Lindsay said to Upson. "The dust isn't so bad there. You slide in under the wheel first, then Somchan." Lindsay talked with Somchan as they drove along, and Upson was a little surprised not to feel jealous. Instead, he felt secure about her and confident that she was his. Nor was he envious that Lindsay could talk to her and he couldn't. He didn't want to talk to her in a language she could understand. What if she found out she didn't like him, or if he didn't like her? What if they confused or bored each other?

Past the airport they came upon a checkpoint, with its gate swung open to let the traffic pass unchallenged. Two soldiers were playing cards in the small guardhouse, seldom bothering to look up as the cars went by.

"They don't fool with cars much," Lindsay explained. "Anyone rich enough to have his own car is probably too powerful to shake down. Mostly they pick on trucks and taxis."

"Can't we get them to stop it?"

"Why would we do that? Our government shakes people down, too, every April. But here practically nobody pays taxes, so the soldiers have to collect their own salaries."

"Still, it gives the PL another talking point."

"The PL might not shake down taxis at roadblocks, but what they do is worse. They ship your ass off for a couple months of porterage, carrying supplies down from Vietnam. And then they grab part of your crops, too, same-same IRS."

Except for Upson's flight to the Plain of Jars, he had never been outside Vientiane before. Mission policy required official Americans to clear all trips outside the city with the embassy security office, but Lindsay had said not to bother. "Better not to stir up those assholes," he said. "They think anything outside the city limits is Indian territory."

The countryside seemed peaceful enough, and in fact, Upson knew, the Pathet Lao almost never set up their B-40 rocket ambushes this near the city. The road was wide and well graded, but the traffic had turned its red dirt surface to wash-board that hammered the old jeepster. Since Lindsay drove faster than anyone else on the road, they kept catching up with the dustclouds raised by other trucks and cars. Soon the red dust dulled Somchan's glossy hair and lay thick on their clothes. Here and there along the road were stands of tall trees, running up sixty feet or more before the branches started. But most of the country on both sides had been cleared for fields and paddy. The soil had been baked gray by the sun. Where water had filled the paddies, the drying mud had cracked into millions of irregular, gray tiles. The bushes and grass seemed dried up and dead. The wind through the windows was like the blast from a heat register.

For miles there were no houses. Then all at once, as they topped a small rise, a desolate city of huts appeared. "We're here," Lindsay said. "KM 30."

"Jesus," said Upson. The hundreds of small huts stood on short stilts. The roofs were thatch, the framework of bamboo poles, and the walls were mats woven from split bamboo. There was no grove of trees, no stream, no pond, no cross roads, no temple or market around which a village might naturally have grown. It was as if the refugee trucks had driven thirty kilometers north and dumped everybody off at the milestone. The trucks must have brought the building materials, too, since there was no vegetation around the camp. Even the garden plots here and there among the huts held only stunted or dead plants.

"They don't know how to make things grow down here," Lindsay said. "Not even themselves, actually. They'll stand all kinds of punishment in the mountains and stay alive. But bring them down a few thousand feet and they start dying off. New strains of malaria and TB, new kinds of bugs in the water. Ever try to keep a baby cottontail alive? He's fine out in the weather, but put him in a box by the stove and he'll get the shakes and die during the night."

They were following Somchan back into the settlement, as she asked directions from refugees along the way. Well into the camp, an old man pointed to a hut indistinguishable from the others. It stood on four-foot stilts; a baby sat quietly in the shade underneath. A man sitting in the doorway called out when he saw Somchan, and came down the ladder to meet her. He walked with a limp and his legs were a dark, unhealthy, bruised color. As Upson drew closer, he saw that the discoloration was caused by tattoos, in heavy, blocky patterns like Mayan designs. The tattooing covered most of the skin, so that the man looked as if he were wearing dark tights down to his ankles. His bare feet were undecorated.

Somchan made a deep wai to the man, her head bowed lower than her joined hands. His bow to her was not quite so deep, but when he turned to Upson and Lindsay, the gesture of respect was exaggerated almost to parody. Lindsay spoke briefly to the man, and turned to Upson. "I told them now that we know the way, we'll go back to the car and get the stuff," he said. "Take a good look around, so that we can find the joint again."

"I never saw those tattoos before," Upson said as they walked off.

"You don't see them much anymore, except on the older guys like Somchan's uncle, there. They do it when you're a kid, with bamboo splinters and vegetable dyes. I talked to one guy, he said it took a couple of days to put his on. Men hold the kid down so he doesn't wriggle too much from the pain."

"Do the designs mean something?"

"Probably once they did. Nobody knows anymore. Or at least they wouldn't tell me."

Back at the car they got out a big red and white cooler holding beer and soda. Somchan had also brought two string bags bulging with papayas, breadfruit, mangoes, and custard apples. "Maybe we should have brought them some kind of gift, too," Upson said. "Poor bastards."

"I don't like to do that," Lindsay said. "These folks have been self-sufficient all their lives, because they've had to be. You give them stuff and they're glad to take it, but it does a certain amount of harm, you know? Bad enough they have to live on rice handouts down here, at least it's institutionalized. Bring them something personally and it's different. Do you see what I mean?"

"I guess I do, yes." Upson still would like to have brought something, though, to make Somchan's relatives happy and

97

grateful. Grateful. Yes, now he could see what Lindsay meant.

When Lindsay and Upson got back, Somchan was holding the baby boy who had been sitting, quiet and content, under the hut. Now he was screaming. When Somchan put him back down on the ground he stopped crying at once. He began smacking his hand into the dust, watching it fly. Lindsay said something to Somchan, and her answer made them both laugh. "I asked her why she was hurting the baby," Lindsay explained. "She said if I wanted to hear the kid really cry, I should pick it up myself and show it my sharp nose."

"Sharp nose?"

"You never heard the kids chanting that when you walk by in the streets? *Farang dang mo?* It means pointy-nose foreigner. They sing a little song—Pointy-nose foreigner, riding his motorcycle to the market, crashed into a tree and that's why his nose is like that."

"Is that right?" Upson said. He felt uncomfortable.

"Face it, Fred. We all look alike."

The middle-aged man with the tattooed legs, Khammone, motioned for them to climb up the four steps of the bamboo ladder leaning against the door of his hut. Upson stepped aside for Somchan to go first, but Khammone made Upson and Lindsay go up before her. He himself came last. Although bright sparkles of light came through the thatch roofing, the inside was still so dark that it took a moment for Upson's eyes to get used to it. Then he saw a very old man lying in an alcove, smoking a pipe. An old woman with a gray crewcut squatted in the main room, grinning widely. She seemed toothless, but when she spat a mouthful of reddish liquid through a crack in the floor Upson realized that her teeth were just hard to see—stained dark by betel-nut juice.

"Sambai di, taan," the old woman said.

"Sambai di," Upson answered.

"Sambai di, eui-i," Lindsay said, and went on to ask her a question. The old woman's answer made everybody laugh but Upson, who smiled to be polite. "I asked her why she was spitting on the baby through that crack," Lindsay said. "She said it kept the flies off him. When a woman in Laos gets old, she chops off her hair and turns into a hot shit."

There was also a middle-aged woman, and three children.

Presumably she was Khammone's wife and the mother of the little children. Somchan's cousins. The newcomers sat on the floor, which gave with every movement, like a trampoline. It was made of plaited mats, over thin bamboo poles lashed together with vines. Upson was afraid that the floor couldn't hold so much weight, but nobody else even seemed to notice the swaying. One of the cousins, a little girl of four or five, came over and stared at Upson from a safe distance. There was something of Somchan in her, he thought. His smile encouraged her to come closer. She reached out and touched his forearm lightly, and then jumped back, giggling at how brave she was. When Upson still smiled, she touched his forearm tentatively again, and then began to pull gently at the light-colored hairs on it. After watching for a minute, the other two children joined in the game.

"That's why I grew this mustache originally," Lindsay said. "To give the kids something weird to play with." Once over their shyness, the children sat on Upson's legs and leaned against him, as they examined his strange fur with friendly curiosity. They chattered to him in perfect confidence that he understood, and they laughed when he answered them in his funny way, with nonwords. Upson felt overwhelmed with love. He tickled one of the children in the ribs and said "Nakadiem," as he remembered Somchan saying to him. The children looked at him in surprise, the way they might look at a water buffalo that had come out with a recognizable word. Then they went off into helpless laughter. As soon as they showed signs of recovering, one or the other would say, "Nakadiem," and they would burst out all over again. They stopped for good only when Lindsay said something to them that ended with the word "Pepsi."

Somchan and the children had soft drinks from the cooler. Everyone else had sixteen-ounce cans of Budweiser from the American Community Association commissary. To judge by the gestures, Khammone was surprised by their size. "It's a nonstandard part," Lindsay told Upson. "There's a whole cottage industry based on aluminum cans, making mousetraps and lamps and stuff out of them. But they're all twelve ounces."

The conversation seemed to turn to the war. With his hands, Khammone described a plane circling, and the other ones coming in faster, diving and zooming away. His wife added

99

details, and so did the old people. They sounded cheerful and unconcerned to Upson, like people describing a football game or a visit to the amusement park.

"Whose planes is he talking about?" Upson asked.

"Nobody in Southeast Asia has planes except us," Lindsay said. "Right from the beginning, Hanoi had it figured out that a thirty-seven-millimeter antiaircraft gun is a whole lot cheaper than an F-4 fighter-bomber."

"I meant was RLAF flying them."

"No, they know that RLAF flies the T-28s. What he's talking about are the little OV-1s, the spotter planes, and then the F-4s and F-105s following up."

"How many attacks is he talking about?"

Lindsay put the question to Khammone, and the man with the tattooed legs went into a long explanation. At the end he sketched a pattern on the floor with his forefinger, touching the matting here and there as if to poke holes in it.

"He says it started getting really bad just after the rains ended in '68," Lindsay translated. "That was when Johnson stopped the bombing in North Vietnam, and the air force was able to transfer all those resources here. Not that Khammone knows about that, but that's what happened. From then on the attacks came just about daily. All the orchards were destroyed, and a lot of the livestock. People had to hide in the woods during the day and work the fields at night."

"What was he showing you on the floor there?"

"The way they had to cook. Any visible smoke would bring in the planes, so they'd build these little fires underground, with tunnels leading off to be like chimneys. They'd poke holes along the tunnels to let the smoke come out in a lot of little wisps, too small to see from the air."

"Were there any PL or NVA in the village?" Upson was relieved to see Khammone nod vigorously and go off into a detailed reply to Lindsay's translation of the question.

"He says the Pathet Lao came one day with a truckload of supplies," Lindsay translated at the end. "They had what he figures was an NVA officer with them. He was dressed in a PL uniform, but he spoke Lao with a strong North Vietnamese accent and he used chopsticks."

"What does that signify?"

"The Lao don't use chopsticks. Anyway, they left off a bunch of cement bags and stuff under one of the houses. They were going to come back the next week to show the folks how to make a dam with it, but that was almost two years ago and they never did come back. Sounds like one of our own aid projects. The cement turned as hard as rocks after the first rainy season. The steel reinforcing rods are all rusty, but he figures they're still good."

"Reinforcing rods?"

"Yeah, you know. Those long rods you see at construction sites, tied into bundles. They stick them into the concrete when they pour it."

That recalled something to Upson, but he forgot it when the children discovered his glasses. He let them take turns looking through them, which made them shout with laughter at the way the world turned all fuzzy. The child wearing the glasses would stumble around, feeling his way like a blind man. The world was dim for Upson, too, without his glasses. The old woman seemed to be showing Lindsay something, and then he was doing something to her that looked as if he were giving her an injection. Upson motioned to one of the children to bring back his glasses; the child, still laughing, did it right away. With the glasses, he could see that Lindsay was pushing gently at the old woman's upper arm. She motioned for Upson to come over, too.

"She wants you to feel the little pellets from the CBUs," Lindsay said. Upson remembered the cluster bomb unit he had seen during the refugee airlift: the steel cylinder the reporter had almost kicked. "The Lao word for CBUs is *bombi*," Lindsay said. "It's supposed to be a French word." Upson tried to think what the French word could have been, and then it came to him. *Bombe à billes.* Ball-bearing bombs.

The old woman put his hand on the leathery skin of her arm. The flesh was soft underneath, not at all like the healthy, elastic feel of Somchan's body. Not knowing what to do, he smiled and nodded when the woman made his fingers palpate the lump inside her arms. The old woman laughed and poked him with her elbow, as if it were the funniest thing in the world that steel ball-bearings had found their way into her arm. She led his fingers to a second one, and laughed again. They felt like hard little cysts, buried in the loose flesh.

"How did it happen?" Upson asked Lindsay.

"She was out trying to chase their water buffalo under cover when the planes came. The buffalo made it, but she didn't. The old folks and the kids get the worst of it. The old folks can't run so fast, and the kids don't have enough sense to be scared. The planes are almost like a game to the little ones. Sometimes you lose, like Shorty there did."

"What do you mean?"

"Didn't you see the kid's leg?"

Now Upson saw. The little boy wore nothing but a small T-shirt, so that his bottom was bare. He had been so lively and active, playing with the eyeglasses, that Upson had thought the limp was part of his acting like a blind man. But the back of the boy's leg was shiny and uneven, as if someone had begun to sculpt a leg from pink modeling clay and failed to smooth it off. The scar tissue had drawn up into lumpy ridges, so that the leg couldn't straighten out all the way.

"Grandma says to go ahead and touch it," Lindsay translated. "She says it feels really funny, not like skin at all." Upson made himself touch the awful scar. Its surface was hard, like saddle leather. The little boy made a show of grabbing his leg, howling with mock pain, and rolling around on the floor. When the boy finished his comical reenactment of his injury, he hopped back to his feet and laughed. The other children and the grownups laughed, too.

"What happened to him?" Upson asked.

"Napalm. It makes those keloid scars, the same kind you see in the pictures of the Hiroshima survivors."

"Can it be fixed?"

"Probably. You'd have to cut all that shit off and replace it with skin grafts before he could straighten his leg out. I guess they could do it in Bangkok."

"What would it cost to send him down there and get it done?"

"I don't really know. Five or six hundred bucks? Maybe a thousand? Look, Fred, think about it. Who do you start with? How far do you go? We could walk through this camp and find fifty kids worse off than him, in a half an hour. The little boy can get around, just with a little limp. He'll be able to work in the fields when he grows up. You're not Tom Dooley, Fred. What can you do?"

"A little, at least."

"The most useful thing any of us can do, Fred, is do our own jobs the best we can. That's the best way to help the folks."

"It's different for you. Your job is to help the folks."

"Are you shitting me, babes? Your job helps the folks more than mine does. You can keep them from getting burned in the first place."

It was hot and airless in the hut, but Upson was learning not to be bothered by the heat so much. He moved as seldom and as slowly as possible, accepting the heat as part of being alive rather than as something to fight. He had nothing to do but listen to the sound of the others talking. He felt loose and drowsy from the beer. And he felt at peace as he never had, except with Somchan. Men like him had bombed these people, maiming and killing them. He himself might have ordered such strikes for all they knew, and yet they plainly held him blameless. The little boy had joked about his awful burn with no hint of bitterness, vengefulness, or self-pity. The old lady hadn't been asking for sympathy; she had offered up the steel balls in her flesh as an amusing phenomenon, like being able to touch your nose with your tongue. The whole family had a gentle courtesy that went further and deeper than good manners. They seemed to regard the two Americans not as foreigners to be treated politely, but as people who must be about the same as Lao, in spite of the odd way they looked and sounded. Or so Upson imagined, as he lay on the matting, half listening to the buzz of talk. It seemed to him that the family would be acting exactly the same if he and Lindsay had been two Lao friends, dropping in for a visit. Upson felt that the family was his family, and that their country was the country everyone searched for—that peaceable kingdom where the lion lies down simply with the lamb. The time passed. He had more beer. Upson came alert from a semi-doze when he realized that Lindsay was talking in English: ". . . so we might as well head on back."

"Oh, yeah," Upson said. "Right. Sure."

"Leave the empties here," Lindsay said, when Upson began

to put his four empties back into the cooler. "They'll find some use for them. Let's leave the rest of the beer and the Pepsis here, too. The ice, too. They don't get much ice out here. You know what the Lao word for ice is? *Nam kawn*. It means 'water in chunks.'"

Upson took the beer and soda and the plastic bag of ice out of the ice chest. "Save us a couple of cans for the trip back," Lindsay said, getting to his feet at the same instant Upson was. Upson almost lost his footing as he felt something tear loose in the floor from the sudden strain. More and more things gave way. Upson tried to grab for the wall, but found nothing to hold to. Everyone and everything slid toward the center of the room, slowly at first and then faster. When the last support gave way and they were in free fall, Upson had the moment of terror he had known so often in nightmares. But in a split second he thumped safely onto the ground below.

The collapsing floor had let them go only two feet above the ground, dumping everyone into a jumble. Somehow nobody had landed on the baby playing below, who sat silent in the middle of them all, too astonished to cry. A cold can of beer and a handful of ice cubes had landed in his naked lap. When the baby's surprise wore off enough for him to notice the cold, he suddenly wailed into the silence. The old woman pointed to the baby's lap and said something. Everyone, children and grownups, went off into helpless laughter that fed on itself, dying down only to start again when someone repeated the old woman's words.

"What did she say?" Upson was finally able to ask Lindsay.

"Said the pigs ate the kid's pecker."

Everyone started laughing at the baby again, as if they had understood Lindsay's words. Upson saw that the cold had shrunk the little boy's penis back up into his belly, so that only a wrinkled nubbin of foreskin remained. The dust and the water from the melting ice made a reddish mud all over the baby's legs. There was a huge rent in the floor above them, nearly as wide as the hut itself. The floor had sprung partway back into place after getting rid of all their weight, but it still sagged badly. "How much will it cost to fix it?" Upson asked.

"Nothing. They tie everything back together, maybe re-weave part of the floor matting. Two hours at the most. Christ, you could build the whole thing from scratch in a couple of days."

"I thought it seemed flimsy. We were too heavy for it."

"There was something wrong with it, Fred. I've seen these things hold up four or five round-eyes at once, upcountry."

"It held together all right till we came along, though."

"Everything isn't somebody's fault, Fred. Things just happen."

"We're what happens to them."

"Takes two to tango. The Vietnamese happen to them, too. You think these folks would have been any better off if they had stayed back home in Xieng Dat?"

"Is that the name of their village?"

"Xieng Dat, yeah. A little northeast of the PDJ."

"How do you spell it?"

"I don't know how it would be on the maps. The French seem to spell S with an X for some reason. Probably it would be X-i-e-n-g."

"Jesus, I hope not."

"Why?"

"Nothing," Upson said. "I'm probably wrong."

Somchan moved faster and faster, her heavy black hair whipping across her face until she made the little cry she always made at the end, and a shudder shook her body. Her head fell forward, the dark curtain of hair over her face. She made a little wriggle, as if to seat herself more firmly on him, and slumped there exhausted. Upson was still strong inside her. He had drunk enough during the visit to the refugee village so that he felt he could remain at Somchan's service as long as she wanted. At the beginning she had been shy about letting him see her naked, but little by little she had got over that. He admired the smooth, harmonious lines of her shoulders, her arms, her breasts, her belly. He thought of the two of them living in one of the little villages they had passed on their trip to the camp earlier in the day. He saw her walking under the trees in her *pakama*, the prettiest woman in the village, in the world. She would bathe in an orchid-hung jungle glade, her smooth, brown body glistening with water and only him to watch. After they made love in the forest, she would put her hand in his and they would walk back to the village. They would sit together in the soft dusk on the porch of their little house.

"You would be Sheena, Queen of the Jungle," he said to her aloud, "and everybody would envy me because you were mine. Do you know, I feel that now? Even though nobody knows I have you, I feel proud because they would envy me if they knew. I see other men, and I feel sorry for them because they don't know what it is to have you. I feel like a great lover, as if I could make any woman in the world happy because I can make you happy. Do I make you happy, Somchan?"

The girl looked up at the sound of her name. Her breathing had slowed now, and she said a sentence or two. "I never want to leave this place," Upson said. "Here I can say what I was never able to say to anybody before. I can say I love you." Once he had said the words aloud he felt freed, as if now he could say them easily and often. "My only sunshine. You make me happy when skies are gray. I always thought those songs were silly, but they aren't, are they? Oh, how I wish. But at least this is the here and now, and we have it."

He moved a little in gentle question; she moved in answer.

Somchan may have felt it wasn't her place to spend the night with him; she may have wanted to keep the neighbors from talking; maybe the sexes slept apart in Laos, for all Upson knew. He would have liked her to pass whole nights at his side, as he would have liked her to caress him with her mouth sometimes. But these were small regrets beside what she brought to him, and he seldom thought about them at all. He lay alone in the dark, imagining what she was doing in her quarters out back. At last he went to the window, to look. Both her room and the laundry room were lit. A shower pipe ran up one wall of the laundry room, with a large, old-fashioned shower head that hung drooping from the top of the pipe like a sunflower borne down by its own weight. He heard the water splashing on the concrete floor. Somchan must have finished soaping herself; the moonlight picked out suds in the water that was sluicing out of a drain in the side of the building. It ran into the ditch between his yard and Bancroft's. The noise of the shower stopped, and a few minutes later the light in the laundry room went out. Somchan showed in silhouette for an instant in her bedroom doorway, and then all he could see was the line of light under her door. He heard the sound of her tiny radio, voices and music that he would never understand. Next week one of the men from the air attaché's office was bringing Upson a good shortwave radio and a powerful fan from the Udorn PX; he hoped Somchan would like them. As Upson thought of her settling in to sleep, he remembered a line from an old musical comedy song. He had no ear for tunes, but a few of the words had stayed with him and he said them softly aloud: "Good night, sweet someone."

Monday morning, Upson went straight to the wall of his office where the big maps hung. He unlocked one of the panels and slid it aside to expose the section that included the Plain of Jars. Northeast of it, in what the contour lines showed to be a little flat-bottomed valley between two steep ridges, he found Xieng Dat. As he feared, his memory had been right. He noted the village's coordinates and went to his files for the photo he half remembered. The picture wasn't sharp; the pictures in his files seldom were. The papers wrote about satellite and U-2 photography so clear that you could make out a ball on a putting green, lenses of such incredible resolution that you could read newspaper headlines from miles in the air. But the air force's pictures from just a few thousand feet in the air were fuzzy. Could the papers be right? Upson wondered. Could anything really see that well from a satellite's altitude? Eagles? God?

The photo from his files showed a small village built along a stream which ran through the broad valley. He counted fourteen thatched roofs among the trees. Sticking out a little from under one of the houses was a row of indistinct objects. Upson's magnifying glass just brought up the graininess in the photo, making the row even less distinct. He called Major Mulhouse, the man in the air attaché's office who had tutored him in photo interpretation months before.

"Remember the picture of a rocket-storage dump you showed me a couple of months ago?" Upson asked.

"Which one?" the major said.

"The one you said they use in the photo reconnaissance classes as a classic example of a rocket-storage site. A village called Xieng Dat, above and just east of the PDJ. Would the coordinates help?"

"No, I remember it. Didn't I give you a copy, though?"

"You did, but I was wondering if you had any after-strike pictures. Presumably there was a strike."

"Presumably, but it was before my time. That photo goes back a few years. Hold on, let me see what we got. . . . Okay, sorry to be so long, but here it is. The rockets are blown all over the place. Want me to send it over?"

"I'll come by. Thanks, Bill."

When Upson got back to his office again, he laid the prestrike and the poststrike photos side by side. The first showed dozens of bomb craters all around the village—old ones, because water was standing in them. Some were close to the little houses, but there were no direct hits. The second photo, taken after the attack on the rocket storage site, showed three lines of fresh craters, roughly parallel. Upson remembered the man with the tattooed legs making his hands into imaginary airplanes, coming in low between the ridges. Two of the crater lines missed the targeted hut by a good margin, but one of the bombs in the third string had hit right next to it. The rockets lay scattered like jackstraws around the smoking debris of the hut. He was able to get an idea of their size from a twisted bicycle that lay on its side not far from the ruins. He dialed the army attaché's office and got Major Leroy Dutton on the line.

"Leroy," Upson said, "what's the biggest rocket or missile the bad guys use in Laos?"

"In the Nam they use the JT-10, but it wouldn't be worth humping them to Laos for a little tiny war like this one."

"How long are they?"

"All set up to go, about eight feet."

"They couldn't be using another model or something in Laos, could they? About twelve feet long?"

"Negative. The JT-10 is already so big it usually knocks the little guys on their ass when it goes off. Why?"

"I've got some old photos of missiles or rockets, twelve feet long. From MR-II, up the road from the PDJ."

"Let me come by, okay?"

Dutton was there ten minutes later. He was a short, heavily built man, with stiff black hair like an Indian's. This was his third tour in Laos, a country he knew as well as any American ever had. The major glanced at the photograph for only a second, not bothering to use the magnifying glass.

"What kind of shit are they trying to hand you?" he said. "You know what those things are? Bundles of steel reinforcing rods."

"I know."

"And they tried to tell you these were rockets? Christ, didn't those air force assholes ever walk past a construction site?"

"Leroy, they use that first photo back in the States, at the air force photo reconnaissance school. It's the textbook example of what rockets look like, hidden under a hut."

"God help us. You know, except for close air support, I sometimes think we'd be better off over here without the air force at all. Once I was on a Pentagon bombing review panel, met every Tuesday morning to review all the good shit the air force was doing over here. The first Tuesday I said, 'What are these forty-seven pack animals you guys destroyed?' 'Water buffaloes,' the air force guy says. 'Pack animals my ass,' I say. 'It's the dry season. When the ground hardens up, a water buffalo can't walk more than a kilometer or so without going lame.' Next week they killed another fifty or sixty pack animals, water buffaloes again. Every week I told them, every week they'd come in with another bunch of dead goddamned buffaloes."

After Upson's second gin and tonic, his headache from the day's work was almost gone. He decided not to make himself a third; he was too comfortable, sitting in the dark on the porch, to bother. "Somchan, my love," he said, "the secret potion has cured me once again."

She looked up at the sound of her name, and smiled.

"I thought at first the headaches were from eyestrain, looking through that damned viewer all day," he went on. "But if the drinks make it go away, it must be from tension. That's what I deduced, and here's how I deduced it. Tension causes restriction of the blood vessels in the brain, right? I think that's what the *Reader's Digest* says. The heart keeps trying to pump blood through those squinched-up little vessels, and the pressure gives you a son of a bitch of a headache. Whereas alcohol enlarges the blood vessels as everybody knows, which lowers the pressure, which removes the pain, which proves that if alcohol cures it, it must be a tension headache. Somchan, my love, I should have been a doctor. I know more about medicine than I do about photo reconnaissance, God knows.

"Today was an exceptionally good day for the mad bomber. I found out that we bombed your family's ancestral village by mistake. Not me personally. Some former mad bomber. No, I didn't make that particular mistake. I made other mistakes. Knowing full well what rockets under a hut look like, I've approved a good half-dozen strikes on similar rocket dumps, cleverly camouflaged as houses. The PL must have cached those damned reinforcing rods all over the place.

"A long time ago I saw a magazine cartoon, Somchan. It showed two big guys with whips and black hoods, down in this dungeon. One of them was saying, 'The way I look at it, if we didn't do it, somebody else would.' Funny, huh? Except the hell of it is, the guy was right. Somebody else would. Maybe me, but I'd be responsible and humane about it. I wouldn't heat the irons quite red-hot, and I'd slack off the tension on the rack a little when nobody was looking. Probably later I'd write a memo. That's what I did today. I wrote a memo."

Something in his voice made Somchan come over to him.

She took his hand in hers, and smiled to show him that every-thing was all right.

The memo had read: "The attached photographs show Xieng Dat, in Xieng Khouang Province, before and after a strike which occurred approximately two years ago. Photograph #1 purportedly shows a cache of NVA or PL rockets protruding from under the structure in the lower left-hand corner. Photograph #2 shows the destruction of the structure and the rocket cache under it. The purported rockets, however, appear to be about 12 feet long. This length was arrived at by comparison with the damaged bicycle also visible in Photograph #2, assuming the bicycle to be five feet in length. Major Leroy Dutton, Assistant ARMA, agrees with me that the supposed rockets appear to have been bundles of steel reinforcing rods. Several of the bundles were broken open by the explosion, and were clearly composed of rods both thinner and longer than any rocket known to be used by the enemy. In view of the fact that Photograph #1 is currently used as an example of a rocket cache in USAF photo reconnaissance courses, it is recommended that such use be modified or discontinued as appropriate. This is a matter of some urgency, since a number of strikes have been recently approved by the undersigned officer which it now seems probable were not on military targets. We risk further repetition of such incidents if photo-interpretation personnel continue to be trained in courses that include use of the photograph in question."

Upson put his free hand on top of Somchan's and smiled back at her. "It was an excellent memo," he said. "I referred to the bombing of villages as 'incidents.' "

The next afternoon, Annie Cutler brought a copy of the memo back to Upson. On the top, the deputy chief of mission had written, "Good memo, Ambassador concurs. Original sent to Costikyan for appropriate action." Upson wondered whether Brautigan meant that the ambassador concurred with the memorandum's recommendation, or concurred that it was a good memo. And he wondered whether he should have mentioned the existence at KM 30 of eyewitnesses who could confirm that the photo showed steel reinforcing rods. But the afterstrike photography made the fact obvious enough. If Mike Costikyan still needed convincing, though, Upson could always cite the witnesses. He picked up the phone and got through to the air attaché.

"Fred Upson, Mike," he said to the colonel. "Was that memo Jerry sent along any use to you?"

"Damned straight it was. I sent it on down to Seventh Air Force, along with my implementation recommendation."

"Good enough. It just seemed to me like something that should be called to their attention."

After the colonel hung up, he muttered something his sergeant couldn't make out. "Beg your pardon, sir?" he said.

"Civilians, sergeant. Fucking civilians."

"I know what you mean, sir."

"Did that memo on rocket-storage dumps go forward?"

"Yes, sir. A couple hours ago."

Colonel Costikyan figured Brautigan had only sent the memo along to keep his in basket clean. But against the slight chance that Brautigan or the ambassador really cared, the air attaché had forwarded the thing to Seventh Air Force with a handwritten covering note: "Bill: Recommend non-implementation. Photo evidence non-conclusive. Non-military utilization of steel re-inforcing rods in MR-II highly unlikely anyway. Best to Midge and the kids, Mike." This would leave Costikyan free of any possible blame for inaction, since Bill Farley knew enough to toss out the personal covering note.

This goddamned Upson kid is getting almost as bad as Gus Thompson, Costikyan thought. Thompson, you never knew who he was working for, us or goddamned Ho Chi Minh. The ambassador had his shit together, but civilians like Thompson and Upson and even Brautigan sometimes were fucking up this war to a fare-thee-well. Not a one of them could get it through his head that if the commies were going to swim like fish in the ocean of the civilian population like Mao said, then what you had to do was dry up the ocean. Simple as that. Suppose Upson was right about those rockets, for example. What did he think the commies were going to use steel reinforcing rods for anyway, up there in the boonies? Either bunkers, or some kind of USAID-type project to win the hearts and minds. What a bleeding heart like Upson could never understand was that dam or bunker, *either one* of them ought to be bombed. Did he think the commies were up there building dams because they're good guys, or because they want to get the peasants on their side, so they can win the war? Unlike us, for Christ's sake. What was the whole point of the rules of engagement, if not to make it fucking impossible for the good guys to win?

Lindsay had introduced Upson to a tin-roofed soup kitchen next to the embassy motor pool, and Upson had taken to going there most days around noon for noodle soup and weak iced tea. The proprietor was an Italian in his fifties, a former corporal in the French Foreign Legion who had stayed on in Southeast Asia after Dien Bien Phu. Sometimes the Italian would sit down with Upson, since almost all his other customers were motor pool drivers, mechanics, and mission guards who spoke no French. This made Upson feel he belonged, like the regulars in certain bars who all seem to know the bartender and each other.

"I feel like sweeping you off your feet," Upson said to Annie Cutler at noon the next day. "Let me take you to Giovanni's for lunch."

"I must have passed this place a hundred times without seeing it," she said when Upson showed her the Italian's tiny soup kitchen. "I wondered why I never saw you in the ACA snack bar."

"Takes too much time out of the day to go up there," Upson said. Giovanni took their order, and translated it for the Thai woman he lived with.

"Your day is long enough as it is," Annie said. "You're

getting to be like poor Gus Thompson. He used to work twelve- or thirteen-hour days, seven days a week. They did him a favor when they eased him out of here. His health was going."

"I'm going to have to start coming in weekends, too. Otherwise I can't keep up."

"The man who had the job before Gus worked nine to five, on the dot. He was promoted to FSO-4 and his next posting was to Rome."

"Don't think I'll get to Rome, do you?"

"I thought you would at first. But then something changed, didn't it? Not that it's any of my business."

"No one thing changed, Annie. Little things piled up. I guess maybe I'm not on the team anymore. As they say."

"Oh, you're still on it. But just barely."

Upson looked at her, wondering whether there might ever have been anything between them if Somchan had not come into his life. Annie was older than him, probably in her late thirties. She had a strong face, more handsome than pretty, with lines beginning to show. And she had a child, which was somehow intimidating.

"It's funny," he said. "In Morocco there was a guy who wasn't on the team. A USIS guy down in Marrakech who was always raising hell because he claimed the king was using PL 480 grain illegally to pay soldiers on the Algerian border instead of workers on irrigation projects. He was probably right, but I always thought he was kind of a jerk to make so much noise about it. I liked the ambassador there. I like the Foreign Service. I liked my teachers in school and college."

"Well, it's not too late," Annie said. "You're still on the team, and you can stay on it if you want to."

"And go to Rome?"

"And go to Rome."

"I think I'll have to start coming into the office on weekends instead, Annie."

"We all do what we have to do. Just watch out, though. Don't give them anything to work with."

"How do you mean?"

"Gus got two or three warning citations for security violations when the marine guards found classified material on his desk that he forgot to lock up overnight. It didn't make any real difference, since the whole suite of offices is a secure area. But they made sure it got in his file, and people kept bringing it up in a kind of a kidding way, only not really kidding. For the rest of his career, people will be saying, 'Gus Thompson, oh, yeah. Wasn't he that guy who got into some kind of security trouble, someplace or other?' "

The bitterness in her voice surprised Upson. He wondered if there had been something between Annie Cutler and Gus Thompson. The bitterness made him feel safe in asking a question he would not otherwise have risked.

"It can't be intentional, can it, Annie?" Upson said. "You don't think they're conscious murderers, do you?"

"No, it's more dangerous than that. They're all children."

Walking Annie back across the parking lot toward the embassy, Upson was struck by something. Even a few weeks ago he wouldn't have said "they." He would have said "we." But wasn't the right word still "we"?

The man climbing up to light the first rocket of the festival gave perspective to the bamboo scaffolding, which Upson could now see was as high as a three-story house. The structure was tilted away from the Lao bank, so that the rocket would fly toward Thailand, nearly a mile away across the dry riverbed. Upson remembered his father on the Fourth of July, pushing the little red sticks of cardboard rockets into the rectory lawn, lighting the fuses at arm's length, and then jumping back while the things whooshed off into the night sky, trailing sparks. The rockets for the Lao rocket festival, *Boun Bang Fai*, were not much different in design. But they were so big that some of them had been brought in on flatbed trucks, and then carried down to the riverbed by dozens of young men. The men had now leaned the first one against the bamboo scaffolding, ready for firing. The tail was a light bamboo pole, to hold the contraption off the ground and to steady it in flight. The rocket tube itself was of bamboo as thick through as a drainpipe, reinforced with rope to contain the power of the gunpowder charge inside. Shiny wrapping paper and streamers decorated the device.

The man on the scaffolding down below stretched out a cautious hand toward the giant rocket. The distance was too great for Upson to see the lighter in the man's hand. But he could tell the instant the rocket's fuse caught by the way the man yanked back his hand and scrambled back down the scaffolding to the safety of the ground. The huge crowd standing on the bluffs in front of the Laan Xang Hotel fell so silent that the hissing of the fuse could be heard clearly. It got louder and louder, until it seemed that the charge had caught and the rocket must take off. But then it fizzled out. The rocket leaned against the scaffolding, failed and motionless, while black smoke poured out its tail.

"Number ten," said Somchan, who was at Upson's side.

"It's number ten, all right," he said. "Too bad." The crowd laughed and jeered as men climbed up the scaffolding to take away the disgraced rocket. Another was put in its place. Rocket followed rocket. Some flew true, burying themselves like javelins in the sandy riverbed hundreds of yards away. A few more misfired completely. Some wobbled, their tails making crazy loops until they crashed. Some barely managed to clear the launching tower before falling to the ground. Acrid gunpowder smoke soon reached the bluffs and stayed there, with no breath of wind to spread it. The air was fiercely hot, like the inside of a closed car in the sun. Upson felt sticky and smelly and oversized beside Somchan, who wasn't perspiring at all. Nor did the heat seem to bother the rest of the crowd, which groaned or cheered or laughed at each launching.

For the first time, Upson wished he shared a language with Somchan. He wanted to ask her what people were doing, what everything meant, which rocket belonged to which village, which one had been made by the monks of her own wat, whether the Lao were fully conscious—as he suspected they were—of the symbolism of firing rockets during a fertility festival.

A line of dancers came snaking toward them—young men dressed in women's clothing. The dancers wore heavy makeup and filmy scarves on their heads. They were drunk and happy, beating on drums as they sang and danced. One of them was working an arrangement of jointed sticks that made a large, red phallus thrust up and down at the girls in the crowd. Women pushed yellow carts full of sugarcane for sale. Food stalls were set up all over, shaded by red and white nylon cut from parachutes. There were fruits, sweets and salads, chicken livers and bits of pork grilled on bamboo skewers, the little cubes of chopped pork which Upson had eaten on the Plain of Jars, and a hundred other strange things that he had no way of asking Somchan about. He stopped in front of one stall and gestured for the girl to order them whatever she wanted. The vendor filled a plastic bag with orange soda from a bottle, stuck in a plastic straw, and fastened the mouth of the bag around the straw with a rubber band. Somchan offered him the first sip. It was warm and repulsively sweet. *"Sep-sep,"* he said—the Lao word for delicious. When she smiled her shy smile, he felt a surge of protectiveness so strong that he would have put his arms around her if they had been alone. She wore her best clothes for the festival—a silk, ankle-length skirt with an embroidered hem and a sleeveless blouse of white cotton. Her hair was coiled up formally on her head instead of hanging loose. But on her feet she wore her everyday rubber-thonged sandals, and she looked to Upson like a little girl dressed up in her mother's clothes.

Further down the line of stalls they came across a booth with a sign saying *Lao National Radio*. One of the men in it was doing a burlesque of an announcer, using a huge, papier-maché phallus striped red, white, and blue as his microphone. The man he was interviewing was made up to represent the U.S. ambassador, with stars and stripes on his top hat, a large, false nose, a sign saying "Ambassador" around his neck, and stuffing under his coat to make him look fat. The real ambassador was lean, but Upson had been struck once, at a large party, by the fact that virtually every American there was overweight. He supposed that fatness would be part of a Lao's general impression of the American physical type.

The announcer would ask his questions and then reverse the big phallus so that the mock ambassador could answer into it. The crowd roared with laughter each time one of the men put the red, white, and blue penis to his mouth. Upson smiled at the irreverent boldness of the performance, since most of the Lao

National Radio's funding and programming came from the U.S. embassy. Somchan was laughing along with the rest of the spectators at the questions and answers.

A man came out of the crowd, cavorting and bobbing in a ridiculous way. He wore a feathered headdress with an enormous beak like a toucan's sticking out of his forehead. His face was painted red, white, and black, giving him the menacing look of an Indian on the warpath. He pecked grotesquely with his beak at the announcer's phallus, and cocked his head in the quizzical way of a bird. The announcer handed the phallus to the birdman, who began speaking into it. Whatever he was saying made the crowd laugh. He was elaborately careful to look elsewhere, so that Upson only realized what the subject of discussion must be when people in the crowd began to sneak glances at him and Somchan. She was blushing, but since she still wore her shy smile, Upson assumed it was all in good fun. At first he smiled, too. But there was an ugly edge in the man's voice, and in the laughter of the crowd. The birdman paused and found enough courage in the crowd's amusement to face Upson and Somchan with an insolent, challenging smile. Upson didn't know whether to hold his ground or retreat. What could he do, unable to talk, if he stayed? What would he be retreating from?

A voice came from behind them, cutting flat and contemptuous into the silence. The announcer, looking ashamed of himself, reached out and took back the red, white, and blue phallus. The birdman seemed angry, but said nothing. The voice spoke again, this time in English, and Upson recognized it as Dick Lindsay's. "Come on, Fred," Lindsay said. "Let's get out of here. Walk slowly, and smile."

As they left, the silence broke. The crowd was laughing again, but now at the man with the beak growing out of his forehead. "What did you say to him?" Upson asked.

"I said he must have the balls of a bird, too, if all he's brave enough to do is insult young girls."

"What was he saying, Dick?"

"Nothing. What was she doing with an American, how much did he pay her, stuff like that."

"It was rougher than that, wasn't it?"

"Yeah, but don't worry about it."

118

"The son of a bitch."

"Forget it, Fred. I'm telling you."

"Why should I?"

"Maybe she jilted the guy once. Maybe he's her brother or her uncle. Maybe he's just some punk off the wall with a big mouth. We just don't know. But no matter who he is, you get in a fight with him in the middle of the rocket festival with the whole town watching, and the embassy will ship your ass home in forty-eight hours."

Upson had never been in a fight, anyway, and couldn't imagine how it would be hitting someone. He felt like a failure, dirtied, inadequate, and unable to protect Somchan, but he had no idea what to do about it. He let Lindsay lead them to an outdoor restaurant, where they only managed to sit down because some people were just leaving. A huge banyan tree spread its limbs over the tables but gave little shade, because most of its leaves had fallen off from the drought. The trunk was white-washed up to waist height. At the base of the tree was a shrine, a brick column with a little roof of rusty, corrugated iron. Under the roof were offerings of wilted flowers. The nearby ground and the deep fissures in the tree trunk bristled with burnt-out red joss sticks. A boy squatted a few yards away, hacking at the green husks of coconuts with a machete till he had exposed enough of the nut so that he could lop off its top. When he had done two or three, a girl would take them away to the service counter and pour the thin, grayish milk into big glasses filled with crushed ice.

"Look at the crowd," Lindsay said. "The only way we'll ever get served here is do it ourselves."

When he had gone off after two beers and a Pepsi, Upson turned to Somchan. "I'm sorry, my darling, my sweetheart," he said. "Sorry, sorry, sorry. I stood there grinning like a damn fool and all the time you didn't know what to do and you had to stand there and smile and take it because I was too stupid to understand he was hurting you. Sweet Jesus, I wish it had been me he was humiliating. I wish I could take away the memory of it all from you."

She looked up at him, not smiling, and answered him softly. He imagined that he understood her—that she had understood him, too, and was now forgiving him. He wanted so badly to take her hand, even if the Lao didn't touch in public, that he had started to reach for it when he heard the voice of the real American ambassador beside him.

"Well, Fred," Ambassador Simmonds was saying, "how do you like your first rocket festival?"

"Fine, sir. Fascinating." The ambassador's wife was with him, a round, soft, self-important woman from South Carolina. Phil Casey called her the Iron Honeysuckle.

Upson got to his feet, and so did Somchan. "Uh, Mrs. Simmonds," he said, "I'd like you to meet Somchan. Somchan, this is Mrs. Simmonds. Ambassador Simmonds." Somchan made a very deep wai, but said nothing. "Somchan doesn't speak English," Upson explained.

"Oh, I just envy you so, speaking Lao," Mrs. Simmonds said to Upson. "I just try and try, but I never seem to get anywhere."

"Well, I don't speak it, really," Upson said. "Only a few words." He saw the ambassador's wife inspecting Somchan, her eyes resting an instant on the girl's rubber-thonged sandals. Mrs. Simmonds, he knew, must be seeing her in comparison to the wealthy Lao officials' wives who came to her embassy parties. Somchan had no gold bracelets or earrings, no gold belt, no Seiko ladies' watch, no silk blouse or sash, no high-heeled shoes, no strands of pearls around the hair coiled neatly into a bun on the back of her head.

Just then Lindsay came back with the drinks. "Hello, Mrs. Simmonds, Mr. Ambassador," he said. "Will you join us? All they've got left is warm beer, but if you can stand it with ice in it, I can get a couple more glasses."

"Another time, Dick," the ambassador said. "We're on our way to the PM's reception."

"So nice to have met you, dear," the ambassador's wife said to Somchan, who smiled helplessly with embarrassment. "I love your little cotton blouse, so simple and cool. Silk is so hot in this climate, I don't know how people bear it. Tell your little friend I love her blouse, Fred."

"I will, Mrs. Simmonds."

"Bye-bye, then. Bruce, we'd better be going."

Early next day, Lindsay telephoned Upson at his office. "I'm out at Wattay, Fred," he said. "About to leave for Sam Thong, be up there a week. I wanted to catch you before I took off. Listen, I ran into the ambassador's wife again at the Millers' reception last night, and she made kind of a point of asking who that sweet young lady of Fred's was. I said she was your maid, and we ran into her at the festival. Probably doesn't amount to anything, but since she bothered to ask, I figured you should know."

"Thanks, Dick."

"Stay loose, babes. My pilot's out there warming up, so I'm off to the fourteenth century."

Upson thought nothing more about it, until two days later a mimeographed memo showed up in his box. It was addressed to, "All Members, U.S. Mission," and it read: "The U.S. Mission to Laos, while large in comparision to many others, is small enough so that the conduct of each one of us reflects on all the others. Every official American should therefore exercise special care in observing the same social distinctions the Laotians themselves do with regard to local employees, third country nationals (TCNs), and domestic personnel. These correct relations are particularly important when U.S. officials are in the public eye, as at parades, sporting events, carnivals, festivals, and other public gatherings."

Why, the lousy, rotten sons of bitches, Upson thought when he read the memo. He was ashamed and afraid and angry all at once. The ambassador's wife must have seen him talking intensely with Somchan, seen his hand start to reach for hers. And later she learned from Lindsay that Mrs. Bruce Kingdon Simmonds had been introduced to a domestic servant, with God knows who looking on. Upson buzzed Annie Cutler on the intercom. "Annie," he said, "where did this weird memo on fraternization come from?"

"I imagine the ambassador. The DCM drafted it, though." Brautigan did all the drafting for the ambassador, who hated to write.

"Did the DCM say what the hell it was all about?"

"I wondered, too. But he just said it was general guidance for the troops."

"Very odd stuff," Upson said.

"Isn't it?"

He hung up, remembering what Annie had told him about Gus Thompson's security violations. What should he do now? If either the ambassador or Jerry Brautigan felt strongly about the matter, they certainly would have brought it up with him directly. Going through the charade of a mission-wide memo must be a way of convincing the ambassador's wife that action had been taken, whereas none would be. Upson guessed that both men were embarrassed at having to be involved in such a silly business at all, and certainly didn't take it seriously enough for a direct confrontation. If this were the case, should he escalate the matter by confronting *them* directly? If he challenged them, they could look innocent and say the memo had nothing to do with them. If he apologized, he would be apologizing when he had done nothing wrong. The ambassador's wife was the one who ought to apologize. She was Somchan's inferior in every way that could matter to a rational man. But Upson could hardly say that, and would therefore say nothing.

Still. The sons of bitches.

Upson had begun to work weekends, as he had told Annie Cutler he would. He spent the Saturday morning after the rocket festival checking strike requests, writing justifications for his disapproval of doubtful targets, and drafting requests for poststrike photography on a selection of last week's strikes. This would probably lead to nothing, but would at least let the air force know that somebody cared.

When he had finished these routine matters, he turned back to a request that had puzzled him the day before. It was to attack a ford near the Pathet Lao capital of Samneua with something he had never heard of, called an EOGB. All the air attaché's office knew was that it was a new weapon and that the letters stood for Electrical-Optical Guided Bomb. At last Upson got through to an air force major down in Udorn who knew more about it. They were large bombs—one thousand to two thousand pounds—guided to their target with the aid of a TV screen in the plane's cockpit. They were designed for targets like fords, roads, and runways, that only a great deal of explosive power could destroy. The prototypes cost about two hundred thousand dollars each. After Upson hung up, he wrote out a refusal of the strike request on five grounds: the missile was too costly; no solid intelligence showed the ford to be of military importance; it was too near Samneua, a politically sensitive area which was not validated; the missile would probably miss; even if it didn't, the hole in the riverbed would just fill in again by itself, or be filled in again by the Pathet Lao. Unassailable logic. He locked the draft in his drawer, to be typed by Annie Cutler Monday morning.

Colonel Costikyan decided not to call Upson directly. It was better to work around an obstruction than to waste energy meeting it head-on. The air attaché called the deputy chief of mission instead. "Jerry, what is all this shit about the Samneua ford?" he asked. "How can we fight a war this way?"

"Don't you think Fred might be right on this one, Mike?" Brautigan answered mildly.

"Right? What's right? Jesus, we can't be nickeled and dimed to death. What is Fred anyway? A goddamned accountant?"

"Two hundred thousand bucks is a lot of money, Mike. Even in a war. You told me your rule of thumb was a dollar a pound for ordnance. For the price of that one missile, you could drop how many two hundred fifty-pound bombs? Let's see now. I work it out to eight hundred of them."

"Come on, Jerry, you can't figure it that way. We've already bought the goddamned thing. It's just a question of how to get the best use out of it."

"Exactly."

"How about if we redo the strike request for a Bullpup, Jerry? They're a hell of a lot cheaper."

"Go ahead. Send it on up and we'll see if my tiger lets it get through."

"I'll do that little thing."

"Mike, I'm curious," Brautigan said. "What's the difference between the EOGB and the Bullpup, aside from the money?"

"Basically, the Bullpup is controlled by the stick in the plane, and the EOGB is a lot more sophisticated. Radar in the plane slaves onto the target and guides the thing in automatically. And you can stand off further with the EOGB, so you don't have to risk getting so close to the target."

"But they both leave pretty much the same kind of hole?"

"Sure."

"What I'm getting at is that there wouldn't be any way to tell from a poststrike photo which kind of missile had been used, would there?"

"No way."

"I thought that might be the case. Well, try resubmitting your request, only for a Bullpup this time, and we'll see what happens."

"Roger that, Jerry. I read you five by five."

Brautigan sat at his desk doodling for a few minutes after the call. He drew what he always drew: a naked female torso. The woman's face was hidden by her hair, because Brautigan couldn't do faces. The hands and the shoulders never came out to suit him, either, but the breasts were just right. When he had finished, he obliterated the drawing with big loops and whorls, so that Annie Cutler wouldn't come across it. He began to tap on his desk with the point of his pen as he thought about Fred Upson. Upson's long hours and weekend work were unhealthy and unnecessary. The sin of scrupulosity, the Church called it. If Upson worked in the field and spoke the language, the most likely diagnosis would be that he had gone bamboo—begun to identify more with the local culture than with his own. It was a shame, whatever was happening to Upson. He was potentially a good officer—bright enough, hard-working, and anxious to please. In another job he could be very useful, but in this one he had become a problem.

Upson had to be backed up, of course, as in this business with Costikyan. Otherwise the ambassador would lose a little bit in relative strength. The constant question in the mission was whether the State Department was to run Laos, or whether the

CIA or the Pentagon would gradually take over. The battle was one of perceptions, and it had to be fought day by day in a dozen tiny skirmishes like this one just finished. Mike Costikyan had to know that he couldn't simply overrule the judgment of a member of the ambassador's immediate staff with a phone call to the DCM. But the colonel also had to be reassured that the embassy remained basically on his side. Now Costikyan knew he could safely switch missiles and try out his new two hundred thousand dollar toy, as soon as Upson approved the redone request. Nothing had been written down or even spoken directly—but Costikyan was an old bureaucratic knife-fighter who could read between the lines. Moreover, he would know that the ambassador could always dig the truth about the missile-switching out of Seventh Air Force, if the need ever arose to pressure the air attaché. And the new missile would probably miss anyway, just as Upson predicted. By proving that the embassy had been right in the first place, this would strengthen its position in any future disagreements.

Brautigan thought the situation had worked out pretty well so far. Upson might still have to be eased out of his job— probably would—but that, too, could be managed in a way that would satisfy everyone.

Upson considered asking Annie Cutler simply to retype his original refusal of the Samneua strike request, changing EOGB to Bullpup throughout. That was what Colonel Costikyan had done with his new strike request, which was otherwise identical with the first one. But Upson decided that to follow suit would be needlessly provocative, and perhaps even childish. Instead he restated his original objections, although in somewhat different language.

"Ah, so," Annie Cutler said when she saw his draft. "The battle is joined."

"The battle damned well better be won. The DCM backed

me up before and I don't see why he won't again. Just changing to a cheaper missile doesn't invalidate my other four reasons for disapproval."

"Gee, Fred, you're cute when you get mad."

"Lay off, Annie, will you?"

"I'm sorry. I didn't mean to make fun of what you're doing. You know I'm on your side, Fred."

Upson could hear the whir of her typing from his office. In a few minutes, she brought in the memorandum of disapproval for his signature. "I'll put it on top of the boss's pile," she said. "That way he'll see it first thing when he gets back from lunch."

Brautigan buzzed for Upson an hour later. "I wanted to get a little more of your thinking on this Samneua thing," Brautigan said, scratching at his already tousled head as if he were totally perplexed. "I'm a little bit on the spot on this one, and I have to figure out how to get off."

"I tried to lay it out pretty fully in the memo, Jerry."

"Oh, I know that. I understand the points you made, and in fact I agree with them. That's why I let the original disapproval go on forward to AIRA."

"What's changed, then? Costikyan's new request is precisely the same as the last, except for a different bomb. All my other objections still stand."

"I know they do. And as I say, basically I agree with them. It's only that Mike Costikyan called to bitch, and I'm afraid I might have given him the impression that cost was our major objection. Now that he's brought the cost down, it's going to be a little awkward going back to him with another disapproval."

"Well, it's your prerogative to overrule me."

"Sure, but I don't *want* to overrule you. First I basically agree with you. Second, I don't want to give AIRA the idea that this office won't back up your judgment."

"What do you want, then, Jerry?"

"Well, it would help us in our dealings down the road if you could see your way clear to approving the request, and then I could pass it along with your signature."

"Do you think it's a good request?"

"No, I think it's pretty weak. You could very well be right, that the tracks in the photos were made by carts hauling stuff to market and not by military traffic. And the other points you make are sound, too. But it goes beyond whether the request is a good one, Fred. The point is that it's not really a *bad* one, either. No dwellings or structures in the area. Nothing but the river and they can't hurt that. Probably can't even hit it."

"It's too near Samneua, Jerry. It's needlessly provocative." Like Costikyan's damned retyped request, he thought.

"Technically, it's in a validated zone," Brautigan said.

"Just barely. If they miss the river and hit on the east bank, they're in nonvalidated territory."

"In this particular case, though," Brautigan said, "it won't do any real harm if they do miss. And a miss that we had predicted would strengthen our hand down the line, sometime when it might be more important. Do you see what I mean?"

"Yes, I see what you mean."

"Good, that's fine." Brautigan lowered his head and examined the backs of his big, freckled hands. "You know, Fred," he said, "we haven't really been such sons of bitches here in the front office, have we? We've always backed you up pretty well, haven't we?" He raised his head again and smiled. "You don't feel you're out at the end of the trapline, abandoned? Do you?"

"Oh, no. Not at all."

"The ambassador has always gone with your judgment, and so have I. It's just that you've got to let the other guy think he's winning one now and then, or he'll want to quit the game and go home. And unfortunately we don't have any F-4s. The balls and the bats belong to him."

"On the other hand," Upson said, "if he wants to play baseball at all, ours is the only game in town."

"And it's our job to keep it that way. Our game, and everybody willing to play by our rules."

Brautigan's open, friendly smile made Upson feel that the two of them, Fred and Jerry, were in an adventure together—a secret plot to trick the world into acting sensibly, for once. Upson nodded when the deputy chief of mission said, "Oh, listen, would you initial your approval on this Samneua thing and give it to Annie on your way out?"

When Upson had gone, Brautigan made himself turn to the budget requests stacked on his desk. Discretionary items, recurring expenses, fixed expenses, leases and rentals, official in-country travel estimates, stuff to make the eyes glaze and the attention wander. But he had to go through it one last time, in case the ambassador had any questions during the budget session they were to have in half an hour. Not that the ambassador was likely to. The budgetary process was so boring that he was happy to leave it to his deputy, who was happy to have it left to him. Those dull columns of figures were the tools with which you controlled an embassy. The man who could approve your wife's remodeling projects or your own request for additional staff was a man you would be anxious to accommodate in all things.

After Brautigan had gone over the figures a final time, he carried the stack of requests into the ambassador's office. The ambassador was at the big map on the wall, moving around little paper flags in accordance with the latest intelligence on the locations of various military and paramilitary units. "I've got the budget stuff together, Buck," Brautigan said. "If you want to take a look."

"It's all right, isn't it?" the ambassador said. "No problems?"

"No problems."

"Then you go ahead and handle it, okay?"

"Good enough."

The ambassador moved the last flag that needed moving, a little square of yellow paper standing for a special guerrilla unit. "Jerry," he said, turning to his deputy, "what the hell is this Samneua request that Upson's been sitting on, apparently? Mike Costikyan was bending my ear about it earlier."

"No problem," Brautigan said. "I worked it out just a few minutes ago, as a matter of fact. I'm surprised Mike felt he had to mention it to you." And not just surprised, the DCM thought. What made Mike think he could get away with an end run around the DCM's office? Could Costikyan possibly be interpreting Fred's stubbornness as a sign that the deputy chief of mission was losing control of his own staff? If the air attaché sensed this

128

kind of weakness, might it have tempted him to try going over the DCM's head?

"Well, fine," the ambassador said. "As long as you've got it under control. That goddamned Upson. For a while after he came, I thought we had that situation licked."

"It's a hard balance for a relatively inexperienced man to strike, Buck. You have to maintain your authority over the air force, but still leave them alone enough so they can get the job done."

"Well, by God, *somebody* must be able to do it. Upson's getting to be nearly as big a pain in the ass as Thompson was. We may have to do something about him."

"We may, Buck, but I'm inclined to go with him a little while longer rather than train somebody new. He's got pretty good sense, basically, and he still may work into the job."

"Christ, I hope so. You know what he's like, him and Thompson both? They're like those union troublemakers that slow down the line by obeying every little nit-picking regulation to the letter. What do they call that?"

"Work to rule."

"Right, work to rule. Slow down the line deliberately. All they send me out anymore from Washington is a bunch of goddamned shop stewards. Work to rule, for Christ's sake."

"I'll sort it all out, Buck."

"I hope so. Goddamn shop stewards. Christ."

Captain Harry Sedgwick tried to do everything with precision. Otherwise the data would be no good, and pilots could die when they used new ordnance with inappropriate delivery parameters over the Ho Chi Minh trail or in North Vietnam. It was one thing to evaluate the operational effectiveness of new weapons in the relatively benign atmosphere of northern Laos; it was another when they were shooting back at you with the heavy stuff. Before leaving Udorn he had checked the coordinates from intelligence against the maps so that he would know for sure where the ford was, in relationship to the dirt road called Route 6, the bend in the little river, and the town of Samneua just east of it. Samneua was the Pathet Lao headquarters, he knew, and was off limits to the bombing, presumably for political reasons. Those reasons were probably stupid, but still Captain Sedgwick never bombed in off-limits zones. A few of the pilots, though, made a game of coming as close as they could to Samneua with their bombs. They made enough mistakes in the game, assuming they really were mistakes, so that many of the town's buildings had been destroyed over the years. It was the kind of game that would appeal to the pilot who flew in the back seat of Captain Sedgwick's F-4. His GIB—Guy in the Back—was Lieutenant Albert Bouteiller. The lieutenant called himself "Boots." He wanted to get out of this chickenshit ordnance-testing business and go to Vietnam, where he could really put the boots to Charlie. Once he had told one of the mechanics that the greatest feeling in the world was when you strapped that big F-4 onto yourself. Bouteiller might be competent, but he was what you would definitely have to call an asshole.

The sky was bright blue with little puffs of pure white clouds here and there. Captain Sedgwick rolled in on the target area, banking the plane carefully so that it headed directly at the ford in the river. At the moment the F-4 was serving as a camera mount, allowing the target area to appear on the little television screen in the cockpit of the GIB, whose view to the front was blocked. Captain Sedgwick had his own screen in the front cockpit, and checked it against the scene in front of him.

"Okay, I've got the target in the reticle," the captain said into the intercom, once he had maneuvered the plane so that the cross hairs on the gunsight combining glass were superimposed on the televised image of the target.

"Roger that," Bouteiller answered. "I've got it, too."

"Okay, there's the bend in the river. The target's two hundred meters north of the bend."

The GIB would put his cross hairs over the target now growing rapidly on the screen, and slave the TV camera in the missile's seeker head to the image on his own screen. The EOGB, once it was clear of the plane, would steer itself automatically to its target. During the moment it would take for Bouteiller to be sure that the computer had digested all the information necessary, Captain Sedgwick checked to make sure his altitude was just at ten thousand feet. It was. He looked out of the cockpit for a final check of the target area, and said, "Oh, shit."

"What's the matter?" Bouteiller's voice said. "Haven't we got the lateral extension?"

"Sure, we're in the envelope. But it looks like people on the bank."

"Fuck 'em, they should have stayed home."

"They're kind of hunkered down right at the edge of the river, looks like. I'm going to take it on down, clear 'em out."

"You're the boss."

"Damned straight I am."

Captain Sedgwick went in on them low and fast, holding it up on one wing with a little top rudder so he could see below. The figures were women washing clothes, as he had thought they might be. The women ran in panic toward the protection of some nearby trees. "All right," he said. "They're scattering." He pulled his plane up and around in a miles-wide circle, to regain his optimum delivery position. "Okay," he said at twelve thousand feet, four miles out, "let's reacquire the release parameters, and get this show on the road." Once again, he rolled in and put the ford on his little television screen.

"I've got an insert," Bouteiller said when he had his cross hairs on the target. The "Clear to Release" light went on in Captain Sedgwick's cockpit; he settled his thumb on the pickle button that would release the bomb.

"I'm down the chute," the captain said. "Delivery angle look good?"

"Right at thirty," Lieutenant Bouteiller said, and began to count off the altitude. "You got ten . . . nine . . . eighty-five . . . ready, PICKLE!"

Captain Sedgwick pressed the pickle button and felt the thump that meant separation had occurred. "The bomb's off," he said. "Keep an eye on it, Boots. I'm off to the left." The captain rolled toward one wing and pulled back on the stick, putting five and then six Gs onto the airplane, and added power as soon as the nose lifted toward the horizon. The Gs made it difficult for Sedgwick to move his head sideways so he could see what was happening below. Bouteiller wouldn't be able to move his head very well either, but he would already have been looking back, as instructed, at about seven o'clock.

"Son of a bitch is waffling," Bouteiller reported. "It's going to the left. Son of a bitch missed."

"Where did it hit?"

"A little east of the river, just on the edge of that bunch of trees there."

Captain Sedgwick hoped the women had kept running all the time he had been circling around for his second approach. That way they would have been out of danger, since most of the weapon's blast effect would have been in an upward cone. He hoped none of the women had taken cover as soon as they reached the shelter of the trees. Probably they had all made it to safety. Most likely they had.

"Goddamn it, anyway," he said.

"What the hell, we don't make 'em, we just shoot 'em off," came the voice of the GIB. "Your egress heading is two-three-five."

Two days later Upson got the after-action report he had requested on the Samneua strike. "Malfunction of the Bullpup missile," the report said, "caused it to impact on the east side of the river adjacent to a wooded area. Despite this bank of the river being unvalidated as a target, it is believed that the wooded area in question was uninhabited although technically in violation of the rules of engagement. No disciplinary action against the pilot is recommended, as repeated efforts on the part of the referenced officer to redirect the missile were unsuccessful due to an apparent guidance system malfunction."

Upson took the report in to the DCM, who scanned it and grinned. "You had that one figured just right, didn't you, Fred?" he said.

"At least they missed it with a cheaper missile. I suppose that's something."

"Nothing I think I'd mention to the air force, though,"

Brautigan said. "Mike would claim they wouldn't have missed if we'd let them use the expensive model." Brautigan examined the poststrike photos which accompanied the report. As Mike Costikyan had said, the hole looked just like any other crater, but bigger.

The Foreign Broadcast Information Service came in by teletype, on endless rolls of teleprinter paper. Ed Morton in the political section was supposed to read through these translated broadcasts from all over Southeast Asia, even though there was too much for anyone to get through. He often thought that the best way to paralyze North Vietnamese intelligence would be to bomb Hanoi with every classified document America had in Indochina. And every communist analyst would be faced, as Morton himself was, with more useless garbage than he could digest in a lifetime. Morton would let the FBIS stuff accumulate for several days on his desk, long rolls of paper piled in loose pleats that sometimes reached a height of two feet. At last he would force himself to skim through the translations—endless and repetitive broadcasts from both sides of propaganda in Kha, Khmer, Kachin, Yao, Hmong, and half a dozen other tribal languages. Morton never bothered to read the output of the several clandestine stations financed by the CIA, and only paused rarely over items from Hanoi or the Pathet Lao. Two weeks after the attack on the Samneua ford, though, Morton's eye was caught by a few sentences in an old Pathet Lao broadcast. "The cowardly capitalist aggressors," it read, "savagely attacked the neutral capital city Samneua repeatedly yesterday. The aggressor warplanes bombed and strafed civilian targets more than once, although the American imperialists shamelessly and repeatedly deny that they attack the peaceful capital. The woman Phailin was mercilessly killed by the neocolonialist air pirates while firing back courageously at the capitalist aggressors."

Sometimes there was a kernel of truth in the communist

propaganda broadcasts, which was why Morton was supposed to glance over them. He suspected this was one of those times, since it was unusual to see anything as specific as an actual name in the transcripts. Nor was there anything inherently improbable about the report; the air force had strayed too close to Samneua before, and would certainly do so again. The item might conceivably be of interest to the bombing officer, though. Morton tore it out, attached a buckslip marked *FYI, Ed,* and tossed it into his out box for delivery to Upson.

When Upson was a little boy, his father had taught him a trick to stay calm. The Reverend Upson showed his son how to feel his pulse, and how his heartbeat slowed down if he held his breath. "See, son? his father said. "If your heart goes slower, you won't be so upset."

Upson held his breath before he went into Brautigan's office, but it didn't work. "What's wrong, Fred?" the deputy chief of mission said on seeing Upson's expression. Upson handed him the Pathet Lao broadcast, which Brautigan took in at a glance. "What a damned shame," he said.

"What a damned shame? That's it? What a shame?"

Brautigan came out from behind the barrier of his desk and put a hand, broad and heavy and reassuring, on Upson's shoulder. "Come on, Fred," he said. "Let's sit down." They sat at a low coffee table with rattan armchairs around it, the broadcast transcript on the table between them.

"We killed the woman Phailin right in this room," Upson said. "Admit it."

"Of course I admit it." Upson felt off balance, as if a door had unexpectedly swung wide open the instant he began to push it. "She died by accident," Brautigan went on, "but we sent the plane up there with the missile that went haywire. And either one of us could have stopped that plane from going up there, so we killed her right in this room, yes."

"What does that make you feel like, Jerry? It makes me feel like a murderer."

"I feel the way I told you. That it's a shame."

"Jesus Christ."

"Fred, listen me out. By the standards we're both applying right now, a lot of people have been killed in this room. And in other rooms all over the mission, both by accident and on purpose. And in other rooms in Hanoi, and Samneua, and in Moscow and Peking and Washington, too. It's what happens in a war. The end product is dead people."

"The woman Phailin."

"Dead civilians aren't the intended product, but they're an occasional byproduct. If the missile had gone straight, she wouldn't have been hit. But there's waste, confusion, error, carelessness. Callousness, indifference, cruelty. Your job is specifically to cut down on those things. But you make mistakes, too."

"Just like the missile did?"

"Just like the missile. We both made a mistake this time, me more than you. And we'll make mistakes again."

"Not this mistake, I won't. I'll never sign off again on a request I know is wrong."

"One you know is wrong might be right," Brautigan said. "One you're sure is right might be wrong. Nobody can do any job perfectly. You just do it the best you can."

"If a job's worth doing, it's worth doing right. Is that it?"

"I suppose."

"And if a job isn't worth doing? What about that, Jerry?"

"Your job is worth doing."

"I mean the whole job. The air war."

The deputy chief of mission looked down at his freckled hands on the table for a moment, and then gazed at a point over Upson's shoulder. The fingers of his right hand drummed soundlessly on the table. "All right," he said at last. "I see what you're saying. I don't agree with you, but you've come to your conclusion for decent and honorable reasons. Could you bring yourself to stay on the job for just another couple of weeks, though? We've got a Junior Officer Trainee coming in on the twenty-fifth, fresh out of FSI. I was going to send him up to Sam

135

Thong, but it was just to get his feet wet. They don't really need him up there."

Upson looked at the DCM in surprise. He hadn't thought the thing through as far as asking for reassignment, but he wasn't disposed to protest. Again the door had swung open unexpectedly, this time before Upson even knew whether he would have pushed. But he was relieved to find that he had somehow stepped through it.

"This new JOT should be able to handle the job," Brautigan said. "Don't you think so? Somebody with your amount of experience was wasted in it, anyway. The job's 90 percent clerical. In the military, they'd have an enlisted man doing it. I've had it in the back of my mind for a long time that you could do the mission a lot more good in the political section, but I didn't dare switch you. As long as you seemed satisfied here with us, I was afraid you might misread reassignment to mean we weren't satisfied with your work."

As Upson left the office, he didn't much care whether they were satisfied with his work or not. He was just grateful that the decision had been reached, even if inadvertently. It was the decision he would have had to come to anyway, eventually. At least he thought it was.

Once Upson had left Brautigan's office, the DCM telephoned Dennis Goldman, the head of the political section. Brautigan respected Goldman's ability, although he found it hard to like him. The Ambassador called Goldman, in private, "that smart Jew."

"Remember that new slot you were asking for, Dennis?" Brautigan said when the secretary had put him through.

"I remember all right, Jerry. But I had pretty much given up hope."

"There's always hope. What do you think of Fred Upson?"

"I see." It was the kind of remark Goldman often made, always in a carefully neutral tone. He saw too damned much.

"He's a good man, Dennis, and wasted where we've got him. He had damned good OERs as a political officer in Morocco." This was true; Upson's Officer Evaluation Reports from his superiors in Morocco had been excellent.

"You don't have to sell me on him," Goldman said. "I'll be

grateful to get him. Who are you thinking of for Mad Bomber? Not one of my other guys, I hope."

"There's a kid coming in, fresh out of the Foreign Service Institute. He was slated to go up to Sam Thong, but they can get along without him. It was just to get his feet wet, anyway."

"You'll be able to wet his feet for him down here," Goldman said. "I have every confidence in you, Jerry."

When Brautigan went in to tell the ambassador what he was planning, he found Simmonds with his hands clasped behind his back, standing before the huge map full of pins and little paper flags. "You know something, Jerry," the ambassador said, "I wish there was some way we could take one of the networks up to Site 87, let them see how Vang Pao's old uncle has been holding out for seven years on that hilltop. Show those newsies how full of crap they are when they talk about CIA mercenaries. You know what those little guys get from us? Seven bucks a month. Some mercenaries."

"It's a shame we can't get the real story across to the public now, isn't it?" Brautigan said. "But someday it will all come out."

"Meanwhile, though, all the people back home know is what they get from commies like Bill Bailey. I can't believe Punch Sulzberger knows what kind of people he's got out here. Maybe I should write him a letter, Jerry. Think it would do any good?"

"I doubt it. As I understand it, they feel that they have to give the news department pretty much their head."

"Probably the goddamned unions. They get into everything. What have you got for me, Jerry?"

"Just these couple of things for signature, and I think I may have worked out something on the air force liaison business."

"I hope so. All we ever seem to get in that job is bleeding hearts. I thought Upson was going to be a good man at first, but Mike says he's turning the position right back into a goddamned bottleneck."

"Fred's a good officer, Buck. Just wrong for that particular job. Goldman has been wanting another reporting officer, and he thinks Fred could handle it."

"Why not? Stick him off in a corner of that liberal think-tank Goldman runs over there, where he can't do any harm. Who takes over the bombing, though?"

"We've got the young fellow coming in from FSI. They can do without him up in Sam Thong."

Looking back, Brautigan knew he should have filled the job with someone fresh from the Foreign Service Institute in the first place. Nobody wanted to make waves in his first job. And it was a good learning position for a young FSO, like being aide-de-camp to a general. Upson's transfer would make everybody happy: Colonel Costikyan, Goldman, the ambassador, the new young officer, and Upson himself. The best solutions were the ones that gave everybody something he wanted.

Two days later, Upson was checking coordinates on a map when he came across a name that looked familiar. Phil Casey had once told him about a village in government-controlled territory which the air force kept mistaking for a communist-held village many miles away. Hadn't Casey said that there were mountains just north of each village and a small bridge over a nearby river? The air force kept blowing up the wrong bridge, until the then-ambassador put a stop to it by cabling Washington that he planned to mark the friendly bridge with balloons. The name on the map was Muong Phine; Upson thought he remembered it as the name of the village the air force should have been bombing. The other, he recalled, was supposed to be down south somewhere, above Savannakhet. Upson searched the maps of that area till he found a village called Phouei Sai, which would have looked very much like Muong Phine from the air. He turned to the back files to see if Phouei Sai was the village, and if Casey's story had been accurate. There was a folder for Phouei Sai, but it was empty except for a note in the handwriting of his predecessor, Gus Thompson, which said *See Miscellany File.* Upson had been too busy, right from the first day, to do more than familiarize himself very generally with the back files he had inherited. But he couldn't remember a miscellany file, and now he looked more carefully. No folder in any of the steel filing cabinets was marked *Miscella-*

neous; he had just about concluded that Thompson had taken the file with him when he finally found it. The file was unmarked and thick, at the back of the bottom drawer of a cabinet whose records dated back so far that Upson had wondered if he should send the whole lot upstairs to the code room for shredding in the big machine. The only thing that led him to pull the file at all was that it was the only one in the drawer to lack a label. But it must have been Thompson's miscellaneous file, because one of the envelopes in it was marked Phouei Sai.

All the documentation of the attacks on the village was inside. There were even records of solatium payments to the surviving relatives of bombing victims, since the bombs on two occasions had missed the bridge and hit the village. Casey had been right on the former ambassador's cable, too. It read: ADVISE ALL USAF PERSONNEL THAT IN FUTURE THE PHOUEI SAI BRIDGE WILL BE MARKED BY PINK WEATHER BALLOONS SUSPENDED ABOVE IT. THESE BALLOONS MAY BE USED AS A CHECKPOINT TO INDICATE TO ALL PILOTS THAT THEY ARE 61 MILES FROM THE CORRECT TARGET, AND CAN NOW TURN TO THE CORRECT HEADING WHICH IS . . . Upson had half suspected Casey was making up the story of the cable, since it was so preposterously remote from anything the present ambassador would dream of sending.

He began to go through the rest of the envelopes in the thick file, becoming more and more amazed. That evening he stayed late, as he usually did, but it was not to keep up with current work. He was running off copies of the material Thompson had collected. Now and then the marine guard came by on his rounds, but he would see nothing unusual in Mr. Upson working late again. At last Upson put the copies he had made into his briefcase, replaced the originals in their unmarked resting place, and secured the bar lock on the classified filing cabinet. Then he carried his briefcase out of the embassy, feeling the way he had during his only venture into shoplifting—as a nine-year-old walking out of DeLeo's Drug Store with a stolen Hershey bar in his pocket.

After a late supper, Upson went out to sit with Somchan on the dark porch. Upson thought of the planes coming in from Cam Ranh Bay, Yankee Station in the South China Sea, Sattahip, Sakhon Nakon, Ubon, Udorn Thani, across Vietnam and Cambodia and Thailand, refueling from tankers four miles up in the air, guided by giant C-130 motherships called Moonbeams in the south, Alleycats in the north, all of the bombers on their way to Laos to blow it up.

Here everything was quiet and at peace; the pilots were under orders to go around Vientiane, so that no jet was ever heard. A radio was playing Thai music far away. Insects buzzed. Now and then came a dry, brief, scurrying sound as a chinchuk lizard darted after a moth on the ceiling of the porch.

The briefcase sat on the floor beside Upson's chair. It held accounts of air attacks on American field personnel, on CIA installations, on friendly villages and troops. Twice the bombers had managed to miss the whole country of Laos, blowing up villages in Thailand by mistake. The air force had reported the destruction of an enemy helicopter on the ground sixteen different times, the last four after it was already known to be a South Vietnamese aircraft to begin with, missing in Laos since 1967. Once a flight of Phantom jets had mistaken General Vang Pao, his staff aides, and his top CIA advisors for the enemy. The pilots strafed the group with explosive shells, but missed. Samneua, off limits as the Pathet Lao headquarters, had been whittled away until little of it was left standing. Thompson had collected reconnaissance photos going back over the years which showed the process, crater by crater.

"It's all Wizard of Oz stuff," Upson said to the girl in the shadows. "We've set up this elaborate sham to convince ourselves of our own virtue. But the rules of engagement aren't much more than the rubber glove the doctor uses when he pokes his finger up you. I guess I knew that ever since we went to see your people out at the camp. Isn't it strange, though, that I only became really convinced today, when I saw it in official, classified documents? The whole damned mumbo jumbo, with cipher locks and barred code rooms and shredders, we're like a bunch of little kids with a Captain Midnight secret decoding ring. We only believe what we see in the classified traffic. But now I have to believe, and what am I going to do about it? I guess Thompson didn't have the answer, either. He just collected the stuff and left it sitting there. God knows why I copied it. Presumably to document my case when I set out to change everybody's mind. But whose mind? The ambassador's mind can't be changed. Jerry Brautigan's won't be changed. The secretary of state?

Theoretically, any foreign service officer has the right to send his views directly to Secretary Rogers. Lots of luck. But I had something like that in mind when I was copying the stuff, to show you how irrational I am. Kissinger, I thought. He's the man. I'll take this stuff home and mull it over and draw up an indictment of the air war so logical, so eloquent, so morally compelling that Henry Kissinger will be brought instantly to see the light, like Saul of Tarsus. Sure. The serfs in Russia used to think, if only the tsar knew all the awful things they're doing to us, he'd put a stop to it. But of course the tsar knew all along, Somchan, my love. He gave the orders."

Somchan answered him with a sentence or two. Little by little she had begun to talk herself, during their times on the porch—never more than a few sentences, and only when she heard her own name. Upson nodded, as if he had understood her perfectly.

"The truth is," he went on, "that I don't really know why I copied those papers. Maybe as insurance, for the same reason Casey thinks he pimped for the columnist. But I doubt it. I don't really know what I'm going to do with them, if anything. I don't know if I should have jumped at the chance to get out of the bombing job, because I did jump at it, like a coward. I think I just gave up. I think I just got tired of swimming upstream, Somchan. It's not my nature. I know I'm tired now."

Somchan knew, too. She came over in the dimness and began to work the muscles of his shoulders with her strong hands. Before they went to bed, Upson put the thick envelope of copied documents on a shelf in his closet, under some folded sheets.

T. W. Jackson was described as a businessman on the passport he gave to the Lao immigration officer at Wattay Airport. This was true, since he owned an apartment building in Washington and two motels in Florida. But he was also Ted Jackson, the syndicated columnist. He used only his initials when traveling in search of a story, because he preferred to poke around unnoticed as long as he could. The photo that appeared with his column was fifteen years old and a poor likeness to start with, so that almost no one ever recognized him from it. Jackson knew Laos from ten years before, when he had come to cover the Kong Le coup. Then all the newsmen stayed in the Hotel Constellation, and so Jackson told the cabdriver to take him there this time. He doubted that Maurice, the proprietor, would remember him after a decade. Maurice didn't.

The hotel still seemed to be a headquarters for journalists, because the drawers of a wooden filing cabinet at the far end of the bar were labeled *Reuters, UPI, AP,* the *New York Times,* and various other news organizations. The cabinet evidently served as a message center. "Do you know Bill Bailey of the *New York Times*?" Jackson asked the Vietnamese behind the bar.

"I'm Bailey," said the tall, thin young man who had been sitting alone at a table when Jackson walked in. "What can I do for you?"

"Harvey Hazelton told me to look you up, that you'd know what's going on," Jackson said. "I'm Ted Jackson."

"The Ted Jackson column?"

"That's it. I've only got three days here and I want to get to as many of the right people as I can before the embassy finds out I'm in town. Harvey said you could tell me who to see."

That night, at Bailey's suggestion, Jackson took Dick Lindsay to dinner in one of the private rooms at the Tan Dao Vien. "Order whatever's best and don't worry about the price," the columnist said. "I love Chinese food."

Lindsay ordered elaborately and expensively. "I'm glad to talk to you, Mr. Jackson," he said when he was done. "But I don't imagine I'll be able to tell you anything that'll be much use to you."

"Ted, call me Ted. Hell, my mother did. Listen, Dick, I made my reputation protecting sources. I even went to jail over it once. Nobody will ever know you talked to me."

"That's not the point. Anything I'm free to tell you, I'd tell any newspaperman who asked. But whatever I'm not free to tell you, I wouldn't tell them and I wouldn't tell you."

"I understand that. I'm not necessarily looking for classified information. Bailey told me you were generally knowledgeable, that's all. I don't want you telling me anything that would make you uncomfortable."

"Don't worry. I won't."

"My interests are just general."

They talked during dinner about the communist offensive just completed on the Plain of Jars, about General Vang Pao, about the gold and the opium trade. Jackson kept away from direct questions about CIA involvement, and Lindsay told him nothing that hadn't been in the papers dozens of times. A Chinese waitress stood in the corner of their private cubicle, removing empty dishes and topping off their glasses from liter bottles of Beck's beer. At the end, Jackson said, "Dick, this has been terrifically helpful, really. It's all old stuff to you, but it's new to me and most of my readers. Let me just show you one more thing and ask you about it before we take off. Let's see if I've got it here." Jackson dug out the transcript of a Senate hearing the year before, and pointed out a passage to Lindsay. "There's Ambassador Simmonds telling the Senate we don't bomb villages in Laos. Let me ask you straight, not for attribution. Have you ever seen a bombed village here?"

"Well, I won't answer you straight. You'll have to find out for yourself."

"Is there any way I could get up there and look?"

"You don't have to. The people are down here."

"What do you mean?"

"We emptied off the population of the Plain of Jars last fall with C-130s. No secret, it was on television. The villages are still up there, but the villagers are all down here. If they were bombed, they might remember."

"Where are they?"

"Hire a taxi and tell him to drive north on Route 13 till you get to the milestone at thirty kilometers. Get out and introduce yourself."

"Nobody will stop me? No roadblocks? No guards or gates?"

"You'll be right in the middle of the camp."

"Well, I'll be damned. Easy as that?"

"A lot of things are easy as that here. You newsmen always want to talk to the Americans, but the Lao are the ones to talk to.

They're pretty primitive. Most of them don't even know their country's been classified."

Two days later Jackson telephoned the press attaché from the only phone in the Hotel Constellation, which was kept behind the bar. You had to speak so loudly to be heard over the government phone system that everybody nearby could listen in.

"Ted Jackson calling, Mr. Casey," the columnist said.

"I heard you were in town. What can we do for you?"

"I wish I had the time to come by and see you, Mr. Casey. I understand you're a good man."

"Jesus, don't let the embassy hear that. I'm in enough trouble as it is."

"Really? What kind of trouble?"

"A little joke, that's all. What can I do for you, Mr. Jackson? Somehow I doubt if you want my standard military briefing, with the maps and the extensible pointer."

"Ted, call me Ted. Hell, my mother did. Listen, I wondered if there was a chance of seeing the ambassador this morning. I know it's short notice, but my plane is leaving at eleven."

"I can call over and ask, if you want. It'll be a waste of time, though. I can give you a hundred percent guarantee he'll be too busy to see you. But I'll call if you say so."

"Maybe I'll just go over and knock on his door. I wanted to call you first, though, to go through channels. It's true, incidentally, that I heard you were a good man."

"It's also true that I hope you won't pass the news on to the embassy."

"The friend of my enemy is my enemy?"

"You said it, not me."

Bill Bailey was sitting over his coffee at a table a few feet away. "Good luck," he said after the columnist hung up. "Simmonds hasn't seen a newsman for more than three months, and then it wasn't a real newsman. It was the special correspondent for the CIA, Harrison Bottsford."

"Most people see me," Jackson said.

At the embassy, Jackson gave his card to the Thai receptionist. "Would you take this in to the ambassador's secretary?" he said. "And would you tell her that I'd like to see her for thirty seconds? No more than that. I have a very important package for the ambassador, and I want to hand it to her personally."

In a few moments Annie Cutler came out. "The ambassador's secretary is out sick today, Mr. Jackson, but I'm filling in for her. Souphet said you had a package?"

Jackson nodded, and handed her an envelope along with a small package. "The package is a dub of a tape I made the other day," he said. "It's for the ambassador personally, and so's the envelope. The envelope is an English translation of the tape. It proves the ambassador lied to the U.S. Senate last year."

"I'll be sure he gets them personally, Mr. Jackson."

"There's a message, too. Please tell him the Jackson column runs in six hundred twenty-three newspapers, with a combined readership of a little over thirty-five million. When I call a man a liar in front of that many people, I don't take the responsibility lightly. I always give him a chance to tell his own side. That cassette shows beyond a doubt that the U.S. has been systematically bombing inhabited villages in Laos for many years. Ambassador Simmonds told the Senate under oath that the U.S. never bombed inhabited villages. If he wants to explain himself, I'll be glad to listen. I'll wait here five minutes. It's nine twenty-one now."

"I'll pass that message on to the ambassador, Mr. Jackson," Annie Cutler said. Her face showed nothing, but secretly she was amused by the columnist, as she was by most men.

"Christ on a crutch," the ambassador shouted when she gave him the message, verbatim. "Get Brautigan in here. Jerry! Oh, there you are. Take a look at this stuff. How did this son of a bitch Ted Jackson get in-country without us knowing about it, anyway?"

"Punderson mentioned it at yesterday's country-team meeting, but you weren't back from your Pakse trip yet. It was in the minutes."

"You should have told me. I don't have time to read the goddamned minutes."

"I'm sorry. I guess I should have."

"Who did he talk to?"

"Casey hasn't been able to find out, except that he was seen with Bailey."

"Casey wouldn't tell us anyway. He's on their side. USIS is a bunch of goddamned pussies. Jerry, I've got to see this lousy bastard, don't I?"

"It'll be bad either way, but I think it'll be a little worse if you don't see him."

"Tell Annie to give me five minutes and bring him on in, then."

When the secretary showed Jackson in, the ambassador was seated behind his desk, apparently working on some papers. "Come in, Ted, come in," he said, rising. "Let's sit over here where we can be comfortable. Jerry, do you mind leaving us alone? You might tell Annie to bring some coffee on in, too. Didn't we meet at the Metropolitan Club once, Ted?"

"It's possible. I've been there, but I'm not a member. I don't join clubs."

"That's probably where it was, then. Cigarette, Ted?"

"I gave up twenty years ago. I don't want to waste your time, Mr. Ambassador, and I've got a plane to catch at eleven. Did you have a chance to look at the transcripts? I marked the relevant parts."

"Glanced at them, yes. I was wondering who translated for you."

"A young man named Harold Finkelstein."

"Finkelstein. Let me just give you a word of warning about Finkelstein. You should know that he's an agent of Hanoi."

"Really? He told me he used to be with International Voluntary Services, which is under contract to the U.S. government over here, as I understand it. It's a damned good story if Hanoi is using IVS to infiltrate spies into Laos. What documentation can you give me on it, Mr. Ambassador?"

"Well, nothing on paper, I'm afraid. My intelligence people pick up a lot of stuff we can't put out publicly, or we'd compromise our sources. But it's useful to us in-house to know these things. I just mentioned it to raise a warning flag, Ted. I wouldn't put too much confidence in Finkelstein's translations."

"I don't. That's why I brought the tape dub and the transcript to you. If your people have any problems with the translation, just notify the State Department Office of Public Affairs and they can call me back in Washington. I won't run anything for a week. I'm also having an independent translation made when I get to Washington, and I'll make a copy of the tape available to the Senate Committee on Foreign Affairs, too. But I doubt if there'll be any substantive difficulty. I told Finkelstein I was going to have the tapes independently translated and transcribed back home, so I imagine he was pretty careful. Now can we get to the allegations . . ."

Half an hour later, Ambassador Simmonds was confident he had done the best job possible of convincing Jackson, cold and suspicious bastard though he was, that the American mission was doing everything it could to avoid civilian casualties. As by God it was, within reason.

"I'm glad we had a chance to talk this over," he said as he walked the columnist to the door. "Next time let us know when you're coming, and we can lay on transportation up-country, show you some of our sites, even. Who knows? By this time next year, maybe we can even take you up to the Plain of Jars."

"I don't need to go up. The people are all down here."

The U.S. Information Service's daily wireless file carried the full text of the Ted Jackson column on Laos. The teletype machine for the file was in the anteroom of Phil Casey's office, so that he was the first one in the mission to see the story. He ripped the copy off the machine and took it down the hall to Earl Punderson, the public affairs officer. "Take a look at this, Earl," Casey said. "Jackson really shoved it into us and broke it off."

"Oh, Jesus," Punderson said when he had skimmed through the column. "Phil, I don't want to be the one to hand this to the ambassador."

"Oh, no you don't, Earl. Not me."

"Get Jeannie in, then, and have her hand-carry it over to him right away."

The column began:

"VIENTIANE—I have turned up irrefutable evidence that

147

the United States Ambassador to Laos, Bruce Kingdon Simmonds, lied to the Senate last April when he swore that American warplanes were not bombing unarmed civilians. I have just talked to dozens of those civilians and they tell a very different story—one of around-the-clock bombing of peaceful villages, farms, orchards, and even, incredibly enough, Buddhist temples. The maimed and crippled survivors of the U.S. bombing—many of them horribly scarred by napalm—give an account directly opposed to the one bluff, tough-talking "Buck" Simmonds gave a Senate investigating committee under oath even as the bombs were falling halfway around the world. A young, Lao-speaking American, Harold Finkelstein, helped me get the true story. I have made tapes of our interviews with refugee survivors available to the Senate Foreign Relations Committee, and those tapes stand unchallenged by the U.S. Mission in Laos. Here is the tale they tell . . ."

The column ended: "Incredibly, the embassy that spent billions of dollars bombing Laos has never spent a nickel to find out from the survivors just where those bombs were falling."

"What are we going to do, Phil?" Punderson asked when the secretary had left to take the column down the street to the embassy, three blocks away.

"Deny we were ever in Philadelphia."

"What does that mean?"

"Nothing, Earl. Forget it."

"For God's sake, Phil. I've got to go over and face the ambassador in a few minutes. What do I tell him? What do I advise him to do?"

"Sit tight and shut up, that's all. Cable Washington to say, in effect, that we do the best we can and we'll try to do even better. Mistakes sometimes happen, though, but we try to be sure they don't happen again. Flat denials would just make it worse. Unless we can prove he's wrong, we better just shut up and take our lumps."

"But he *is* wrong, Phil."

"Is he? You think the refugees were lying to him?"

"Phil, that bastard Finkelstein must have hand-picked them. He probably took Jackson to a few selected refugees."

"Do you believe that, Earl? Jackson's a pretty sly old fox."

"It had to be that way, Phil. Maybe there are mistakes

sometimes, but how could it be wholesale, the way Jackson says? What about the rules of engagement?"

"What about the Protocols of Zion? What about the tooth fairy? Come on, Earl, who still believes the air force?"

"If you're not going to believe the air force about this, Phil, who are you going to believe?"

"The refugees."

"All right, then, goddamn it. The refugees. We'll go out and poll the refugees and prove the son of a bitch is lying."

"Don't suggest that to the ambassador, Earl. I'm telling you as a friend."

"Why not?"

"Because we're wrong on this one, and a poll will prove it. We'd just be shooting ourselves in the foot, and the ambassador won't forget whose idea it was."

"Phil, we're not wrong."

"Okay, we're not wrong. If we're not wrong, it's a swell idea."

"The more I think about it, the more I like the idea," the ambassador said. He was too angry to sit down, and kept making quick forays as he talked, changing direction when he came up to a piece of furniture or one of the walls. Earlier he had jabbed with a ballpoint pen at the column to indicate some particular passage. The point had torn through the paper and gouged the polished teak of his desk.

"Maybe you're right and I can't sue the son of a bitch, but at least I can show him up for the lying cocksucker he is. Notice how he ran right to Fulbright with his little tape? Fulbright probably sent him out. There's another son of a bitch for you, always playing politics with national security. Okay, goddamn it, Earl, you go ahead and do it."

Brautigan had been listening in worried silence. He knew there was no hope of heading the ambassador off, not when he was in this mood. There might be a chance of talking him out of it later, once he had cooled down, but even that was doubtful. The deputy chief of mission was already thinking of ways that the poll could be managed and contained.

"Get moving on it right away," the ambassador was saying to the public affairs officer. "And find out something else for me, too. How do you think that bastard Jackson found out about the refugees in the first place? Who told him they were out there?"

Brautigan's memory flickered for a moment over the old report from security on the visit to the refugees by Upson's maid. He couldn't remember the details, but they were certainly irrelevant, anyway. "I don't think he would have had to talk to anybody special," the DCM said. "The networks covered it when we flew the refugees out, and it's no secret where the camps are. They could have told him over at the Ministry of Social Affairs. All he had to do was think of the question and it would be easy enough to find the answer."

"Well, maybe so," the ambassador said.

Still, Brautigan thought, the point was an interesting one. How had Jackson come to think of the question? In the DCM's experience, journalists showed very little enterprise and imagination. They would badger the American press attaché for news of the war, but never think to interview wounded soldiers at the hospital in Vientiane. For years the streets had been full of Meo tribesmen, refugees from the areas where the CIA was carrying on its most secret paramilitary operations, and yet no newsman ever seemed to interview them. Although most radio transmissions between Vientiane and the Plain of Jars had been in the clear during the fighting there, no reporter ever bought a single side-band receiver to listen in. Jackson had done an unusual thing, then.

Brautigan kept the thought to himself, of course, because the ambassador, in this mood, might go off in some even crazier direction. It should prove possible to control the problem of a refugee poll, but the damage would be too great to contain if Simmonds took it into his head to track down Jackson's embassy contacts with lie detectors, or something equally stupid. Brautigan tried not to think of the ambassador as a fool. Simmonds was energetic, forceful, aggressive, unafraid—all traits that were admirable and too often in short supply among senior State Department officers. But Simmonds was impulsive, simplistic, and short of judgment as well. Brautigan often found himself in a babysitter's role, trying to make sure that the ambassador didn't hurt himself.

"All right then, damn it, let's get moving on this thing," the ambassador was saying. "Keep me informed."

"Yes, sir," Punderson answered. The ambassador always made him afraid, and his head hurt from too much scotch the night before, and he would never have suggested a survey if he thought for a minute that he would be the one charged with carrying it out. He had assumed that USAID would be the logical ones; they handled refugee stuff, after all.

"What do I do now?" the public affairs officer said to Brautigan once they left the ambassador's office. "President Nixon remembered how Kennedy used those USIS polls against him in 1960, and now we've cut way the hell down on polling, Jerry. I think we've still got a small polling operation somewhere in Africa, maybe. Nairobi? I'll have to find out, Jerry. Maybe they could send me somebody on TDY."

"I'd rather keep the whole thing in-house," the DCM said. "We start bringing in people from Nairobi and we lay down a paper trail—requests back to Washington, personnel actions, travel orders. Too many people wind up knowing about it, and pretty soon the whole thing is out of control."

"But the only Lao-speaking officer I've got is Barry Gleason, Jerry," Punderson said, "and he can't spare the time from running the Lao-American Association."

"He can spare the time. Earl, let me give you some news. The ambassador won't be thinking about how the Lao-American Association is coming along when he writes your OER. He'll be thinking about how well USIS performed on this poll."

Actually, as both men knew, Brautigan would be writing Punderson's officer evaluation report, for the ambassador's signature. Public affairs officers were evaluated annually both by their ambassadors and by their USIS area directors back in Washington.

"This is a touchy thing, Earl," Brautigan went on. "Jackson is smart, and he's mean as a snake, and he knows a lot of people. If we take him on based on a poll, we have to be sure our facts are straight. Do you want to tell Gleason that, or do you want me to talk to him?"

"No, I'll talk to him, Jerry. Tell him what?"

"What I just said. That we're dead if we try to fake this thing in any way. He has to be able to back up his findings. Have him keep close check on whoever does the interviews. Follow up behind the interviewers himself now and then, asking the same questions a day or two later."

"What for?"

"So he can be sure the answers the interviewers say they got are the ones they really got. The interviewers will probably be local employees, and we don't want them telling us only what they think we want to hear."

"Jerry, why couldn't Gleason just do the interviews himself, in the first place?"

"Come on, Earl. He won't have time to do anything but spot-check to keep everybody honest. The ambassador wants this in two weeks, and you can't get any statistical reliability if you've just got one man, interviewing a few dozen refugees at the most."

"I don't see how much reliability we can get, anyway, Jerry. Polling is a whole science. You need pros for it."

Brautigan bent his head, clasped his thick hands together, and squeezed until the joints cracked. Then he let his breath out. There was no sense getting mad at Punderson; it would just confuse him. The thing to remember was that stupid people didn't know they were stupid; they thought they were acting perfectly reasonably.

"Earl," he said gently, "don't worry about all that. Just get as good a sample as you can in the time available—as many people as you can, from as many different places. You can draw on the whole mission for your interviewers. We'll just pull them off their regular jobs for a week or so. Keep the questions simple. Name of your village. Population. Was it ever bombed? How many times? When? By whom? Make sure you get that one in, because a lot of these incidents will probably turn out to be T-28 strikes by the Royal Lao Air Force. The RLAF guys don't have any rules of engagement. It's their country, after all, and we can't very well tell them where they can't bomb. They get paid by the sortie, too, so they drop as many bombs a day as they can. So put in a question about what kind of plane, too. Fast-movers, it's us. Slow-movers, it's RLAF and we can't do a thing about it. Ask about enemy military presence in the village before or during the strike. Well, you get the idea. Set everything else aside and get moving on this. Okay, Earl?"

Punderson felt better. It didn't sound too hard, now that the DCM at least had explained what he wanted for a change. He could safely turn it over to his deputy, and just ride herd as the project progressed.

Upson read the title on the cover of the report his new boss had handed him. " 'An Attitudinal Survey of the Air War in Laos, 1967–1971.' What the hell is an attitudinal survey, Dennis?"

"Read the executive summary," said the chief of the political section. "It explains everything."

Upson turned to the second page, and read: *This report contains the findings of a survey of 243 refugees from the MR-II area of the Royal Kingdom of Laos concerning their reactions and attitudes toward aerial bombardment carried out during the 1967–1971 time frame in connection with armed reconnaissance flights carried out at the request of the Royal Lao Government. It is to be stressed that this survey is neither comprehensive nor conclusive, but rather attitudinal in that its parameters only measure on the basis of a statistically inadequate sample what are basically subjective, or attitudinal, responses of the few individuals sampled rather than an objective, or scientific, evaluation of the air war as such. With these reservations in mind, the survey seems to indicate that a majority of the respondents claimed familiarity to some extent with aerial bombardment, having experienced it one or more times in their localities of previous residence. A majority of the limited sample of individuals also alleged to have witnessed or had knowledge of casualties supposedly caused by such bombardment, as well as damage to structures. It was not possible in the limited time allotted for the survey and in the absence of trained, professional personnel to compare these subjective recollections with the more objective evidence available from USAF and other intelligence sources, which would undoubtedly put these findings in a more accurate perspective. Without such cross-verification of the accuracy of the refugees' statements relative to their experience, they must be considered nonfinal. Determination of whether they warrant further investigation by qualified personnel is outside the scope of the present study.*

"You don't get the impression that it's much of a report, do you?" Upson said to Dennis Goldman.

"No, you don't get that impression. But you should. Wait till you find out what Punderson means by 'a majority of the respondents.'"

"I thought that guy over at the Lao-American Association wrote the report. What's his name? Barry Gleason."

"He did. But Punderson wrote the executive summary. Let me write a bureaucracy's executive summaries, and I care not who writes her reports."

Upson leafed past the section on methodology used, to the beginning of the report's actual findings. "I see what you mean," he said. "That's a majority, all right." Of the 243 asked whether they had personally experienced bombing in their villages, 241 answered yes.

"Read through the rest of that, will you, Fred?" Goldman said. "Then bring it right back to me, because I've got to give it right back to Jerry. They're holding it pretty close, for reasons which will become apparent to you. But I'd like to get your personal impression of it, speaking as the former Mad Bomber."

The findings of the report were worse than anything Upson had imagined. Every village had been bombed, usually repeatedly. The villagers seldom reported that communist soldiers had been nearby, or even military targets. Houses, crops, orchards, and livestock had been destroyed almost everywhere, although human casualties were lighter than Upson would have expected, given the huge number of strikes. He remembered Lindsay's remark, months before, that it didn't take a peasant long to become smarter than the U.S. Air Force.

Upson thought of his own experience in the bombing job. The requests for target validation that he had routinely approved day after day were, for the most part, clearly in unpopulated zones, or zones of military activity. Some of the requests he picked out of the stream at random for further verification turned out to be doubtful or plainly improper. But most of them, to be fair, turned out to be permissible under the rules of engagement. And yet the bombing reported by the refugees had been so commonplace that the system must have massive defects. Perhaps the fully validated zones had civilian populations after all. Perhaps some pilots dropped their bombs wherever they felt like it, regardless of validated coordinates. Perhaps some forward air controllers were calling in strikes on targets of opportunity without reference to the rules of engagement. But even all these taken together would hardly account for the intensity of the bombardments. He took the report back in to Goldman.

"I can see why they're holding it close," Upson said. "Do you think it's still this bad?"

"You mean was it this bad when you were the Mad Bomber?"

"I guess that's what I mean."

"Probably. After all, Gus Thompson had the job during part of the time covered by the survey, and he was a much bigger pain in the ass than you were."

"I never tried to be a pain in the ass."

"In that job, you hardly have to try at all before they ease you out."

"I could have stayed."

"You're still not quite sure what happened to you, are you? But if you turn your head, it'll fall right off. Brautigan is really very good."

Upson's face grew hot. He knew he must be blushing, something he hadn't done since high school.

"Welcome to the turkey farm, Fred. It's not so bad over here. Sort of like one of those independent eating houses in college. We may not be in the fraternities, but we have each other. If you do good work for me, I'll take care of you as well as I can. Which is pretty well. When I do your OER in August, it'll be based on your performance in the political section, not on how you got along with the Generalissimo."

Upson knew that some of the junior officers called the ambassador that, but he was surprised to hear it from the chief of the political section. Goldman was a Foreign Service Officer 2, only one step from the top grade. Upson himself had been promoted up to FSO-5 during his tour in Morocco, and had hoped to make 4 during this tour. "Jerry already did an OER on me," he said. "I just got it yesterday. Apparently he had to do one covering the part of the rating year when I worked over there."

"How did you make out?"

"He said I lacked judgment."

"That's pretty rough. Like saying a running back can't run. Judgment's the only thing you've got to sell."

"How can I appeal it, though?" Upson asked. "It's like having a bad attitude in school. You can never prove you don't have one, because it's the teachers who decide what one is."

"Have you signed off on his evaluation yet, Fred?"

"Not yet."

"I'd go ask him, very politely, to explain what he means, so you can do better in the future. He can't make it any worse; he's already blown you out of the water for promotion for at least the next three years, even if your next bosses think you're Metternich. And maybe he'll soften it a little if you go in and see him. Jerry doesn't really like confrontation."

Neither did Upson, and he was uneasy later that afternoon while waiting by Annie Cutler's desk for Brautigan to be free. "Is it that damned OER?" she asked. "I typed it, is how I know about it. But nobody else has seen it."

"Yes, that's it."

"Well, his light's out now, so he's off the line. You can go on in. Good luck."

Brautigan nodded toward a chair and said, "Sit down, Fred. What can I do for you?" He didn't come out from behind his desk to sit in one of the other chairs, as he usually did.

"I just wanted to talk to you before I signed off on my OER, Jerry."

"You don't have any problems with it, do you? It's a damned good report."

"Well, most of it is. I was just wondering about here under 'Work Performance,' where you say, 'This young officer occasionally displays poor judgment in the discharge of his duties.' I don't know just what you mean by that, so I don't know what I should be doing differently."

"Fair enough, Fred. First off, let me say that I wasn't kidding when I just said it's a damned good report. You ought to see one or two of the OERs *I* got when I was your age. If I had

156

let myself get discouraged, I'd be selling life insurance for a living today."

He paused and smiled. Since it seemed to be expected of him, Upson smiled back. "The fact is," Brautigan went on, "you've got a long and successful career ahead of you in the foreign service, and you're making a mistake if you think this report is going to change that. It's a fine report."

"Except for that one part."

"I had to put that in, Fred. The whole system breaks down if you don't evaluate officers as honestly as you can."

"How did I display poor judgment, though? What are some examples? That's what I want to know."

The deputy chief of mission clasped his big hands together behind his neck and leaned back in his chair. "All right," he said, "let's take the business of the strike on the Samneua ford . . ."

"But I was right, Jerry. They missed the damned ford and blew up an innocent woman. My judgment wasn't poor. My judgment was vindicated."

"Your judgment on the strike request itself, sure. That's not in question. I shared that judgment myself, you'll recall. I'm talking about your judgment in the whole matter. Let me give you an example. When I was in the army, every spring there would be a certain day when you changed into summer uniform. Up to that day, you wore your wool uniform even if it was hot; from that day on you wore khakis, even if it was cold. Now obviously on certain days and in certain places, that rule looked wrong and stupid. That's always the case when you apply general rules to particular cases. But you have to have general rules in any large organization, or it's no longer an organization. That means, though, that there's a certain amount of stupidity and injustice and even immorality built into all large organizations. Do you begin to see where I'm going?"

"Not really, no. I was *supposed* to judge particular cases. That's what my job was."

"That's true up to a point. But there has to be a certain amount of play in any large machine. If you engineer the tolerances so close that they approach perfection, you may have a beautiful machine. But it'll seize up when you try to run it. The important thing is the operation of the whole machine, Fred, not the theoretical perfection of one little part of it."

157

"You mean I showed poor judgment by doing my job too well?"

"Let me try again. The machine we have here is an unusually complicated one, with a lot of parts that normally wouldn't mesh too well. It's important that the ambassador maintain his control over those different parts—the CIA, USAID, the military attachés, and so on. Otherwise, the Pentagon would pour a half-million troops into Laos and pave most of the country over for runways. But the ambassador can't *coerce* those different parts, or elements, of the mission. If the machine is to work, each of them has got to cooperate, and they can withhold that cooperation in a thousand little ways without ever disobeying a direct order. So if somebody wants to try out one of their little toys and there doesn't seem to be too great an objection to it, it's best in the long run to let them go ahead. As long as you say yes in such a way as to let them know you still exert final control. And I think we did that, you and I. Does that make sense to you?"

"It seems like a pretty subtle point to base a bad OER on."

"It's not a bad OER, Fred. But let's not argue that. If the language disturbs you, let's take another look at it. Maybe I was too broad. Why don't we sharpen it a little bit? Suppose I put, 'This young officer occasionally displays poor judgment in that he assigns more value to conscientious performance of his own job than to the performance of the mission as a whole. I am confident that he now understands this shortcoming, and will correct it.' How's that?"

"It's still pretty rough. It's the phrase 'poor judgment' that I object to. Along with 'young officer.' "

"You are young, but I'll knock that word out if it bothers you. There. I can't go any further than that, though. I'll have Annie retype it, and I hope you'll decide to sign off on it. You still have the right to appeal, but my private advice to you is that appeals are always a dirty business. They can hurt you a lot worse than a bad report in the long run, and this isn't a bad report. Believe me, it isn't."

Upson took the emended report back from Brautigan and looked at it. The handwriting seemed oddly small and precise to have been formed by fingers so thick. Upson didn't think the DCM would change the report again, for better or for worse, and so he decided to go ahead and ask the question that had been on his mind.

"This may sound crazy, Jerry, and it probably is crazy. But I'll ask it anyway. Is there something else to this poor judgment thing? Maybe something that shouldn't be in the 'Work Performance' section, but in the 'Personal Qualities' section instead?"

"I don't follow you at all."

"I was talking about that strange memorandum that went around just after the rocket festival, the one on fraternizing with the natives."

"I still don't see . . ." Brautigan said, and then he burst out laughing. "Oh, my God, no. Oh, Fred, you're off on a totally wrong track. Don't let it get out of this room, but I'll tell you what happened. I imagine you guessed part of it already, or you wouldn't have asked."

"I figured the memo was directed at me, yes."

"It was directed at calming down the ambassador's wife. Your gal, all right?—your maid or cook, whatever she is, the gal with the relatives out at KM 30—anyway, Mrs. Simmonds had to suffer the awful ignominy of being introduced to her in public. A servant, can you imagine? She thought that was a terrible outrage and the ambassador ought to do something about it, and by God, the ambassador did. He had me send around that stupid memo to get her off his back. I hoped you wouldn't even make the connection. You hadn't done anything wrong; you just ran into this gal at the festival and Mrs. Simmonds just happened by at the wrong moment. The ambassador knew that. He was there. He certainly didn't want to call you on the carpet for nothing at all, but at the same time he wanted to cool off his wife. No, that silly little business had nothing to do with it. Nobody blames you."

Upson had hardly paid any attention to most of Brautigan's explanation, except to wait until it was finished. "How do you know she has relatives at KM 30?" he asked.

"Oh, hell, that's just nonsense, too. Mancuso over in the Mission Guard's office hasn't got enough to do, so he has his guards picking up gossip about servants or something. There was something in one of his weekly reports that your cook took a trip out there to see some relatives, that's all. The only reason it stuck in my mind is it seemed like such a stupid thing to put in a report."

Brautigan came out from behind his desk, held his hand out to Upson, and smiled a warm, open smile. "What do you say, Fred?" he said. "Friends again?"

"Sure, Jerry," Upson said, shaking his hand.

"This is a lousy job I have, Fred, it really is. I don't want to be a prick, God knows, but sometimes the job makes you one. I've tried to make you understand. I hope you do, a little, anyway."

"I guess I do. A little."

"I was so much like you when I was your age. Always the class rebel."

"Class rebel?" Upson had never thought of himself as a rebel, had never much liked rebels, didn't think he had become one.

"In the good sense, Fred. Always asking the questions that need to be asked. Keeping everybody on their toes."

Back outside the office, Upson gave the reworded version of his officer evaluation report to Annie Cutler to be retyped. "Congratulations, sort of," she said. "At least he made it a little bit better. You should have seen the one he gave Gus Thompson. It was so bad Gus didn't even bother to go in and pound on the desk. He just filed a formal appeal and requested transfer."

The deputy chief of mission, behind his desk again, remembered how Upson had been at first. Bright and quick, if not brilliant. Anxious to do well and get ahead. A steady, reliable, and useful ally. Maybe there was enough difference in their ages and ranks, Brautigan had thought back then, so that they could become friends instead of wary colleagues. Brautigan missed having friends he could talk with easily and openly. His only real friend, a boy he grew up with, had been killed in the Korean War.

But Upson had changed. The Upson of a few months back

would not have come in to complain in the first place, and would certainly not have made that crack about showing poor judgment by doing his job too well. Upson seemed to be spinning ever so slightly out of control. Maybe the very nature and structure of the Mad Bomber job changed its occupants for the' worse. Maybe it would happen to this new young officer, too, unless the responsibilities were redefined, or modified, or shared more widely. Perhaps a committee structure, or something.

It was interesting, too, that Upson had brought up that stupid memo on fraternization. True enough, the thing had been circulated solely to placate the ambassador's wife. But if Mike Costikyan had been the one with the girl, for example, the ambassador would have laughed the affair off no matter what his wife said. Upson, though, was no longer in that small group whose members the ambassador would defend against all comers, even his wife. Brautigan wondered if Upson had sensed that. Certainly he had been correct in suspecting that the charge of poor judgment on his OER was, for a fact, based in part on the incident with the ambassador's wife. It *was* poor judgment to be seen in a social situation with your maid. If the girl had been a prostitute, oddly enough, it probably wouldn't have bothered Mrs. Simmonds so much. The boys-will-be-boys defense would have been adequate. A maid was different, Brautigan knew, although it took him a moment to figure out why. The answer was that the American men who went to Loulou's and the White Rose and the Lucky Bar weren't paying to own the girl; they were paying so that the girl wouldn't own them. Thus prostitutes were an unpleasant fact of life for embassy wives, but no real threat. The unforgiveable sin, to the guild of married American women, was to fall in love with an Asian woman. This made the guild members afraid for their own marriages, and fearful that a perfectly good catch for some American girl might betray his own kind by marrying a member of the slender, soft-spoken, and unfairly dainty opposition. Mrs. Simmonds would not have gone through that whole reasoning process, but she would have sensed intuitively that a young bachelor seen in public with his maid was more likely to be emotionally involved than if the woman were a bargirl. Brautigan doubted that Upson would have the poor sense to be in love with his maid, but that didn't matter. What mattered was that Upson lacked a certain delicacy of judgment, or he would have taken care not to be with the girl in the first place. And yet you couldn't point to this as evidence of poor judgment without sounding petty and absurd.

Brautigan tensed the muscles in his left forearm, and felt the hard bulk with his right hand. Forearms and calves, for some reason, seldom seemed to go to fat. He used to enjoy his bulk and physical strength; now that too much work and too little exercise had made him soft, that old enjoyment was gone. He looked with distaste at his middle, where the belly bulged against the shirt. Brautigan forced himself to think of business again.

For the moment, the problem was that damned Gleason report on the bombing. He pressed a button on his intercom. "Annie," he said, "would you work out the soonest possible time for me to get together with Mr. Punderson and Mr. Gleason?"

"Yes, sir."

There was always that little edge to the way Annie said everything, even "Yes, sir." The smile that worked with men didn't work with her. Nor did it work any more with his wife, not since the Christmas Eve party. Brautigan was uneasy around both of the women he passed his life with, and he had no idea what he could do about it. The buzzer on his phone sounded, and Annie said, "Mr. Punderson and Mr. Gleason will be here in a few minutes."

Punderson would never cause trouble on purpose. But the public affairs officer was so stupid that dealing with him was dangerous—like playing with a bridge partner so bad that he didn't know what his own bids meant. Brautigan knew little about Gleason, except that he had been a Peace Corps volunteer in Thailand before joining USIS, and that he was supposed to be doing a good job at cleaning up the administrative mess he had inherited at the Lao-American Association. The Peace Corps background sometimes was troublesome. Former volunteers were usually fluent in the language, which could lead to an unhealthy degree of identification with the interests of the host country. Annie Cutler buzzed to tell him that the two men had arrived.

"Earl, come on in," Brautigan said. "Barry, we've never really had a chance to sit down and talk, but I understand you're really taking hold over at the LAA. And everybody's impressed with the way you were able to wrap up this survey thing in such a short time. I'm sorry it had to be such a rush job. You must be beat to death. Let's sit down over here. Cigars?"

Punderson took one, as Brautigan knew he would. Punderson would drink a glass of castor oil if a superior officer offered him one, and show every sign of enjoying it. Gleason declined a cigar. Just as well. A cigar, Brautigan felt, gave you a slight psychological edge over the visitor who wasn't smoking one. Once the ritual of cutting and lighting the cigars was over—a ritual from which Gleason had excluded himself—Brautigan leaned forward. "Well, to business," he said. "First of all, how many people have seen the survey?"

"Barry and myself, of course," Punderson answered. "And Phil Casey."

"Why Phil?"

"I thought he should take a look at it, Jerry, and see what kind of a press impact it would have."

"What did he say?"

"He thought it would be a three-day wonder, Jerry. He said the general public probably figures we've been bombing villages all along and doesn't really care."

"He's probably right," the DCM said. "But I'm not concerned with the impact on the media. I'm concerned with the impact on Capitol Hill, and on eventual funding levels."

"The same thing I told Phil," the public affairs officer said. "Gives the politicians another chance to play politics with national security, Jerry."

"So three people at USIS have seen it," Brautigan broke in. "Plus, presumably, whoever typed it. That's four over at your shop. I've seen it myself, and Goldman has, and Fred Upson. So that's three more. Seven altogether."

"Excuse me," Gleason said. "How about the ambassador?"

"I've briefed him on it, but he hasn't read it yet."

"I would think he'd want to see it."

Gleason might be trouble, Brautigan thought. He said, "He does want to see it. He's just been up to his ears lately."

"Christ, you should have been at the ops meeting this morning, Barry," Punderson said. "The poor guy's up to his ears with MR-II going down the tubes."

"Well, I know," Gleason said. "I didn't mean right away. I just meant he'd probably want to take a look at it when he gets a chance, that's all."

Thinking that Gleason might not be so much trouble after all, Brautigan went on. "Well, seven people is a manageable group, if we can keep it at that for the moment. I think you were absolutely on the right track in your executive summary, incidentally, Earl. What we've got here so far is a preliminary piece of work. Suggestive, but without too much statistical validity at this stage."

"But it isn't really statistics, Mr. Brautigan," Gleason said. "Not in the sense a poll is. It's a collection of observations from eyewitnesses, brought together and tabulated. More like reporting, really."

"Barry, I'm not suggesting that you didn't do a good, sound job, because you did. I'm just saying that a statistician or professional pollster could poke it full of holes, fairly or unfairly. Size of the sample, selection methods, wording of questions, a hundred things that none of us would probably ever think of. That being the case, I think we'd be premature if we put the full weight of the embassy behind the report at this time."

"My sentiments exactly, Jerry," Punderson said. "It's a preliminary document." He puffed on his cigar and then twirled it between his fingers, in exact imitation of a mannerism the deputy chief of mission had. For a moment Brautigan was tempted to scratch his crotch, to see if Punderson would do the same.

"My thinking," the DCM said, "is that we should keep the report strictly to ourselves until we can take a good, hard look at it. Maybe do what you suggested earlier, Earl. Get a professional out here on TDY who can tell us whether what we've got is defensible from the statistical point of view, or merely anecdotal."

"I don't see how we could be too far wrong overall," Gleason said. "Even if our methodology was less than perfect, the figures are overwhelming. Practically no village in that whole part of the country escaped being bombed."

"Assuming the refugees are telling the truth."

"Why would they lie?"

"You'd know more about it than me, Barry. But aren't the Lao known for telling you what they think you want to hear? If the Americans are asking questions about the bombing, wouldn't the Lao assume that these round-eyes must want to hear that their bombers are doing a hell of a job, blowing up everything in sight? Maybe that's farfetched, Barry. I'm sure it is. But I just throw it out as the kind of possibility a professional would guard against with cross-checks and dummy questions, and I don't know what. None of us knows, which is my point. We're not George Gallup. We're foreign service officers."

"That's right, Jerry," Punderson said. "That's an art, public opinion polls. Look at the Harris Poll. Those guys make millions."

"The report as it stands gives us enough information to be very concerned," the DCM said. "And I am concerned, when I see the kind of responses you turned up, Barry. But we don't want to get out in front of the White House on this one, God knows."

"What happens to the report, then, Mr. Brautigan?"

"Nothing for the moment. I want to get a few more readings on this thing, firm up our thinking some more, and in the meantime let's just keep it between ourselves, okay?"

"An awful lot of people already know about it, Mr. Brautigan."

"I thought only seven."

"I mean know that I've been working on the thing. Me and sixteen locals. They're already calling it the Gleason report."

"They know you've been working on something, but they don't know what's in it, do they?"

"Not the figures, no. Just that it's a bombing survey of the refugees from the PDJ."

"And you're still pulling it together into final form. It's a big job, still in its preliminary phases. Which has, as Dr. Kissinger likes to say, the additional virtue of being true. You look worried, Barry. What's the trouble?"

"I am worried, I guess. I think we could learn something important from this survey, and I don't think it should be buried."

"It won't be buried, Barry. You have my promise. I mean to

pursue the matter, but very carefully and in a way that won't be open to the slightest challenge. You've got to trust me to use it the most effective way I can. And that may turn out to be strictly in-house or it may not. I just don't know yet. Okay?"

Brautigan smiled his warm smile, and Gleason smiled back.

Bill Bailey's alarm clock was set to go off at five o'clock in the morning, but he woke up just before, and pushed the button to keep the bell from ringing. For a long time, he had thought he had the ability to wake himself automatically a few seconds before the stroke of five. But then one morning he had been lying in bed, wakeful from the heat, and heard the clock make a tiny click, a second or two before the alarm went off. And so it must have been the click, really, that woke him each day.

The reporter's apartment had no air conditioning. He had bought a large floor fan instead, from a restaurant going out of business. He talked about how it was just as comfortable as air conditioning, but the truth was that he woke most mornings with his bedclothes in a damp, hot tangle. Still, he wouldn't have an air conditioner. They were just another example of the ostentatious extravagance, waste, and cultural insensitivity of the official Americans in Laos. Besides, the cost of electricity in Vientiane was extortionate. Bailey had once done a story about how the Americans had bought all the generators for the Vientiane electric plant, and then let themselves be gouged for the product. Virtually nobody else in Vientiane paid the quoted rate. Everybody but the Americans tampered with the meter, or bribed the meter reader, or both. It had made a good little story, even if it had done, as usual, no good at all.

The one shower in Bailey's three-story apartment building was a concrete stall off the courtyard, two flights down. The tepid water felt pleasant on Bailey's skin. He soaped himself, and then shampooed his hair with Thai shampoo, a quarter the price of the American stuff at the ACA commissary and just as good. Before rinsing, he spread a handful of the shampoo lather on his beard and shaved in the mirror he left permanently on the wall of the shower stall. He had no fear that anyone would steal his mirror; there were no American tenants in the building. When his face was smooth he rinsed, and brushed his teeth, and dried himself with a slightly damp towel. Towels never got quite dry in the climate of Laos. Even if you hung them in the sun, they picked up moisture from the air as soon as you took them in.

Back in his small apartment, Bailey got out his flash cards, each with a Lao word on one side and its English equivalent on the other. He worked his way through one pack of fifty until he got them all right three times in a row, and then moved on to another pack of fifty. He had more than six thousand cards, and added fifty more each week.

At the end of exactly half an hour, he put his cards away and turned to the notes and research materials he had assembled the evening before. During the day he supported himself by journalism; evenings and early mornings he set aside for his book. The working title was "Laos: The Last Colony." This was an exaggeration—but a permissible one, in Bailey's view, because the other colonies still remaining were insignificant places like New Caledonia and Belize. The countries of Eastern Europe were not colonies, but rather members of a military alliance much like NATO.

Bailey began his day's real work, which was blocking out one of the chapters on Western involvement in the opium trade. This ran in a straight line from the French colonial government to the Corsican mafia, then to the CIA and its proprietary airline, Air America. The first two stages were the easiest to document, since the French and the Corsicans no longer feared jail if they told the truth about their former roles. In writing about the American stage of this corrupt exploitation, though, Bailey was forced to rely on weaker evidence than he would have liked. The refusal of current participants to talk left him with no choice but to rely on what sometimes bordered on speculation—and yet that refusal itself went a long way towards confirming the guilt of the U.S. Mission. There was a particular irony for Bailey in the fact that most of the CIA's eventual customers were

GIs in Vietnam. Thus Americans were engaged in a criminal conspiracy that weakened the combat effectiveness of other Americans, engaged in a criminal war.

By nine o'clock Bailey had finished his daily quota of a thousand words, and dressed to go out on his reporting rounds. Many of the people in the U.S. Mission were afraid even to be seen with him. This was partly why he made the daily rounds: to get everyone used to him, even if they didn't like him or what he did. Sooner or later some of them drifted into sociability; sometimes one would even develop into a source. Bailey's first stop was at the air attaché's office, which had never produced any news at all for him. Bailey would ask the sergeant in civilian clothes who sat in the outer office what was going on, and the sergeant would say not a damned thing, and Bailey would leave. Once in a while one of the officers would pass on his way in or out, and Bailey would ask the same question. None of them had ever given him anything, either. But this morning, as the reporter was leaving, he heard steps behind him. He held the door open for the man—presumably an air force officer, although he wore civilian clothes, like all of them. "You're the guy from the *Times*, aren't you?" the man said when they were outside.

"Bill Bailey, yes."

"Well, Bailey, why don't you put it in your fuckin' paper that fuckin' USIS—Useless, I call it—is wasting the taxpayer's money putting together some half-ass study of the air war in Laos. Shit, those dickheads don't know any more about war than I know about nuclear physics."

"What kind of a study?"

"Study? I don't know anything about a study."

"What's your name?"

"Me? I got no name. I'm not even in this country."

"Well, thanks."

"For what?" The man swung his leg over a red, 750-cc Honda, started it up, and roared away toward the gate of the American compound.

Bailey turned toward the American Community Association coffee shop, where he spotted a USAID refugee relief worker he had met once or twice. Bailey took his coffee over to the man's table and sat down. After a few minutes' conversation, he said, "How's USIS coming along with that air-war survey?"

"The Gleason report, or poll, or whatever they call it? I don't know, really."

"Poll? Who are they polling?"

"Look, I don't know anything about it really, Bill. I shouldn't be talking about it, okay?"

"Sure. Listen, what's the new director like? Is it worth asking him for an interview yet? Does he seem to be picking up pretty fast on what's going on?"

When the USAID man left, Bailey went next door into the cocktail lounge, deserted at this hour, where there was an embassy phone at the end of the bar. "Mr. Gleason, please," he told the operator.

He heard the phone ring at the other end, and then a voice answered, "Samakhoom Lao-America."

"Taan Gleason yoo, bo?"

"Bo yoo. Taan het kaan yoo USIS la ya hung."

"Tham thamada taan het kaan yoo sai?"

"Yoo ni. Pin nai."

"Taan pai het kaan yoo USIS dai dohn layo, bo?"

"Dai song-sam athit layo."

"Yoo poon, taan het kaan neo dai?"

"Bo hoo. Pai lak sam-sip took-took muh."

Now Bailey knew that Gleason was director of the Lao-American Association, on detail to USIS headquarters for the last several weeks. Every day he went to KM 30, to do unspecified work. KM 30 was the refugee camp that Ted Jackson had visited. Bailey was still angry with himself for having let a visiting columnist beat him on his home ground. It was a stupid lapse to have watched the refugees flown off the Plain of Jars, and then not followed up to find whether they were going someplace accessible, where they could be interviewed at length. But it might be working out for the best, after all. The *Times* would have given feature treatment to interviews with eyewitnesses to the bombing. But if an official government survey came to the same no doubt damaging conclusions, then the story would move to the front page as hard news. Particularly if the mission tried to deny or suppress the survey, which it was sure to do. Bailey already had enough to mount a convincing bluff, and so he called the weakest of the players opposing him.

"Hello, Bill," Earl Punderson said when his secretary had

put him on the line. "What can we do for the *New York Times?*"

"Nothing difficult. I'd just like to get hold of a copy of the Gleason report."

"Where the hell did you hear about that?"

"Earl, you can't go around polling refugees on the bombing without word getting around. It's a small country."

"Well, there isn't any report, per se."

"Why did you ask me how I heard about it, then?"

"What do you mean?"

"I mean if there wasn't any report, you would have said something like, 'What's the Gleason report?' Right?"

"I didn't say there wasn't any report. I said there wasn't any report per se."

"What is there, per se?"

"Not an official report, Bill. I can tell you that in all honesty."

"Let me put it another way. Has Gleason committed any of his findings to paper?"

"Some preliminary notes and data, that's all."

"Can I look at those notes and data?"

"They're not official, Bill. I keep telling you."

"I don't mind. I'm willing to look at them anyway."

"They're not in a state to be seen. They're not finalized."

"So I can't see them?"

"Not yet, not till they're official."

"Are they classified?"

"No, of course not. There's nothing to classify yet."

"Then why can't I see them?"

"Because they're working documents, unofficial. Christ, how can I make it any plainer than that?"

"Do you think they'd be official if they showed that only military targets had been bombed?"

"They'd still be unofficial."

"Don't you think maybe the fact that they show heavy civilian casualties makes them just a little bit *more* unofficial, Earl?"

"No, it doesn't. The data are preliminary and inconclusive and unevaluated. They're not even collated. And that's why they're unofficial."

"But when they're official, I can have them?"

"Certainly. Well, if they ever become official."

"Who makes them official?"

"What do you mean?"

"Is there a board or something that says this particular report assembled by a government employee on government time is official, and that one over there is unofficial? Who sits on the board? What criteria do they use?"

"There's no board. Ultimately, the ambassador makes the determination."

"When do you think the ambassador will make the determination in the case of the Gleason report?"

"I can't answer for him. He hasn't even seen it yet."

"If he hasn't seen it yet, how could he decide that it's unofficial?"

"He knows what's in it."

"And it sounds unofficial to him, does it? Who told him what was in it?"

"Bill, that's internal stuff. I can't talk to the press about who gives what advice to the ambassador, you know that."

"He acted on advice, then, when he decided the Gleason report couldn't be released to the press?"

"Certainly. He didn't just go off hand-cocked."

"Hand-cocked?"

"Of course not. He gave it careful consideration."

"When and if the Gleason report meets the standards for becoming official, who will advise the ambassador of that fact? You, as the counsellor for public affairs?"

"I'll have input, certainly."

"But you won't make the final decision."

"Of course not. The ambassador will."

"I meant the decision on what advice to give the ambassador."

"I don't want to get into the decision-making process, Bill."

"Will it be Gleason?"

"It certainly wouldn't be at that low a level, no."

"So it would be between your level and the ambassador. That leaves the deputy chief of mission, doesn't it?"

"I'm just not going to get into it, Bill."

You already have, Bailey thought as he hung up. Punderson had confirmed that a bombing survey showing heavy civilian

171

casualties existed, and that Jerry Brautigan was trying to suppress it. Bailey walked out of the dark, air-conditioned bar and into the glaring heat of the USAID compound. Outside the gate, Bailey hired a samlor instead of the taxicabs most Americans used. He felt that the pedicab drivers needed the money more than a man who was able to rent or own a taxicab. "Pai sathaan-thoot America," he said, and the driver started off for the American embassy. Bailey watched the flexing of the man's extraordinary calf muscles as he pedalled the three-wheeled machine along. Before the previous ambassador put a stop to it, some of the ARMA officers would hire samlor drivers to race the length of Avenue Laan Xang late at night, after the bars closed and the streets were nearly empty. Betting would be heavy. Bailey had heard, although he could never confirm it, that the winner's reward would be one of the girls at the White Rose, with the American military advisers watching.

At the embassy, the receptionist took his name in and came out only a minute later to show him in to the deputy chief of mission's office.

"That was fast, Jerry," Bailey said. "You wouldn't have been expecting me, would you?"

"Earl called, yes."

"I like that frank admission of the nonessential fact, Jerry. It's a pleasure to deal with you, particularly after dealing with your quick-witted counselor for public affairs."

"Well, the embassy's very much like the *New York Times*. We have to make do with whatever help we can get."

"Can I see the Gleason report?"

"Nope."

"Why not?"

"It's an internal document, for our own use and guidance. It isn't a thorough or a professional enough job yet for us to put it out. We don't trust the figures enough to present them as fact."

"Would you say you were *suppressing* the Gleason report?"

"I wouldn't, Bill, although I have every confidence you will. What I would say for quotation is that the findings are tentative and preliminary, and we have not yet made a judgment on whether they warrant further investigation. If we make such a judgment, and if we determine that the eventual results of such further investigation can be released without compromising security, we will at that point release them."

"Let me see if I've got it. If you ever decide to release the report, you'll release it."

"Bill, you're a quick study."

"Is it classified?"

"Not yet. Nothing to classify at this point. It's just a preliminary working paper. But if . . ."

"If you decide to classify it, you'll classify it."

"Oh, yes. That which should be classified will become classified. That's our role as public servants."

"Suppose you had two reports, Jerry. One of them showed heavy bombing of civilian targets and the other showed no bombing of civilian targets. Which report would be more likely to wind up classified?"

"Hypothetical question. Come on, Bill. We could waltz around on this one all day, but you've got what you came for."

"I guess I do, yes. Okay, now here comes the part where I put my notebook away. Not for quotation or attribution, just for my personal enlightenment."

"I'll always do my best to enlighten you, Bill. You know that."

"I do, oddly enough. Let's start like the lawyers, by stipulating a few things. The other side knows how extensive the bombing is and where it's going on. The U.S. Congress and the U.S. public and every government in the world has known for years that the bombing in Laos has been going on, and now they know officially, because President Nixon just admitted it in his March statement. Why do you think it's still secret?"

"It's not secret, as you just pointed out at some length."

"But there's secrecy. The air war remains classified. You won't give me Gleason's report. The air force won't give me targets or number of sorties flown, even after the fact. I can't go along on missions, I can't go onto the American air bases in Thailand without a public information officer holding my hand. If there's secrecy, Jerry, the purpose must be to keep *something* secret, from *someone*. Can you think of who that could be?"

"No, but I'll bet you can."

"How about Washington, and yourselves?"

173

"We know, and Washington knows."

"No. You know *what* you're doing, but you don't know whether it's working, or how it's working. And you don't want to know. Now that the American ground troops are going home, the bombing is the only way Nixon and Kissinger have to keep the war alive till they can get reelected. If we were allowed to cover the air war, its cruelty and its ineffectiveness would be rubbed publicly in your nose every day. And the whole justification for continuing the war would be gone."

"Well, that's pretty good stuff, Bill. I won't quote you on it, but can I use it on background?"

"Okay, I'm sorry. But isn't that the real reason the air war is kept under wraps, if you think about it?"

"No. The real reason is that avoiding public statements about the bombing helps preserve the Geneva Accords as a workable framework for an eventual negotiated peace."

"Even though all parties to the accords know the bombing has been going on for years?"

"Sometimes pretense is valuable in diplomacy. Face is important."

"And you really believe what you just said? I hope you do, for the good of your soul."

"How the hell did we get into theology, Bill? But since we're talking personally, let me ask you a personal question. Did you ever think of taking the exams for the foreign service?"

"Not for a minute."

"You'd be a damned good foreign service officer."

"I doubt it."

"I don't. If you ever change your mind, let me know. There are plenty of posts where you wouldn't have any ideological problems with American policy, and I'd be glad to give you any help I could. I'm serious about that."

"I think maybe you are."

"I am."

From Brautigan's office, Bailey quietly crossed the lobby behind the receptionist's back and entered the political section without knocking. He kept hoping that someday everybody would be out of the office at once so that he could have a look around, but it had never happened. Today, too, both a secretary and Fred Upson were at their desks. Bailey noticed that Upson

174

had already developed the bureaucrat's standard reaction in Southeast Asia to the sudden appearance of a reporter. The diplomat immediately scanned the papers on his desk for classified documents, and turned over one marked *Top Secret*. Bailey was good at reading upside down, but Upson hadn't given him enough time even to make out the title.

"How's it coming, Fred?" the reporter said.

"Not too bad."

Someday Bailey would try to find out why Upson had been reassigned from the ambassador's staff to the political section, but that could wait for another time. Now he wanted to know about the Gleason report.

"Dennis tells me you're sort of concentrating on the Meo," he said to Upson. "Is that right?"

"Trying to. I've been going through the files as far back as we have them, trying to get some historical perspective on our association with the hill tribes in general. But I haven't got far yet. I've only been over here less than a week."

"Do you come across much about the opium trade?"

"Quite a bit, yes."

"I'm working on that right now. Either two or three chapters of my book, I'm not sure just how many yet, will be on CIA involvement in the drug traffic."

"There isn't any, that I've come across."

"The trail is pretty plain over the years. Who works most closely with the Meo who grow the stuff? Who has the airplanes to move it?"

"If you told me you had proof that individual Air America pilots have gotten themselves involved in the narcotics traffic, I wouldn't faint from the shock," Upson said. "Probably Pan Am pilots have, too. But that doesn't mean that the CIA is in the drug business, any more than Pan Am is."

"Your policies make the traffic possible."

"My policies, Bill?"

"The American mission's policies. The Meo are wards of the U.S. You could certainly get them out of opium growing if you wanted to."

"Well, I suppose we could pressure the government to make opium illegal. Give American narcs arrest powers here. The Seventh Air Force could defoliate the fields. Maybe the U.S.

Border Service could seal off the Mekong, strip-search every traveler leaving the country. I suppose we could do it all right, except then we'd have to cope with all your stories in the *Times* about the way we were trampling on the sovereign rights of a tiny nation."

"All right, I give up. I do, too. The only ones who really have the dedication and the organization to stamp out the drug traffic are the Pathet Lao."

"Of course they have to take over the country first."

"Don't you think they will, Fred? Your efforts here are just a rear-guard action. Seems to me the Gleason report makes that pretty clear."

"What does the Gleason report have to do with rear-guard actions?" Upson asked.

"Oh, just the general ineffectiveness of the air war. From the military point of view, I mean. It seems to work well enough against civilians."

Upson looked up at Bailey without making any answer. The reporter couldn't tell whether he had offended the new political officer, or just made him wary. "What's the reaction in the political section to the Gleason thing?" he went on.

"To my knowledge, we haven't been asked for a reaction."

"What's your own reaction? I'd be interested in that, particularly in light of your old job. Not for attribution, of course."

"Not for attribution, of course, I have no reaction. You'd better ask the press attaché, Bill."

Bailey sat down, uninvited, in the chair beside Upson's desk. "Let me ask you something personal, Fred," he said. "You're a decent man. Bright. They say you did as good a job in the bombing-officer slot as Gus Thompson did."

"Thanks, I guess."

"So what's a nice guy like you doing in a place like this?"

Bailey had found this approach useful once or twice before, in breaking through to embassy officials who seemed likely to be morally troubled by their roles.

Upson looked at the reporter and considered for a moment before he answered. "I'll assume you mean, 'Why don't I come out of the closet?' " he said. "Recognize the war for the criminal enterprise it is. Sign on with Jane Fonda. I'll answer you with a question of my own. When you're talking about U.S. policy with the Indian ambassador, let's say, do you refer to it as 'their policy'?"

"I might. I don't feel that the Nixon administration speaks for me or for most of the American people in its Southeast Asian policies. But I don't see what that has to do with what I asked."

"I'm sure you don't. I'm not even sure I do. But it's your answer, anyway."

When Bailey had left, Upson picked up the phone. Since Dennis Goldman wasn't around, he called Brautigan, as the next person in the chain of command. "The *New York Times* was just in here, Jerry," he said, "asking questions about the Gleason report."

"He was in here, too," Brautigan said. "He must have walked straight across the hall to your shop. Did you get the impression he knew much about it?"

"No. He was fishing."

"My impression, too. Just the existence of a report won't amount to much of a story. As long as he doesn't get hold of it, I don't think he can do too much harm. Anyway, thanks for letting me know."

"Shall I write up a memcon on it?"

"Not worth it. The world can do without another memorandum of conversation. If he comes by again and seems to have picked up any details, I'd like to know about it."

The Hotel Constellation's front room was empty of customers. The Vietnamese barman with the white shirt and the clip-on black bow tie spoke no English, so that Bailey was able to use the phone without worrying about anybody listening in. He dialed the embassy's main number, and waited through what seemed like several minutes of clicks and other noises on the line, until the ancient municipal phone system finally made the connection. The reporter went straight to the point when the embassy operator put him through to a man who had sometimes been helpful in the past.

"Listen," Bailey said, not giving his name, "can you get me a copy of a certain report? Just came out, and I've been having trouble getting my hands on it. Do you know the one I mean?"

"Sure, I know," the man said. "I thought you'd never ask."

Punderson, Brautigan, and Goldman stayed on with the ambassador after the daily ops meeting broke up. "I thought we might as well have our little talk in here," Ambassador Simmonds said. "As far as I can tell, this bubble is the only place in my mission without a leak. Now, gentlemen, *What is the goddamned explanation of this?*" Before anybody could answer, the ambassador went on. "I haven't even read this fucking thing myself yet, and it's all over the front page of the *New York Times*, and the Secretary's on my ass, and Henry's on my ass, to say nothing of the U.S. Congress. The son of a bitch who did this would be stood up and shot if this was the real army. Who did it? That's what I want to know."

"Let me outline to you where we are on that so far, Mr. Ambassador," Brautigan said, keeping his voice as unemotional as a briefing officer's, in an attempt to calm the ambassador down. "Seven people had physical access to the report, including the three of us here. Anyone of the seven of us could conceivably have run off the copy Bailey got hold of."

"Why did he necessarily have to get hold of a copy, Jerry?" Punderson said. "Why couldn't he have picked up a little bit here and a little bit there from people who knew about the survey, and put together his story that way?"

No one bothered to answer Punderson. Bailey's story had been full of precise figures and extensive quotes taken word for word from the Gleason report. It was obvious he had a copy, or had been able to sit down with one for a long time.

"What about lie detectors?" the ambassador said.

"We haven't got one, Mr. Ambassador," the DCM said.

"Vang Pao's got a lie detector. You know what he told me he uses? One of those old, hand-cranked field magnetos. They hitch Charlie up to the electrodes and make the little bastard crank the thing himself."

"In theory we could get security to send somebody in who could run lie-detector tests," Brautigan said. "But we have two congressional requests for the report already and Fulbright's investigators are due out here next week. With that level of interest on the Hill, we'd be murdered if it got out that we were using lie detectors to find the leak. And we have to operate on the assumption that it would get out, under the circumstances. I think the best we can do for the moment is locate the person or persons responsible very quietly and wait to take appropriate action a good deal later, when nobody will make the connection between the two events."

What are we supposed to do in the meantime?" Punderson asked. "Every reporter in town wants a copy of the report now, and what do we tell them?"

"Let me summarize what the ambassador and I were talking about before the meeting," Brautigan said, although he had been doing the talking and the ambassador the listening. But, by now, Simmonds might be made to believe it was his idea, a course of action he had already decided on.

"Briefly, we're in a damage control operation. We have to make the report available to anybody who wants it now, and seem surprised at all the fuss. Say we had every intention of releasing the thing as soon as we had finished reviewing it, anyway. That was the whole point of putting it together in the first place, to follow up on Ted Jackson's charges and see if they warranted corrective action. Then stall for a few days till it drops out of the news. Haven't I summarized your thinking on that pretty well, Mr. Ambassador?"

"Only damned thing we can do at this point in time. But I want you to find out who did this to me, Jerry. I want his name on my desk, one way or another. And I shit you not."

When the others had left, the ambassador kept Brautigan behind in the darkened room with the bright, clear plastic cube suspended in the middle of it.

"Get rid of Punderson," he said.

"You don't think Punderson did it, do you?" Brautigan asked.

"Leaked it? Hell, no. But the whole goddamned thing was

his idea, wasn't it? And then he let it get away from him. He should have kept on top of it every minute, and come to us as soon as it was obvious the way the thing was going to come out."

"All right, Buck," Brautigan said. "It wouldn't look good to ship him home right away, but in a month or so we should be able to manage."

"Nothing in writing, now. Find some way to get word to Frank Shakespeare back in Washington, and he'll take care of it from that end."

"I'll work it out."

So some good was to come out of this whole mess, Brautigan thought. He had wanted to get rid of the public affairs officer ever since his arrival, just on general grounds of incompetence, laziness, and stupidity. But Ambassador Simmonds had pulled strings personally to have the man assigned to Laos in the first place; apparently the two of them had been together on some famous safari in Africa, years before. The DCM wished again, as he had so many times, that just once he might be blessed by serving under an ambassador he could work with, instead of through and around. Although the problem would no longer exist, of course, if he got his own embassy on his next overseas tour. Which might very well happen, if he could only keep his balance during his remaining eight months in Laos.

Instead of heading straight back to his office, Brautigan stopped off on the second floor to see Chuck Hurley, the CIA station chief. Hurley looked like a good-natured Iowa farmer with a wide, smooth, placid face. He was supposed to have a vicious temper among his own people, but to outsiders he gave an impression of soothing, bovine calm.

"Buck seems a little hacked off, doesn't he?" the station chief said when Brautigan came in. "Well, it'll all blow over in a few days, and we can go on back about our business."

"Eventually, yes. But right now he wants red meat. I don't very much like to play detective, Chuck, but I want to make some sort of effort to find out who slipped that damned report to Bailey. Do your folks keep any kind of an eye on him?"

"Not really. We come across his tracks now and then, naturally. When he visits the North Vietnamese embassy, for example, our asset in there tells us about it."

"What does he do there?"

"Legitimate interviews. Buck always wants to make something of it, but our reports are that he confines himself pretty much to journalistic questions with the chargé. And the chargé confines himself pretty much to not answering the questions. I don't know why either of them bothers."

"Who else does Bailey see?"

"Half the town. You. Didn't I see him coming out of our office last week? But we wouldn't take any particular notice of his American contacts, unless there was some specific reason to."

"What kind of reason?"

"Well, suppose he was the target of a recruitment effort by the Russians."

"Was he?"

"No. The Novosti correspondent here is KGB. Yuri Kossinski, you know him? Poisonous little shit. He's never tried to put any American correspondents on his payroll, though. Only non-Americans."

"Why not the Americans?"

"He probably figures that since Russian correspondents work for the KGB, American correspondents must work for the CIA. Little does he know, huh?"

"Chuck, how can I approach this thing? Seven people had access to that report, and the only one I can rule out positively is me. How would you handle something like that?"

"Lie-detector test. With us, it's just routine."

"I could justify that if it were a question of military security. But not for leaking a nonclassified document to the papers."

"Then talk to each of them and see if you think they're lying."

"I already have. I don't know."

"Then go by instinct, I guess. Of your six people, which ones seem likely and which ones don't?"

"Well, I don't know anything about the USIS secretary, but I tend to rule out secretaries as leakers. I don't know why."

"I think you're probably right."

"I can't imagine Punderson having enough nerve to leak something to the *Times*, even if he wanted to. I guess I rule out Casey, too."

"Why?"

"I'm not sure. Phil isn't exactly what you'd call on the team.

But he took on a very confidential assignment for me once, and not a word of it ever got out. I don't know, I guess I think he just likes to talk a lot, but he wouldn't do anything that would basically jeopardize his position. He's not that far from retirement."

"All right, now you're down to three."

"And that's where I'm stuck. Gleason through pride of authorship, Goldman or Upson because of policy differences."

"That's motive. What about opportunity?"

"Any of them could have run off a copy."

"Any of them on friendly terms with Bailey?"

"They wouldn't have to like him to pass it on to him."

"Why Bailey, though? It would have had the same impact in the newsmagazines or the *Washington Post* or *Star*. They've all got stringers here."

"Gleason says he doesn't know Bailey at all, which seems probable. Gleason just got here, and his job doesn't put him in contact with the press. It's hardly conclusive, but I guess it makes him a little less likely."

"And the other two a little more likely."

"That's a long way from being proof, Chuck,"

"Look, Jerry, this isn't a court of law. It's just a management problem. Management-wise, if you're convinced both of them could have done it for reasons of disagreement with policy, what difference does it make which one actually did do it? Get rid of them both."

"That's a little rough, Chuck."

"This isn't Ping-Pong, Jerry. Sometimes it's a little hard to remember down here in Vientiane, but it's a war."

"Even in war there are rules. You don't shoot the whole village just to be sure you get the one sniper."

"Certainly not if you could identify the sniper, Jerry."

"That's what I'm trying to do."

"Wish I could help you."

Back in his own office, the deputy chief of mission told his secretary not to put through any calls unless they were from the ambassador. He drew the woman's torso on his pad, the woman with the perfect breasts and no hands and the hair hiding her face. And he drew her again and again, until the whole page was full. He picked up the phone and buzzed his secretary. "Do me a favor, will you, Annie?" he said. "Bring me in the weekly security activities reports for the last three months, okay?"

"Yes, sir. Is there any particular thing you're after? I'd be glad to go through them and find it for you."

"No, that's fine, thanks. I wanted to look through them. Just bring them all in, would you?"

An hour later, when Annie Cutler next cleared the DCM's outbox, the stack of security reports was in it. Normally he no more than glanced at the reports as they came in. Why hadn't he told her what he was looking for? Before refiling the reports, she took them off with her to the ladies' room and sat down in one of the booths to go through them. The only conceivably interesting entry was the one on Upson's maid: ". . . a potential contact being discovered between the domestic employee of Embassy Officer Fred Upson and her uncle and several other relatives residing in the refugee resettlement area of KM 30. Subject officer is believed to be providing transportation to his female domestic employee (maid) for purpose of visiting her uncle in referenced resettlement area . . ."

She took the reports back to file them. None of her business. She had seen things turning sour this way once before, when she was executive secretary to the chairman of the board of the Telectron Corporation during a takeover bid. Loyalties were suspect. People got hurt, and often not the right ones. It had been a good time to keep your head down and remain uninvolved; it was a good time now, too. Fred was a nice enough kid, but she certainly owed him nothing.

When she got back to her desk, she called him.

"Do you know what it's all about?" she said when she had explained Brautigan's request and the entry about the maid to him.

"If the item all of a sudden becomes relevant now," Upson said, "it must have to do with that story in the *Times*. I'm one of the people who had access to the Gleason report. I didn't give it to Bailey, but I could have."

"It's none of my business to give you advice, Fred, but when everybody gets tense and secretive the way they've been, sometimes it's a good idea to lay everything out on the table. Just walk right into his office and tell him you don't know who leaked the report, but it wasn't you."

"I already told him that, although actually I think I do know who leaked it."

"Thinking isn't knowing."

"No."

"Anyway, I thought you ought to know that the DCM seems to have you on his list. If it helps you in any way to tell him that you know about this security report, feel free. A good secretary can always find a job."

"Annie?" Upson paused, embarrassed by what he wanted to say.

"What?"

"Oh, I don't know. Thank you, that's all." He couldn't very well tell her how sorry he was that she was older than him, and a mother, and had thick ankles, and that he was already in love with a little Lao girl who, for all he knew, might not be nearly as kind and bright and funny as Annie.

"Let me know if there's anything I can do, Fred," Annie said. "Sometimes it helps just to have somebody you can talk things over with."

"I know it does, Annie. Thanks again."

After Upson hung up, he tried to sort things out. Brautigan had known about Somchan's visit to the refugee camp long before the Gleason report story came out in the *Times;* he had mentioned it in connection with the curious memo on fraternization. What new element could have made him call for the report now? The ridiculous allegation that Somchan's family were Pathet Lao? Surely Brautigan couldn't believe that one of his officers would leak a story to the *New York Times* because his maid's relatives were alleged to have communist sympathies. But Brautigan might very well, Upson suddenly saw, connect an earlier visit by Fred Upson to KM 30 with a later one by Ted Jackson. And, if you had once suggested that a columnist visit bombed refugees, why wouldn't you leak a report on those same refugees to Bill Bailey the next time? It didn't make much sense, but what else made any at all?

Upson remembered the day on the Plain of Jars months before, when Phil Casey had talked with Bailey about the ineffectiveness of the bombing. Later, when the reporter was gone, Casey had said something about the *New York Times* being his only way to get messages to Washington. Casey had probably sent another message to Washington, then. Upson kept thinking the same thoughts over and over. Somebody had been bad, and Upson was going to be punished for it even though he didn't do it. Phil did it, Daddy, not me. Did you ever get old enough, Upson wondered, so that you weren't a little boy any longer, in a grown body? Upson felt guilty over something he hadn't done, because he might have done it. The only way out was to tell on Casey, but you couldn't tell on your friends. He didn't know for sure that Casey had done it, anyway. And hadn't Casey, if he had done it, done the right thing after all? Upson didn't approve of what had been done, but he was glad somebody had done it. The thoughts closed in on themselves and clenched, like the python he had seen Christmas day at the market, squeezed into a tight ball with its head in the middle, waiting blindly for whatever came next.

Finally Upson shook his head to break the paralysis, and got up. He would go into Goldman's office and tell him what was happening. It would be something to do, anyway. Some action. The political secretary was just finishing a phone conversation, talking in the fluent French that Upson envied so. Goldman never searched for a word; his hands, shoulders, and facial muscles all became active the instant he switched into French. His accent was, to Upson's ear, indistinguishable from that of a Frenchman.

"Brautigan thinks I leaked the Gleason report, Dennis," Upson started out the instant Goldman hung up.

"He thinks I leaked it, too," Goldman said. He took off his gold-rimmed bifocals and rubbed at the two little red marks they made on the sides of his nose. "He questioned me, he questioned you, I imagine he questioned the people at USIS, too. Probably everybody had the good sense to deny it."

"I denied it. I didn't do it."

"Neither did I, but it doesn't matter much. Supposing Jerry makes up his mind that one of the two of us did it? What can he do to us? He can't put us on his shit list, because we're already on it. He can't give you a bad OER, because he's already done that, too. What's left? Reassignment? From the career point of view, Fred, the quicker you're out of here, the better." Goldman settled his glasses back on his nose, wincing a little.

"Goddamn it, though, Dennis," Upson said, "I don't want to be followed around with the reputation of being somebody who went public because he disagreed with policy. I believe the stuff about working within the system. At least I always have. But here I've been trying to work within the system, and the system seems to be killing me."

"Maybe you're in the wrong system. You have to decide that for yourself."

"What about you, Dennis? Are you in the right system?"

Goldman took off his glasses again, removed a folded linen handkerchief of perfect whiteness from the pocket of his freshly pressed seersucker pants, and began to polish the lenses. "I suppose I'm in the wrong part of the right system," he said at last. "I observe, and wait for my day to come, although I know it never will. And I'll retire with my thirty years in nine more years, without ever having been given any real authority."

"Why not?"

"I picked the wrong line of work. Teaching, one of the professions . . ."

Goldman didn't have to complete the thought for Upson to understand. Independence of thought might eventually be accepted in a gentile but not in a Jew, not in the foreign service.

"That sounds like you're in the wrong system, too," Upson said.

"Oh, I don't think so. I knew what I was getting into, but I went ahead anyway. I like the life, I like the work. It may even be that I don't want real authority. We never know that kind of thing about ourselves. It may be that I'll be happier, years from now, reading my brilliantly prescient old cables and saying, 'I told you so.' "

"If you thought you were in the wrong system, Dennis, would you get out?"

"I don't know. I hope so. Right and wrong aren't such very easy things to figure out. Not just in the abstract, but what's right and wrong for the individual himself."

"The ambassador seems to have right and wrong figured out pretty well."

"The ambassador is a fairly simple organism. Whatever feels good is good. And what's good for Buck Simmonds is good for the country. As a matter of fact, he doesn't see any difference between the two."

"Well, Jerry's not a simple organism," Upson said, "and he seems to have it figured out, too." Upson found himself bending over Goldman's desk, his knuckles pressed on it. He straightened up as soon as he caught himself acting like a student desperate for the one right answer, and sat down.

"No, Jerry doesn't really have it figured out, not yet," Goldman said. "Years ago he put on a mask, with the intention of taking it off once he got where he was going. By now his face has almost grown into the mask, but not quite. Once the process is complete, he'll get where he's going and he'll take the mask off. He'll relax and be himself at last, and know right from wrong with perfect assurance, and never suspect that his face has turned into the mask."

Upson found the image repellent. "How can you think you're in the right system?" he asked, "if that's what the system requires of you?"

"Oh," Goldman answered mildly, "everybody wears masks. You need them, really."

"Let me tell you something about the system that you claim is right for you," Upson said. He was determined to shock something out of the political secretary. But what? An emotional reaction? Moral support? Advice? The answer or at least some clue to it?

"Let me tell you what that system thinks of you, Dennis. Remember when the Plain of Jars was falling and the reporters in Saigon dug out the story that we were using B-52s for the first time in northern Laos? And Washington admitted it, but said it was a one-time thing?"

"I remember it, sure."

"Well, they never stopped. It's still going on. Did you know that?"

"No."

"No way you could have. They've just been routing all the cable traffic on the B-52 strikes up north around the political section. I thought that was kind of funny when I got here."

"Funny ha-ha, or funny peculiar?"

"Both then. Neither now."

"It's not peculiar, certainly. The ambassador doesn't want me running around after him all the time, pointing out that there are no viable B-52 targets up north and that the only long-term solution for Laos is going to be political, anyway."

"It doesn't bother you, then? That the ambassador would keep important information from his own political section."

"Certainly it bothers me, Fred. But not as much as you think it should. Because my view is the correct one. I can't make that view prevail now, but in time its correctness will be generally acknowledged."

"And that's enough for you?"

"It's what one has to settle for."

"Isn't that sort of like what you'd say if your face had grown into your mask?"

"Probably. I wouldn't be surprised if it had."

"Well, mine won't."

"It's nothing to be afraid of, Fred. The process is completely natural and painless. You won't even know it's happening. No one does."

Upson walked out of the air conditioning and cool, fluorescent light of the embassy into the heat of the day, so heavy that the air seemed to have actual body. He began to sweat right away, but he paid no attention. The decision he had just reached made him feel the way he had one time when he was a boy, swimming at a quarry. He and his friends had all climbed up to the top of a cliff, over the deep water. The drop was perhaps fifteen or twenty feet—much higher, anyway, than he had ever jumped from before. He was terrified when his turn came, but the fear went when at last he had jumped and had committed himself to the air. Upson looked at the blue sky; a few puffy white clouds made it seem all the more immense and empty. The flame trees across the street were bare except for their brilliant orange flowers.

When the flame tree blossoms, the white man dies. The Guineans said that, according to a former colleague in Morocco who had served in Conakry. Upson walked to the motor pool, moving slowly as the heat had taught him to do. At first he was going to take a car without a driver, but then he thought, what difference does it make if the driver sees me? He told the man to go to Mekong House number seven. There he went up to his bedroom, reached under a pile of sheets in the closet, and took out the thick envelope of papers he had copied from Gus Thompson's private file at the embassy. Through the window he saw Somchan in the backyard just starting to hang out the wash. At first the thought that she would see his soiled underwear had embarrassed him, he remembered as he saw her pinning a pair of shorts to the line. But he seldom thought about it anymore. The papers in his hand, he went through the kitchen and out onto the back steps. "Sambai di," he called out. "Sambai di, sambai di, Somchan." Hello, hello, hello. She looked up startled, and then waved when he waved at her. He smiled, and she smiled back. "Sambai di, sambai di" he said. "A thousand times sambai di." He ducked back inside when she started to laugh, and went back out front to where the driver waited. Upson thought he would stay on in Laos after it was all over, although he hadn't begun to think of a way he could manage it. He was still in the air; he didn't have to think about swimming until after he hit the water. He directed the driver to the Hotel Constellation. One of the waiters stood outside in the shade of the maroon awning, where two or three motorcycles were parked out of the sun. "Sambai di," Upson said to him. "A thousand times sambai di." The waiter smiled.

Upson only lost his mood when he saw Bill Bailey at his normal seat, facing the front window so he could see who was passing on the sidewalk. In the abstract, Upson had wanted to do it; now, in the concrete, he felt disloyal and guilty.

Bailey looked up from the copy he was correcting and said, "Hello, Fred. What's a nice boy like you doing in a place like this?"

"That's good, Bill. Very funny."

"Something wrong?" Bailey asked.

"I guess not, not really. Not at all. I have to talk to you."

"Want to go in back where it's more private?"

"Here is fine," Upson said. "It doesn't matter."

Jesus, what have I done now? Larry Mancuso thought when the DCM's secretary said that Mr. Brautigan would be on the line for him in a moment. He wondered if something had gone wrong out at the Brautigan residence, and tried unsuccessfully to remember who the guard was out there. He remembered the time the wife of the USAID Director had caught a guard pissing in her flowerbed. Jesus.

"Larry, how are you?" Brautigan's voice said. "How are things over at your shop?"

"Fine, sir, just fine. No problems we can't handle."

"Nothing you need? Nothing I can help you with?"

"No, sir. Everything's fine."

"Look, the reason I was calling, Larry, was one of your weekly security activities reports a few months back."

"Yes, sir, Mr. Brautigan. Something wrong?" He yanked open a file drawer in his desk and pulled out a stack of reports, to have them ready.

"No, no. Nothing wrong. I just wanted to follow up on one item. Do you remember something a few months back on a potential contact between Fred Upson's maid and some relatives of hers out at KM 30 who were possible PL sympathizers? I may have the details wrong, but it's something like that. Do you remember the item?"

"Oh, yes, sir, remember it perfectly well." Mancuso, who had been fingering desperately through the reports, finally found the right one. "What was it you wanted to follow up on, sir?"

"Well, as far as I can recall, there was some mention that Upson might be providing transportation to his maid to visit the camp."

"Yes, sir. I remember perfectly. Believed to be providing transportation."

"I'd like a little clarification on that, Larry. Did he in fact provide transportation? Did he drive her out there himself? Hire a taxi for her? Or what? Can you find out for me?"

"I'll have to go back to my corporal on that one, sir. He may have it already, or he may have to go out and talk to the girl. I should be able to have an answer for you on that one no later than tomorrow, sir, at the latest."

"Appreciate it, Larry. And listen, Larry?"

"Yes, sir?"

"Keep it pretty low-key, will you? It's nothing that Upson has done—it's something else entirely, just something I'm curious about—and I wouldn't want him to think he was the target of any kind of investigation. Okay?"

"I understand, sir. He won't even know we've been around."

I hope he won't, Brautigan thought after he hung up. I'd hate to have to explain to Fred that I wanted to find out whether he had visited KM 30, on the theory that it would then be vaguely possible that he had suggested a similar trip to a columnist I have no reason to believe he ever met, in which case it might be slightly more likely that he would be helpful to the press again, perhaps by passing the Gleason report on to Bailey. As a body of evidence, that lacks a certain solidity. Still, it won't hurt to find out. And Chuck Hurley was right. It isn't a court case, anyway. It's a management problem.

"**O**uday, get in here, goddamn it," Mancuso shouted to his corporal, who appeared almost instantly in the doorway. "Listen, Ouday, we got a real opportunity here. You know opportunity?"

"Yes, sir. Good chance."

"That's right, we got a good chance. The DCM himself has a job for us, and we're gonna do it right or your ass is grass and I'm the lawnmower. Capeesh?"

"Yes, sir. What is job, please?"

"A few months ago you gave me a report on Mr. Upson's maid, how she had some PL relatives out at the KM 30 camp. You remember that?"

"I remember, sir."

"Well, you didn't do the whole job that time and now you're going to finish it."

"That was report of Sergeant Bounlek, sir."

"Then he's going to finish it. You tell him I said so. What we need is to find out if Mr. Upson ever really did take her out to the camp, or if he sent her out there in a taxi, or what."

"Yes, sir. I will tell Sergeant Bounlek to ask her quick."

"We're not going to be caught short again this time, are we?"

"Please, sir?"

"This time we're going to have the answers to any question the DCM could possibly ask, aren't we? We're going to find out if that damned family out there is really PL or not. Whether the uncle is really a wounded PL soldier. When Mr. Upson went there, if he did. Who else the girl maybe saw. How she got out there. Who went with her. Everything the DCM might want to know about, I want to be able to tell him. See?"

"Yes, sir. I tell to Sergeant Bounlek."

Corporal Ouday found the sergeant where he was usually to be found after lunch—asleep in a small storage room off the guards' dayroom. A line of spittle ran from the corner of the sergeant's slack mouth. The sergeant's pants were unbuttoned and partly unzipped, to ease the pressure on his full belly. The sergeant's wide, meaty chest moved gently as he snored. How could it be that a fool like this, the corporal thought, could be the head of theft investigations instead of me? But this might be the "opportunity"—the good chance to correct that situation. The corporal had no idea what a DCM was, but it was plainly a person of great importance. Mancuso, the Bald Pig, would therefore be paying close attention to this business of Upson's maid. And Bounlek was likely to mess it up, particularly if he felt himself to be under pressure.

"Sergeant Bounlek," the corporal said softly.

"Huh? What it is, Ouday? Why are you bothering me?"

"I'm sorry, sergeant, but the Bald Pig told me to find you right away. I told him you were out inspecting the guards, but he was angry that you weren't there. He has a very important job for you. He says it's the most important assignment he's had since he's been in Laos, a job for the ambassador himself. The Bald Pig says it has to be done right away, and you're the only one who can do it well enough."

The corporal explained the assignment to Sergeant Bounlek, who barely remembered the original incident and hadn't known that the corporal had made a report of it. The corporal gave him a piece of paper with all the particulars neatly typed on it in Thai: Upson's address, the names of the maid and her relatives, the name of the guard at the house next door who had first brought the matter to Sergeant Bounlek's attention. Now the whole thing began to come back to the big Thai.

"Sure," he said. "That's the little Lao whore who fucks her boss. The guard next door said he saw them. She probably sucks the American, too. That's what the Americans make their whores do, suck them."

Sergeant Bounlek checked out the white jeep for the ride out to Mekong House #7. He liked driving the open jeep, so that everyone could see him in his beret and his uniform with the sergeant stripes, and the shiny, black nightstick at his side.

Upson emptied the thick envelope onto the table in front of Bailey. Each document had its security classification—"Secret," "Top Secret"—typed or written at the top. "I imagine giving these to you is a felony, actually," Upson said.

"Actually not," the reporter said. "I looked into that once for somebody, in connection with . . . Anyway, I looked into it. You know that form you guys have to sign saying you understand the provisions of Title this and that of the U.S. Code regarding disclosure of classified information? If you go to the trouble of looking up those citations, you find out that every single one of them refers only to disclosure of atomic secrets to a foreign power. Unless you've got the formula for the bomb in there, you're in the clear."

193

"Really? I assumed the law covered all classified information."

"No, there's no federal law in America equivalent to the British Official Secrets Act. That's why they had so much trouble figuring out how to get Ellsberg. He didn't reveal atomic secrets, and giving documents to the *New York Times* doesn't exactly fall under the espionage statutes. He hadn't broken any law."

Upson smiled slightly. The whole mystique of security, the code rooms, the clearances, the cipher locks, the red top-secret stripe at the top of the documents, the FBI full-field checks—all of it, then, was based on bluff. "Well, we don't have any atomic secrets in Laos, at least," he said. "We just drop white phosphorus, CBUs, napalm, herbicides, TNT. The regular stuff."

Upson began to spread out the documents for Bailey. "It's all here," he told the reporter. "You ever hear about the time Ambassador Armbrister cabled the Pentagon that he was going to float weather balloons over a friendly village so the air force wouldn't bomb it by mistake anymore?"

"I heard it as a rumor, a few years back. I could never pin it down."

"Here's the cable traffic on it, right here. The rest of this stuff shows civilian targets hit, the air force out of embassy control, lying about BDA. You know about BDA?"

"Bomb Damage Assessment? Sure."

"This stuff here is about the time they strafed Vang Pao and his entire high command, standing out in the open on a hillside along with our chief spooks up in MR-II. Luckily, they missed."

"Or unluckily, depending on your point of view," Bailey said.

"Luckily, I would say."

The reporter shrugged his shoulders. "Different strokes," he said. "Look, there goes Mancuso's bully boy."

By the time Upson had turned around, the white jeep had passed. "What bully boy?" he said.

"Oh, a guy called Bounlek. A big sergeant, strong as an ox."

"Bounlek," Upson said, remembering the big mission guard at the Brautigans' Christmas Eve party. "Yeah, I think I saw him in action once."

"Once is enough. I don't know where they get these guys. Well, actually I do. Bounlek was kicked off the Thai police in

Chiang Mai a long time back, I heard, for beating a drunk half to death. It turned out the drunk's old man was on the provincial governor's staff."

Upson assembled the papers, squared them away, and slipped them back into their brown envelope. "Anyway, there it is," he said. "The whole business. Falsified BDA. Attacks on our own side, nonmilitary targets, nonvalidated targets, the wrong towns. Sometimes they even get the country wrong. You'll see it in there, strikes in Thailand by mistake. The Gleason report showed some of what happened on the ground. These show how it happened, how the whole thing got to be too big to control, how it developed so much momentum that it just went off on its own. That ought to do it, I would think."

"Do what, Fred?"

"Get their attention back in Washington."

"How much attention it gets depends on you."

"How do you mean?"

"If I run this stuff unsourced, I'll be lucky if I get a two-column head on page one and a jump to inside. But if I can source it to you, a former Mad Bomber, then the thing becomes personalized, don't you see? We could probably make the Sunday magazine, particularly if we run your picture."

"*Magazine?* Are you serious? This is the whole thing, wait till you go through it. Details. Case histories from embassy files. Christ, one time they even bombed Dick Lindsay when he was showing a movie in a nonvalidated zone. Did you know that?"

"I did, as a matter of fact. But it was ancient history by the time I heard about it. Look, let me explain it to you, Fred. You have to see it from their perspective back at the *Times*. They sell news—what's new. The new thing here is that a U.S. government official once in charge of the bombing is resigning in protest over the air war. I assume you're resigning?"

"I don't think so, no. I think I'll make them fire me."

"All the better. That'll make it into a running story instead of a one-shot deal."

"Bill, I haven't properly explained what you've got there. I can see that. This isn't a one-shot deal. This is a major story. A series."

Bailey looked at Upson for a moment before answering. "How can I explain?" he said. "To me, it's a major story. To you it's a major story. To all of us here, it's a major story. But back home it's only a good story, an important story. Not a major one."

"Why not, for God's sake? What more could you want?"

"I'll try again. Look, on March eighth, Nixon admitted the bombing at last, and nobody paid much attention to that part of his statement. It wasn't news that we were bombing, because everybody has known it for years. The only news was that the President was no longer lying about it. The fact of the bombing had already been in the papers."

"The stuff I just gave you hasn't been in the papers."

"Not those particular details, no. But the bombing of civilians has been in the papers for years. The news is that here's official proof of what you've known all along, and here's a government official involved with it who became so disgusted he's blowing the whistle. That's assuming you let me source it to you."

"I might as well. They'd know it was me, anyway. Only two people had access to this stuff. Me and my replacement, and he's a young guy who walks around with a kind of nervous smile all the time. He'd cut his hand off before he'd give you a classified document."

"Okay, then we've got a story. I don't mean to cut it down, Fred. It's a good story. But it won't change the world. Even the major stories don't. The Pentagon papers didn't end the war. The My Lai massacre story didn't end the war."

"Maybe cumulatively they will. Someday."

"Maybe," Bailey said. "But I just don't want you to think that if I put it in the *Times,* the public outcry will force Nixon to stop the bombing."

"No, I imagine you're right, that nothing much will happen."

"Except to you."

"Except to me, that's right. Maybe I can sell life insurance."

Upson remembered Phil Casey's brakeless train, hurtling downhill out of control while the deputy chief of mission ran backward through the cars to slow it down. Not that jumping in front of the train would slow it down, either. No, Upson thought, nothing much will happen except to me.

Sergeant Bounlek parked the white jeep by the front porch of Mekong House #7, in the shade of a tree so that the sun wouldn't turn the seats searing hot while he was gone. He found the maid out back, pinning a pair of men's undershorts to the laundry line. She was a pretty thing. If you were rich, like the Americans, you could buy anything you wanted.

"Are you Somchan?" he asked, very stern. It was good to let them know, right at the start of an interrogation, who was in charge. "The maid of Mr. Upson?"

"I'm Somchan, yes."

"I'm Sergeant Bounlek, head of the U.S. Embassy police. I want to ask you some questions."

"Is something wrong?"

"I hope not, for your sake. Just a few questions. It's hot out here. Isn't there someplace we can get out of the sun?" He was hoping she would take him into the house, where it would be air-conditioned, but she led him instead to her room next to the laundry. Even though the door had been standing open, the little room was stifling. Somchan invited him to sit on the only chair, while she took a place on the bed. She aimed her oscillating fan with the clear, blue blades in the sergeant's direction. The big fan was a gift from her man, as was the powerful radio that would bring in even Hong Kong and Singapore.

"We could go in the house," she said, "but Mr. Upson told me never to let anybody in the house when he's not here. I'm sure it would be all right, since you're with the police, but still, he told me." Her man had never said that, but something gave her the feeling that this huge policeman shouldn't be in the house.

"It doesn't matter. We're fine right here." The "we" somehow made his remark seem too intimate. Nor did she like the way the big Thai was looking her room over, staring harder at everything than it was polite to do. She was glad the door was open. "I guess you know why I'm here, Somchan," the sergeant said.

"No, I have no idea. Is something missing from the house?"

"Don't start off by lying, girl."

"I'm not lying, Sergeant. I don't know why you're here."

"Are you going to pretend you didn't visit your Pathet Lao relatives at KM 30?"

"Khammone and Tongsai? They're not Pathet Lao. They're just farm people."

"Sure they are. Tell me about your trip out there."

"The house fell down," she said. The memory was still so funny that she laughed aloud, even though she was scared. Maybe this could turn into a normal conversation yet, if she acted as if it was one. "The Americans were so heavy the floor broke and we all fell on the baby. The baby got ice in his lap and his little peepee shrunk right back up inside his belly . . ."

The sergeant said, "What Americans?"

"Mr. Upson and Mr. Dick."

"Who's Mr. Dick?"

"I don't know. He speaks good Lao and he has a big, black mustache. He drove us up. Mr. Upson doesn't have a car."

"Whose car was it?"

"I don't know. It looked like those gray embassy cars, but it didn't have the letters or the numbers on it. It was old."

"So you went out there and the floor broke. What else happened?"

"Nothing. We just talked and drank Pepsi and beer. I left some things from the market with them. The floor broke, and we came home."

"What were the things from the market?" He took a notebook out of his breast pocket and wrote down the names and quantities of the fruits and vegetables she had taken out. "Did they give you anything for all that stuff?" he asked.

"No, it was a present. What could they give me? They came down here with nothing. At least I have a job and a home to live in."

"Here? This room?"

"No, my real home. With my mother."

Bounlek wrote down the address she gave him. "Did your relatives give you any messages or papers?" he asked.

"No."

"Did you give them any messages or papers?"

"No. Nothing but a little money. Two thousand kip."

"Where did you get the money?"

"It's my money. I earned it. I make thirty thousand kip a month."

Sergeant Bounlek wrote down the figures. "Colonel Pet is the one who really gave you the money, isn't he?" he said when he had finished. "Tell the truth."

"Who's Colonel Pet?"

"Don't try to fool me. Everybody knows he's the commander of the Pathet Lao battalion here. Or did they give you the money at the Hanoi embassy?"

"Nobody. Nothing. It was my money, I told you."

"You gave them the money and they didn't give you anything for it? Come, on, you've got to do better than that."

"Why should they give me anything for it? They're my aunt and uncle. All they gave me was some of that Pathet Lao money, for my little brother to play with."

"How much?"

"I don't know, a lot. I think thirty or forty thousand kip. It doesn't matter how much it is, though, because it isn't worth anything. The American ambassador said all the money those people had up there, none of it's any good. The ambassador took everything away from them."

"It's illegal to have communist money. I'll turn you over to the police, girl, unless you start answering me honestly."

"I am answering you honestly, Sergeant. Really I am."

"All right, let's see. How did your uncle get lame?"

"How did you know he was lame?"

"Don't worry about how I know. I know everything about you. That's how I can tell when you're lying. Now, what happened to his leg?"

"He hurt it chopping wood years ago. He cut one of those strings you have in your leg."

"He was wounded fighting for the Pathet Lao, wasn't he?"

"Khammone could never be a soldier, because of his leg. He was just a farmer."

"I told you not to bother to lie. You can't even do it well. How do you expect me to believe such bad lies? Do you think I'm fool enough to believe that you gave them good money for their worthless communist money? What I want to know is what they really gave you in return, and why the Americans took you out to see the communist spies?"

Somchan was beginning to tremble. "This is all like a dream, Sergeant," she said. "I tell you what happened, and you twist it to make it all different. They're not spies, and Mr. Upson took me out because he was just being kind. He's very kind."

"I bet he is. You're kind to him, too, aren't you?"

"What's that supposed to mean?"

"You know well enough. So the three of you went up there and gave money to the spies, and took money from them, and then had a party to celebrate. What were you celebrating, sweetheart?"

"Nothing. Don't, you're hurting me." Sergeant Bounlek released the grip he had suddenly taken on her arm, just above the elbow. She rubbed the spot and moved further away from him.

"You might as well tell me the truth, you know," the sergeant said, trying to sound friendly. He had once gone to a lecture by a Thai police captain who had studied interrogation techniques in the United States. The idea was to have two interrogators, one friendly and one unfriendly, but today he would have to play both parts himself. "You haven't done anything wrong, you know," he said. But she sat there silent, looking more frightened than she had before, when he had been tough. What did the Americans know about police questioning? There were police in Thailand before there even was an America.

Bounlek reached to close the door, and the girl moved even further down the bed. The fan hummed softly. The girl stood up suddenly and started toward the door, but Bounlek got there first. "Sit down," he said, putting a hand on her shoulder and forcing her roughly back down on the end of the bed. "I'll do the standing here, and you'll do what I tell you. I'm sick of wasting time with your lies. I want the truth, and I want it now." The big sergeant was walking back and forth in the little bit of free space in the room, full of more violent energy than he could get rid of with his restless moving. His round face was shiny with sweat in spite of the fan.

"Your American lover is through, you know," he said. "The CIA got the whole story out of him. They've fired him for dealing with enemy spies and they're shipping him home to go to jail for the rest of his life. They'll take away his parents' house and big car and make them into beggars. That's what you did to him when you took him to see those spies."

That was better, Bounlek thought. She was really frightened now, almost crying. "It was just a car ride and a picnic," she said.

"Don't waste my time. Everything is in his confession. He told all about the things you two did together, right there in his house. Every single thing. Every time. It's all there. The only way you can stay out of jail now is to tell me everything. Now do you understand how I know when you're lying?"

"But I'm not, Sergeant, I promise you. Let me alone."

"Speak up. I can't understand you when you blubber. Do you deny that you were the American's whore?"

"I told you the truth about Khammone and Tongsai."

"But you were lying when you said you weren't the American's whore, weren't you?"

"I didn't say anything about that. You did."

"Well, he'll never do it to you again. He's going to jail because of you."

"They couldn't do that to him, just for being kind and giving me a ride to see my uncle."

"Kind? Is that the word for it now? Fuck is the real word, isn't it? You let him fuck you, admit it. Stop it, stop your damned sniveling. Admit it. Now!"

"It's no crime," Somchan said, through her snuffles and sobs.

"At last you admit it. How much did he pay you?"

"It wasn't like that, Sergeant. He liked to talk in the evenings. I couldn't understand what he said, but I knew he needed someone to listen. I think he was lonely. He almost never saw any friends. His back was bad and I massaged it for him. It just happened. It wasn't like you say. He was kind to me."

"Don't say that word, say the real word. Say he fucked you."

"No, please don't, please don't." She tried with all her strength to push away the big hands coming toward her.

"You bitch. You filthy cunt. Look what you did." She had somehow torn a button off his uniform shirt, leaving a little rip in the fabric. The unfairness of her attack when he hadn't meant to hurt her flooded him with rage. His heavy hand shot out and she stopped her screaming. A good, solid slap to the side of the head always jarred their brains and made prisoners shut up. Bounlek examined the rip in his shirt and rage filled him again, mixed with excitement.

"Now you've asked for it, you slut," he said. His fingers worked at his belt and his fly. "You'll pay for it by showing me how you suck the American. You like that, don't you? Sucking? There it is, go ahead. I want to see what it is the Americans like so much."

The sight of the thing, just a few inches in front of her where she sat stupidly on the bed, brought Somchan out of the shock of the slap.

"No," she cried. "No, no, no. I never did that to anybody. Please, I can't." She twisted away, crying, to escape from him.

Bounlek put one hand over her mouth to gag her and with the other he seized the tip of one of her breasts, clamping it between his broad thumb and the knuckle of his first finger. He gave it a savage, twisting pinch, as if he were trying to tear the nipple off. She screamed into the palm of his other hand, and he let her go.

"Bitch," he said. "Look at that. You slobbered all over my hand like a dog." He wiped the palm of his hand on her hair. "Now open your whore's mouth, or I'll open it for you." She opened her mouth obediently.

What an ugly slut she was, working clumsily away at him. One side of her face was all puffy and red, she was blubbering and snorting, her eyes were swollen and her cheeks all wet with crying. Even her nose was running, like a sick baby's.

He looked away so he wouldn't have to see her ugliness— just feel what she was doing to him. At the end he grabbed her hair and held her head in place, so she wouldn't cheat him at the last minute.

Then he let her flop down on the bed, sobbing, while he did up his pants. He began to worry that she might try to cause trouble for him, but then he thought of what to do. "I know where your mother lives, whore. Remember that. If anybody hears about this, I'll send my men there some night. They'll poison the dog so he won't bark and then they'll pour gasoline all around underneath and throw a match. Understand?"

Somchan nodded her head, not looking at him, hoping only that he wouldn't hurt her again. When she heard the motor of

202

his jeep and knew he was gone, she ran next door to the laundry and rinsed her mouth and spat, and rinsed and rinsed. But the taste stayed no matter what she did. It only went away when she vomited into the laundry tub, in heaving spasms that kept on even after there was nothing more to come up.

When the heaves stopped at last, Somchan sank to her heels in front of the laundry tub and rocked back and forth, grieving. Because the sergeant had dared to do those things to her, she knew she would never see her man again. The sergeant must know she would never have a chance to tell her man what had happened. Maybe he was locked up somewhere in the window-less embassy, or maybe they had flown him home already. Probably he was in handcuffs, the shiny handcuffs that the Americans gave to the city police. And she herself was the one who had ruined her own man even if she didn't understand how.

Somchan knew what she had to do about it, but she didn't know if she had the courage.

The house was dark when the embassy driver let Upson off that evening, which meant that Somchan had gone to the movies, or to visit friends, or whatever she did on the evenings she disappeared. Upson was sorry she wouldn't be there for him to talk to, so that he could try to sort out what he had done, and why, and what came next. But there would be an endless number of other evenings. He showered and changed shirts while his TV dinner was heating in the gas oven. After eating, he made himself a gin and tonic and went out to the porch to sip it in the dark. He badly missed having someone to talk to. After a while he went inside and telephoned Dick Lindsay. "Would you have a chance to drop by this evening?" he said. "Something has come up that I wanted to ask you about." From the phone he could see out the window to Somchan's quarters. Her door was open, which seemed a little odd. Once he had hung up, he went down the stairs and across the yard to her room. "Somchan?" he said, but there was no answer. He found the light and snapped it on, feeling a little guilty over invading her privacy. Everything seemed to be as usual, except for a chair which lay on its side. He set it up on its legs, put out the light, and closed the door behind him.

Back inside, he opened a can of tuna and mashed it up with mayonnaise to make a dip. His mother always felt there should be something set out when drinks were to be served. Upson supposed, thinking back on it, that this made her husband's drinking seem more acceptable—like a social event. But the Reverend Upson would eat only one or two of the hors d'oeuvres, or none at all. Upson had just set out the crackers and the dip in the living room when Lindsay arrived. "Hi, Fred," he said. "Where's Somchan?"

"I don't know," Upson answered. "Out to the movies or something." Lindsay probably suspected they were lovers, then, to have been surprised at not finding her in the house during the evening.

"What's up?" Lindsay said. "What was it you wanted to talk about?"

When Upson had told him, Lindsay said, "So it's all over, isn't it? You've really burned your bridges. Even Gus Thompson didn't do that."

"The funny thing is, Dick, that Thompson was the one who got all the stuff together. He had collected it in a hidden file marked 'Miscellaneous,' and then never did anything with it."

"Probably too final for him. Being a source or a leak, that's one thing. But actually passing documents, that's heavy. I don't know why there should be a difference, but there is. Maybe it's because there are real objects involved, so it's like stealing something."

"Did I do the right thing, Dick? That's what I still don't know."

"I don't know, either. What's right is different for everyone. I guess I've convinced myself that staying on is right, since that's what I've done. But you're not the first one to jump ship. I can remember three or four over the years who got fed up and resigned. None of them quite as spectacularly, though. The reporters aren't going to let you go gentle into that good night on this one, babes."

Upson hadn't thought about the probability of interviews, maybe even a press conference. "Oh, my God," he said. "I'll just have to stonewall them."

"How can you give the documents to the *Times* and then stonewall everybody else?"

"Well, I don't have any other copies, and the embassy certainly won't let me make any more."

"What about when they want to know why you did it, what you think about the bombing, whether the rules of engagement work?"

"I'll have to stonewall, Dick. No comment. Let the Gleason report and the documents speak for themselves. I'm not going to blow this thing up beyond that."

"Why not? You made your bet, you may as well ride with it all the way."

"I don't know. Question of taste, maybe. I passed on the documents because I thought they should be public, but I don't want to make it look like I'm a hero."

"Why not resign and just get on the next plane, then? Why hang around and make them fire you?"

"I want them to have to put it on the record that they fired me, and why. They do too much by remote control. I want them to be accountable for once."

"They can be pretty rough, Fred. They'll claim they let you go as Mad Bomber because you weren't up to the job, couldn't handle the responsibility, made the same kind of mistakes you're blaming everybody else for now. So you went sneaking to the *New York Times* to get even."

"It wasn't like that at all."

"Wasn't it? They can add the facts up any way they want to, and that's the way they'll want to. This ain't beanbag. The ambassador said that once, when we told him about the Meo burying prisoners up to the neck and leaving them to die."

"At least the ambassador believes in what he's doing, doesn't he, Dick? None of the rest of us does, not all the way. It must be so restful, to believe."

"A lot of the military guys believe."

"It's different with them. They believe in war generally, and they don't bother over whether they believe in this particular one or that one. They've given up their power of decision to somebody else. They let the government point them, and they just shoot whatever they've been aimed at."

"That would be restful, too," Lindsay said.

"You'd think so. But they all seem to want to shoot more, or use different bullets, or be aimed somewhere else." Upson looked around his small living room with its embassy furniture, and out at the porch where he had spent so many hours talking in the dark to Somchan. "Do you think there's any chance they'd let me take over the lease on this house?" he asked.

"No. Are you kidding?"

"I guess you're right. But we can find someplace else."

"We?"

"Somchan and I."

"So you're not going?"

"No. I'm going into the office till they order me not to, and I'm going to stay on the payroll as long as I can. I have leave time coming and I'll draw out my retirement. With my savings, it'll be a year or a year and a half before I have to worry about money."

"Then what?"

"I don't know. It seems to me that worrying about 'then what' can get you into more trouble than it keeps you out of."

"Maybe so. Well, good luck, then."

Lindsay got up to go, and then paused in the doorway. "Fred," he said. "What are you doing Saturday night? Maybe you and Somchan could come over to the house for dinner and a few beers. You've never met Dang, have you?"

"I think we'd like to. I'll let you know tomorrow. And thanks, Dick."

"For what? Talk to you tomorrow, okay?"

For holding out a hand to Somchan, Upson thought once Lindsay had gone. For helping them to take the first step out of hiding. Upson had never met Dang, Lindsay's Thai wife. There must be a whole different society, of Americans with Asian wives. He—they—would be in it now. They would be free to go wherever they wanted, whenever they felt like. He saw Somchan beside him on the street, her sweet, pretty face and her slim figure, her gentle smile, her glossy black hair in a neat bun on the back of her head. He would buy her Lao silver and silk so fine that no ambassador's wife would ever sneer at her again. He imagined how their evening would be Saturday, the two couples eating and talking in the Lindsays' house. As part of the permanent cadre—like Lindsay, like Bailey, in his different way—Upson would of course have to learn Lao. He was no longer afraid that it might spoil things if Somchan and he could understand each other; now he looked forward to the day. He could meet her family, learn what her life had been, tell her about his. She would teach him to speak, and they would laugh together at his mistakes. He went to bed feeling as he used to on the Christmas Eves of his boyhood: glad to sleep because it would swallow at one gulp the time between this moment and next morning.

In the few days left before the *Times* would run the story and Upson would lose access to the files of the political section, he wanted to learn as much as possible about the Meo he had been assigned to study. Next morning, then, he began working through old reports on stock rustling by General Vang Pao's troops, a subject that ordinarily would have held his interest. But he kept thinking about Somchan, who had not appeared at breakfast, either. Although she spent the night away often enough, she had never failed to be back the next morning. It worried him that the chair had been tipped over, the more he thought about it. Her room was always neat, and it would only have taken her a second to set the chair back on its feet. Still, you couldn't read too much into that; still why *hadn't* she picked it up? He called home for the third time since coming to work. Again, no one answered. Upson put the phone down and went into Goldman's office. It was half past eleven.

"Mind if I take off for twenty minutes or so?" he asked the political counselor. "I left some stuff at home and I have to pick it up."

As he drove home in a cab, Upson wondered why he had told Goldman the little lie. Why not say he was worried because his maid hadn't shown up? Why not say he was worried about his lover, as a matter of fact? There was nothing to hide anymore.

No more officer evaluation reports, no more career to endanger, no need to consider what the embassy wives might think.

The house was still empty, everything unchanged from the way he had left it. Through the kitchen window he saw the door to Somchan's room, standing open. He was almost sure he had closed it last night. And he thought, although he was less sure, that it had still been closed while he was eating breakfast. Upson went down the kitchen steps and toward her quarters, brushing through the lines of laundry in such haste that a pair of shorts came loose. He didn't stop to pick them up. He stood still in the open doorway, trying to make sense of what he saw. The room had been cleaned out except for the few small things he had given her. They had been left all together in the middle of the bare kapok mattress: the six-dollar Meo bracelet, the short-wave radio, and the big fan with the blue plastic blades from the PX at Udorn. The cheap metal wardrobe, where her clothes used to hang, stood empty. Why would she have left him, when they were so happy? It made no sense. Why had she waited till this morning to take her things? Nothing fitted together.

The bright sunlight outside was more bearable than the stifling, airless heat inside her room. Upson saw the Thai guard next door, in the yard of his CIA neighbor. The guard saluted when Upson came up, and said, "Hello, sir. What's your trouble?" Upson remembered the strange greeting from the time he had talked to the man about Somchan's relatives at KM 30.

"No trouble," he said. "I'm looking for Somchan. Do you know where she is?"

"No, sir, not know," he said. "Maybe with mama-san."

"Mama-san?" Upson asked. He was confused. He associated mama-san with madames, Madame Loulou. What could the man mean?

"I think maybe mama-san come, one, two hour ago. Come with many families."

"What mama-san?"

"I think maybe mama-san Somchan."

"Somchan's mother came, is that it? And her family? The family from KM 30?"

"I think maybe Vientiane family, taan."

"But Somchan wasn't with them?" To be sure the guard

understood, Upson said very slowly, "Family come. Mama-san come. Somchan no come?"

"No come."

"Did she leave a note with you? Note. Message. Paper?" She had used the Thai guard to send him the note about wanting to visit KM 30, after all.

"No, taan. No leave nothing."

Now that Upson thought of the possibility of a note, he wondered if he might not have overlooked one. "Wait here," he said to the guard. "Wait here a minute, okay?"

"Okay, taan. I wait." The guard was grinning.

Back in her room, he picked up the fan and the radio, but found nothing under them. He looked under the pillow and in the old wardrobe, and under the bed, in case a note might have fallen to the floor. There was nothing. He was back outside in the blazing sun, wondering if he should look in the house, when a sour, unmistakable smell came to him from the laundry room, next to Somchan's bedroom. When he opened the laundry door, the acid stench poured out full strength. Upson made himself go inside the tin-roofed room, heated hot as a sauna by the sun on the tin roof. A hum was coming from inside the laundry tub. When Upson approached, swarming hundreds of fat, black flies buzzed up in brief alarm and then settled back down on the vomit. He went back outdoors and closed the door quickly behind him, to trap the flies and the smell. The Thai guard was waiting, still grinning.

"Where does Somchan live?" Upson asked. "House Somchan. Where?"

"I not know, taan. I think maybe better you ask Sergeant Bounlek."

"Why would Sergeant Bounlek know?"

The guard shrugged his shoulders. "Sergeant Bounlek come here, speak Somchan yesterday. Maybe him know."

"Bounlek? Why would he speak to Somchan?"

"I not know, taan. Sergeant Bounlek speak Somchan, no speak me." The Thai guard still had the smile on his face, as if all this was amusing. Upson wanted to shake him, make him stop smiling. "Better taan speak Sergeant Bounlek," the man said. "Better like that."

"Yes," Upson said. "Thank you."

He hurried back into the house, batting impatiently at the laundry that hung in his path. The embassy operator rang the security office's extension for him, but at first no one answered. Upson was about to give up when finally someone came on the line. "U.S. Embassy Security Office," the voice said. "Corporal Ouday speaking, sir."

"Is Mr. Mancuso there, please?"

"Sorry, sir, Mr. Mancuso go to lunch."

"How about Sergeant Bounlek?"

"Sergeant Bounlek also go to lunch, sir. Only me in office."

Upson identified himself and told the corporal what he wanted. There was a wait, and then the voice came back on: "Somchan live in Wattay Noi, sir. Near airport."

"What's the street number?"

"No street, sir. Many addresses in file like that, sir. Only That Luang, Wattay Noi, like that. No street."

"When does Sergeant Bounlek come back from lunch?"

"Maybe one hour, sir. Maybe two. Sometimes he eat very much."

"Christ, that's wonderful."

"Yes, sir?"

"Nothing. Nothing."

Upson had the cab driver drop him off on the Wattay road, in front of a miniature golf course. No one was playing golf on the little ramps and bridges, all painted green to look like a fairway. The sun had bleached the real grass, alongside, to the color of straw. Water buffalo had passed along the road in front, leaving behind them large splotches of greenish brown.

The small clubhouse at the rear of the mini-golf course looked empty, and so Upson crossed the road to a small café with an open front and a roof of rusty tin. Maybe Somchan was a common name, like Mary. One of the secretaries at the embassy was called Somchan. He thought how hopeless it would be for a foreigner with no English to walk the streets of an American city, asking for Mary. A man behind the counter had just sold something wrapped in a banana leaf to a child.

"Sambai di," Upson said. Hello.

"Sambai di, taan."

"Somchan?"

The man answered something Upson couldn't understand.

"Somchan. Do you know a girl called Somchan?"

"Oh, you're American," the man said. "I thought you were French. A lot of French come in, from the army camp across the street. I am Filipino. I fight with the Americans in the war."

"Yes, I'm with the embassy."

"I used to work for Air America. No more. Now I have a store. Over there is my Lao woman."

The woman was burping a small baby. Another, larger baby sat on the dirt floor beside her chair, playing with an empty condensed milk can. The woman smiled with sweet incomprehension at Upson, who smiled back an instant too late to be natural. The Lao always caught him by surprise when they smiled from embarrassment or confusion.

"Cute babies," he said.

"The little one is mine," the Filipino said. "She already had the other one. I'm Johnny."

"I'm Fred."

"Have some iced coffee, Fred? Some Ovaltine?"

"Not now, thanks. I have to find someone. A girl named Somchan who lives around here. I don't know her last name."

"Probably she got no last name. These people don't have last names like us." He spoke for a moment to the woman with the babies.

"She says there used to be a girl called Somchan near here, only she call herself Susy. She worked at the Lido, but she doesn't see her for a long time."

"It's a different one, then," Upson said. "This Somchan works for me."

"You're looking for her because she steal from you? These people steal. Lao not so bad, but Thai steal a lot."

"No, I'm just afraid something might be wrong with her. She didn't come to work."

"She don't come to work, you better off to find another girl. My wife's cousin is a good girl, works hard."

"Somchan always comes to work. That's why I'm worried she might be sick."

The Filipino talked with his wife for a moment. "She says she heard there was a girl named Somchan over behind the French military mission. Go down there, turn right, maybe somebody know her."

Down the road, Upson came to a wooden archway over the entrance to a side street. The words painted on the archway were so cracked and faded from the weather that he could barely make them out: *Mission Militaire Française*. Now that the Americans had taken over, all the French army did was train officer candidates at the Chinaimo military base on the other side of town.

The side street to the French mission had been paved, but much of the asphalt had crumbled. A drainage ditch ran along one side, its green water almost hidden by the weeds that overhung it. In fifty yards or so the road forked, one fork going toward a collection of low bungalows with straw-colored lawns and beds of dusty red and yellow flowers, motionless in the heat. Upson took the other fork, away from the French bungalows. The paving ran out and there was thick red dust underfoot, soft as flour. Down the road on the left was an open area with a small concrete-block construction in the middle. It looked like something someone had begun to build, and then abandoned before its shape and purpose could become clear—a waist-high base of some sort, with a smaller structure on the top.

A crowd of people, far down the road, was coming Upson's way. Some were monks in saffron robes; others wore white, the color of mourning. They came nearer. The monks wore sandals and carried purses over their arms. They shaded their shaven heads with black or white or red umbrellas. The monk in the lead held the end of a long bolt of white cloth. Other monks, and women in white, and people in ordinary clothes, followed him. Each had a hand on the strip of cloth, which was fastened to a four-wheeled cart. A large box was on the cart. The box seemed to be decorated, but Upson couldn't make out the details yet.

The procession came nearer.

The two or three monks nearest the cart were the ones actually pulling it with the long strip of cloth; the others along its thirty-yard length were just holding on lightly. The decorations on the box were flashy gold paper, cut out in the shapes of temple roofs and shrines. The box was of plain, dark wood, and something was on top of it.

They came nearer. The thing on top of the box was a framed photograph, the tinted formal photograph of Somchan that didn't look like Somchan.

His mind began to run around looking for a way out. He had seen Somchan only yesterday morning. They couldn't have set up a funeral this quickly. The face in the photograph he had seen in Somchan's room wasn't really of her at all, never had been. Probably it had been a sister or a cousin all along. The photograph was too far away to be sure, anyway. The studios must make them by the thousands just that way, with the silk sash across the white blouse and the hair pinned up high by silver ornaments, and the garish hand-tinting like a mortician's makeup.

The cart stopped beside the concrete-block structure. Now that he was nearer, Upson could see that the structure was a shell, with the superstructure open on one end. Heavy chunks of split firewood filled the inside. Two of the women in white had trouble undoing the knot that held the bolt of cloth to the cart, and a young monk had to help them. The women began to fold the cloth carefully, folding it over and over on itself. Upson thought of the marines outside the embassy at the close of each day, folding the big flag so neatly. When the women were done, they put the framed photograph face up on the bolt of cloth and went toward the shelter. The oldest monk was already inside, kneeling on a rush mat. A large bowl, of cheap silver-colored alloy, was in front of the old monk. The women laid the cloth beside the bowl, which held a cone-shaped construction of flowers. Kip notes were pinned to it, little flags of money the mourners were offering to the monks. The old monk, the *acharn*, began to chant. He chanted on and on, as the mourners sat motionless on their mats. The air above the tin roof of the crude pavilion shimmered from the heat, but none of the mourners seemed to be sweating. Upson remembered when his body would be slick with sweat and Somchan's would be dry except where he had lain on her. He was sweating now, in the sun. His shirt was sticking to him. The chanting went on.

"Hello, sir."

Upson saw a boy in his teens beside him, carrying schoolbooks.

"Hello."

"I study the English language at the Lao-American Association. I am happy to meet you. My name is Khamseng. What is your name?"

"My name is Fred."

"I am happy to meet you, Fed."

"Whose funeral is this, Khamseng?"

"Thank you, sir. I am fine."

"Listen. Please understand. Who is dead? What person is dead?"

"Dead?"

"Dead." Upson pointed to the coffin. "Who?"

"A girl."

"What is her name?"

"Her name is Somchan."

"When did she die?"

"When?"

"Yes."

"Tomorrow."

"Tomorrow?"

"No, no tomorrow. Yesterday."

"How did she die?"

"She want to die."

"She wanted to die?"

"Yes, want to die. She kill she."

The boy pointed to a tree, and made the motion of putting a noose around his neck. Upson had to know. He found no paper in his pockets, and so he took a five-hundred-kip note from his wallet. He drew a crude tree on it with his black plastic U.S. government ballpoint pen and drew a little stick person hanging from the tree. He put a skirt on the person.

"Yes," said the boy. "She do like that." He smiled at Upson, pleased to have made the American understand. Upson couldn't let himself cry, because the boy wouldn't go away. They stood

214

there together, watching the old monk chant, and the mourners make their responses.

Upson tried to believe that it could have had nothing to do with him, the suicide. She had a whole life apart from him, must have. But he knew it had to do with him and her together, and the embassy somehow, because Bounlek had been around. Why?

The praying ended. The monks and the mourners got up from their rush mats and left the tin-roofed pavilion. They gathered around the bottom of the concrete-block burning ghat, while six men went to the coffin cart. They lifted the box to their shoulders and carried it up to the top of the bier, and set it level on top of the logs. One of the men slid back the coffin top. There was a short discussion among them, and then the man slid the top closed again.

"I see dead girl already one time," the boy said to Upson. "She like this." He made a twisted face, with his tongue out. "Nobody no want look, no good."

The six men got down, and other people, men, women and a few children, climbed up to take their places on the bier. One of the women held the photograph of Somchan. "Mother of girl," the boy said. Somchan's mother looked like a hundred old women Upson had seen in the market or in the fields. He could see nothing of Somchan in her.

A skinny Chinese with a camera had climbed up with the others. He wore an oversize sun helmet, like the ones Upson had seen in pictures of Japanese occupation troops. The Chinese had on a white shirt, too large and loose for him. His arms, sticking out of the short sleeves, were frail as chicken wings. He was telling people where to stand and what to do, and then he was taking pictures of each of the persons on the bier, as they took turns holding Somchan's picture in front of them. When he was done, everyone climbed back down but one man. The man held a coconut, its green husk hacked open on the top. He slid the coffin lid open and poured the milk of the coconut in. Upson imagined the cloudy gray liquid running over Somchan's tormented face.

When the coconut was empty, the man dropped it onto the logs beside the coffin and slid the coffin cover closed. He moved to the other end of the bier and lit a candle. He set fire here and there to the logs at the foot of the coffin. Once the fire was going well, he tossed the candle into it. Mourners followed him up onto the bier one after another, each carrying a lighted candle to drop onto the logs all around the coffin.

At first the smoke was thick and black and greasy, from the kerosene that soaked the logs. When that burned away, the smoke turned white and thin. The flames shot up yards into the air, pale and almost invisible in the bright sunlight. The fire made a steady roar, like a fierce wind that never varied. A lick of that clear flame, Upson thought, and her hair would be gone all at once, scorched from her head and her hidden places. The smoke began to blacken again. Somchan had been added to the fire, to the clean blaze of the logs and the coffin's dry wood. Upson thought of the liquids boiling and the fats bubbling and the eventual charring and then the final clean ashes and it didn't seem so bad. A quick dissolution into air and ash, to cheat the slow and stinking rot.

What was unbearable was the absence of Somchan from the world. No one else would ever make the little sound, almost like a cry of fear, that she made at the end of their lovemaking. She would never again be on the porch with him in the dark, listening to the things he could say only to someone who didn't understand. She would never again sit at the kitchen table, a pencil clumsy in her hand, practicing her alphabet. Once he had come across her in the backyard, singing to herself. When she saw him, she put her hand over her mouth and giggled and ran into her room to hide, as if he had caught her naked.

The fire roared, now and then making dull, heavy noises as the logs settled. The smoke was thin and white again. Upson imagined a fiery ribcage, the bones glowing red.

Much of the crowd had already left. Somchan's mother and the man who had poured the coconut milk and the rest of the family group finally turned away from the blazing pyre, too. The mother, carrying Somchan's picture, headed toward Upson. The man who had poured the coconut milk was talking urgently to the mother, even pulling at her arm, but the mother kept coming. Upson could not move. He stood and waited, frightened, like a puppy that knows it will be punished.

The mother stopped in front of him and began to talk loudly, just short of a shout. The schoolboy beside Upson said something back, and then the woman started again. At the end she pointed to Upson.

"She say Somchan too poor," the schoolboy said. "You give too much peasants."

"Peasants?" The boy might have said "presents," but Upson had never given Somchan much of anything.

The mother was talking again. At the end, the boy said, "She say Somchan have small life before she go work you, she only small person. But now she have no life. Why you no leave alone? Sir, I think this woman very crazy."

"Tell her I'm sorry."

The boy translated, and the mother answered something short.

"She say she sorry, too."

The man who had been pulling at the mother finally got her to turn and go. Only a few people were left, to tend the fire till the end.

Upson walked the mile back to his house. He went to his bedroom and lay face down across his bed and let himself cry. His sweat gradually dried in the air-conditioned coolness, so that his shirt felt cold on his back. Somchan's skin always stayed dry and smooth in the heat, except for her upper lip. But he knew she suffered from the heat anyway, because she liked the dark coolness of the bedroom in the middle of the day. He had come home from work at noon one day to get something he had forgotten, and found her in there, listening to her radio. She giggled and rolled away when he reached for her, and then she let him catch her.

Now the phone rang. He wanted to let it keep ringing till it stopped, but he picked it up right away. "Yes," he said. "No. I'm coming back in. I felt a little sick, that's all. Some kind of bug. He did? But I sent the bimonthly report to Mr. Brautigan two days ago. I remember signing off on it. The one with the kind of greenish cover, right? Check with Annie; I know they've got it."

Upson sat on the edge of the bed after he hung up, without the will to move. He felt guilty about the fan, the bracelet, and the radio because of what Somchan's mother had said. Altogether they hadn't cost a hundred dollars, but then Somchan's monthly salary was sixty. His own monthly salary was something like fifteen hundred.

217

At last he made himself go to the closet, to change his sweaty shirt. As he took it off, he smelled the smoke on it. The new shirt from his drawer was fresh, washed and ironed by Somchan. "Oh, Jesus God, Jesus God," he said to himself in the dim room. He went to wash his face, so that no one at the embassy would know he had been crying.

Instead of going to his office in the embassy, he went to the security office in the compound across the street. Larry Mancuso, the security officer, was playing with a little wooden framework which had five stainless steel balls hanging from it. "Ever see one of these?" Mancuso said. "My kid gave it to me for Christmas. What it is, they use them in labs and stuff to show you about inertia. Watch how it does."

Mancuso drew one of the steel balls back on its string and let it go. The ball clicked into the four others slung in the wooden cradle, but only the last ball in line moved. "See how those little bastards in the middle just hang there?" Mancuso said. "Something, huh?"

"Larry, my maid is dead."

"Oh, yeah? What a pain in the ass, huh? Well, we keep a maid list. I can have one of my guys bring somebody around, you don't like her, we'll send you somebody else."

"Larry, she committed suicide."

"Oh, yeah? You never think they'll do that, they always smile, you know? But a lot of times they'll kill themselves when their husband takes a number two wife."

"She wasn't married. I want to find out why she killed herself, Larry."

"What can we do, Fred? Unless there's American property involved, something like that, we haven't got any jurisdiction."

"I understand that. But I thought Sergeant Bounlek might know something that would give me an idea."

"Why would Bounlek know anything about her?"

"Because he was out to the house talking to her yesterday. And a few months back you people were looking into whether she had links to the PL."

"Who told you that?"

"The DCM told me."

"Yeah, well, that would be an ongoing investigation."

"What does that mean, ongoing? She's dead."

"We don't have any report as to that effect, though."

"I just told you, Larry. I saw her cremated not two hours ago."

"What I mean, we don't have any official report as to that effect, so her file would be in the ongoing investigation file and we can't release any information about ongoing investigations. To protect the privacy of the individual involved."

"Larry, she's dead."

"Even if she's dead, the file would be classified anyway."

"I'm cleared."

"It's need-to-know, Fred. Didn't you get the security briefing?"

"Listen, pull the file and look at it yourself, okay? Tell me if there's anything in there that would give me an idea on this thing. And let's get Bounlek in here, too."

"Let me see if we've even got a file." Mancuso pressed a button on his desk and a Thai came in, wearing corporal stripes on the gray blue uniform of the mission guard service.

"Ouday, run see if we got a file on Mr. Upson's maid, what's her name?"

"Somchan," Upson said.

"Somchan."

"Okay, boss."

"The name thing makes it hard to keep files," Mancuso said. "None of them even had last names till the French came in and they couldn't keep any decent records with maybe a couple hundred people called Somchan or some damn thing. So they had everybody make up a last name. Did you know that?"

"I heard something about it."

The corporal came in and handed a file to the security officer. "Nothing in here," Mancuso said, once he had glanced over the four or five pages inside. "She had PL connections like the DCM told you. Maybe she was worried that we found out."

"But everybody in this country has PL connections, Larry. Nobody would kill themselves over that. Look, probably Bounlek did the actual investigation, right? Let's get him in and see what she told him yesterday."

"It'll make you feel better, I'll get him in. If he's around." Mancuso rang for the corporal.

"Ouday, see if Sergeant Bounlek's around, will you?" the security officer said. "Tell him I want to see him."

When the corporal had left the room, Mancuso said, "Take a look at the arms and shoulders on Bounlek when he comes in. One time we went over to Nong Khai after this thief, Bounlek walked right through a closed door, took the guy's knife away, and brought him back tied up like a chicken. If I could ever get the big son of a bitch to learn English, I'd make him a lieutenant. But the only thing he knows how to say is, 'Hi, boss.'"

In the outer office, Corporal Ouday had telephoned the guard room for Bounlek. Ouday hoped Bounlek was in trouble.

"What does the Bald Pig want now?" Bounlek asked when he came.

"I don't know, Sergeant. He's in with Mr. Upson, and he asked for the file on Mr. Upson's maid."

"Why, that goddamned little whore. She must have complained, and she begged for it. She didn't want me to leave afterward."

Corporal Ouday opened the door to the inner office for Sergeant Bounlek. "Hi, boss," the sergeant said.

"Look at the arms on him, for a Thai," Mancuso said. "You come on in, too, Ouday, so you can interpret for this big son of a bitch." There were chairs, but the two Thai remained standing in front of Mancuso's desk. "Ask him why Mr. Upson's maid would have committed suicide," Mancuso said.

Ouday didn't know the word *suicide*, but he linked the word *committed* with crime. "Excuse me, Sergeant," he said, "but the Bald Pig wants to know what you did to the girl."

"Nothing that the little whore wasn't practically begging for, like I told you."

"Sir, Sergeant Bounlek say they have nice talk. She cooperate very good."

"Okay, fine. But why does he think the girl might have killed herself?"

"Killed herself?"

"Yeah, suicide. You understand?"

"Yes, sir. I understand everything very good now."

Ouday went on in Thai. "Sergeant, the Bald Pig wants to know why the girl is dead?"

"Dead? She was alive when I left. I only hit her once, and not even hard. She wanted it, tell them that."

"Sir, Sergeant Bounlek say maybe she kill herself because of boy."

"What boy?"

"Just some boy. Sometimes Lao girl do like that."

"Ask him if she actually said anything about any boy," Upson said. "I want names, details, anything he remembers."

"Sergeant, I'm sorry, but the American says how could it be that she wanted it? He says she left a note behind and it says you beat her until she went to bed with you."

"That's a lie. I only hit her when she wouldn't take it into her mouth, the way they do for the Americans."

"Sir, Sergeant Bounlek say probably he wrong. He say if she have boyfriend, why she make fuck with him?"

"What?" Upson said. "With who?"

"With him. With Sergeant Bounlek."

"No, he's lying. She wouldn't have done that."

"Sergeant, I'm sorry, but Mr. Upson says he doesn't believe you."

"So what? She was nothing but a Lao whore who fucked anything that walked. She was fucking Upson. It's all in my report, there, so the Bald Pig knows I'm telling the truth about her no matter what the other one says."

"Mr. Upson, sir, the sergeant say he is sorry, but your maid go fuck with everybody. Also with him."

"He's a liar. Tell him he's a liar."

"Sergeant, he says the girl would never have gone to bed with you willingly. The note she left says you hit her."

"Then she lied in the note. I only cuffed her that once, when she wouldn't suck me."

"Mr. Upson, Sergeant Bounlek says she go fuck with him, never mind. He only have to hit girl a little bit because she no want to suck him."

Upson came up out of his chair, crying out without knowing it, and hit at the sergeant's face. The sergeant ducked so that the blow landed on the side of his neck. He stepped into Upson's attack and wrapped both arms around him.

"Hey, hey," Mancuso shouted. "Take it easy."

Upson jerked back and forth, but he couldn't break loose from the sergeant's powerful hug.

221

"Take it easy, everybody," Mancuso said. "Let him go, Sergeant. Tell him, Ouday. Then both of you get out of here and wait till I call you."

Upson stood shaking while the two Thai left the office. His eyes were blurred with tears.

"Sit down and take it easy a minute," Mancuso said. "Christ."

Upson sat down. Nothing had happened when he hit the sergeant, the first time he had ever hit a man. It had been like hitting the side of a tire, like a dream where you punch and kick and do no damage. He imagined the big Thai with Somchan, his hands in her hair, forcing her mouth onto him.

"Your first shot, you should go for the stomach," Mancuso said.

"What?"

"Always go for the stomach with your first shot. What it does, it brings their guard down."

Upson was clasping his hands so hard together that they turned pink and white from the pressure, and trembled. He said nothing.

"Take it easy," Mancuso said.

"Take it easy," Upson repeated in a dead tone.

"Listen, we got to get together on what to say," Mancuso said. "Sure as shit, Bounlek will file a grievance on this. Top of everything else, I got the goddamned employees' association to worry about."

"A grievance? A grievance? Are you crazy? He should be in jail."

"For what?"

"For rape. For murder. Why do you think she killed herself? You heard him."

"What he says now and what he'd say to a court are two different things."

"We heard him."

"Who heard him? Did you understand him? What we heard was Ouday."

"The girl is dead, Larry. She's dead."

"Listen, Fred, let me tell you something. In this country, you could shoot somebody down in the middle of Samsenthai Street with fifty witnesses around, and for a couple hundred bucks in the right places, you could take a walk."

"You're not going to do anything, are you?"

"Come on, Fred. What kind of an outfit do you think I run? It makes it harder because you hit him, but Bounlek was definitely out of line and he's going to get punished for it if I possibly can."

"Punished how?"

"Listen, there's a lot of things I can do administratively."

"Administratively? You mean you put a letter in his personnel file?"

"Look, what's the use going public on this? We don't handle it in-house, everybody gets hurt. It comes out you had a little something going with the girl, right? Nothing wrong with it, I'm just thinking how it would look."

"Would you dock his pay? Would you go that far?"

"Come on, Fred."

"Come on, Fred. Your goddamned storm trooper rapes a young girl and sodomizes her and drives her to suicide. Don't you care, Mancuso? Don't you care at all?"

"Come on, Fred, be reasonable. What can I do? The girl is dead."

"Be reasonable, the girl is dead. That's what you said, isn't it?"

"Take it easy now, Fred."

"You son of a bitch. You lousy Nazi son of a bitch."

"Take it easy."

"I'm going to see the ambassador."

"So see the ambassador, Upson. You got a right."

When Upson had slammed the door behind him, Mancuso said a word aloud, to himself.

"Asshole."

Upson walked from the security office across the street to the embassy. He went past things he hoped he would never see again: the little unmarked office of the CIA's Air America liaison officer, the soup kitchen kept by the ex-Legionnaire, the marine sentry box outside the windowless bunker of an embassy. Upson was trying to keep himself from spilling over, as if he were a glass filled to the brim. Nodding but saying nothing, he carried himself carefully past the pretty Thai receptionist. Then came the door to his old office, Annie Cutler at her desk saying, "Oh, my God, Fred, what is it?" Jerry Brautigan's office, standing open, and the closed door to the ambassador's office. Upson opened it without knocking.

Jerry Brautigan was bent over Ambassador Simmonds, pointing out something in a set of charts laid out on the teak desk. Both men looked up at Upson, where he stood in the doorway with his hands trembling.

"What's the matter, Fred?" the deputy chief of mission said at once. "What is it? What's wrong?"

The sympathy in his voice was what finally made Upson spill over. Tears ran down his cheeks and the words came rushing out without form or thought. "Wrong? Wrong, wrong! Murdering bastard sons of bitches! Reach out through the walls, can't you? No windows, and kill anybody. She was only a good little girl, only a maid, when did she ever hurt you? When did anybody ever hurt you? Would you hang her up and burn her yourselves, with your own hands? Are you brave enough for that, you bastards? Would you burn a girl yourselves?"

Upson stopped, his throat so choked that he couldn't go on talking. The muscles in his face were slack, and he sobbed and gasped.

"Annie, get hold of the clinic," Brautigan called out the door. "Get somebody over here fast."

The deputy chief of mission started across the room toward Upson. His big, freckled hands were half-raised, as if he meant to take Upson into his arms. Worry was on his face, and in his voice. "It'll be all right, Fred, you'll see," he said. "I don't know what it is, but try not to worry. We'll work it out somehow."

As soon as Brautigan got within reach, Upson punched at him and kept punching. The big man hardly seemed to move at all, but none of the blows landed on him. "Don't, Fred," he said gently. "I used to box in college."

Upson let his hands fall and stared for a moment at Brautigan. Then he turned and rushed out the door.

"What the hell was that all about?" the ambassador asked. "Was that what a nervous breakdown is?"

"I don't know what it's all about," Brautigan answered, although he was afraid he did. That idiot Mancuso, what had he done?

"What a disgusting thing to watch," the ambassador said. "Man must be sick. Have to get him out of here in a hurry."

"I'll take care of it, Buck."

"I never knew you used to box, Jerry. What weight?"

"Light-heavy, back then."

"I'll be damned. Were you any good?"

"Fairly good, nothing great. Junior year, I was second in the New Englands."

"Not bad," the ambassador said. "Damned good, actually."

About the Author

JEROME DOOLITTLE was a member of the American mission to Laos. He has served as speechwriter for President Carter and as director of public affairs for the Federal Aviation Administration. His pieces have appeared in *Esquire* and other national magazines. He is the author of *The Southern Appalachians* and *Canyons and Mesas*. This is his first novel.